**Ellender York has nightmares . . .
but everything she dreams is real.**

TWO YEARS AFTER A SPLIT-SECOND DECISION on a dark country road results in tragedy, Ellender is ready to start over. Not everyone thinks she should be allowed to. Someone wants retribution and will stop at nothing to make her pay.

Attorney Grace Reagan is one month away from maternity leave, and happy to have an intriguing, if odd, case to take her mind off her personal life. She's having a longed-for baby with a man she can't stand, and she's in love with a man she's afraid of losing. Ellender's story is a welcome distraction . . . until it starts to unravel.

Is Grace's new client a victim or a liar? And what happens when a killer emerges from the shadows of Ellender's dreams?

Come back to the Eastern Shore for another round of murder and mayhem in the Land of Pleasant Living!

DEATH and CONSEQUENCES
An Eastern Shore Mystery

THE EASTERN SHORE MYSTERIES

Squatter's Rights

A Commission on Murder

Bad Intent

Death and Consequences

A Little Christmas War (Short Read)

The Eastern Shore Mysteries Box Set, Books 1-3

Readers' reviews for the Eastern Shore Mysteries

For *Squatter's Rights*:

"… Cheril Thomas is a masterful storyteller and had me guessing the whole time."

"… The characters are fun and clever… an engaging page turner…"

"I loved this book, couldn't put it down, such great characters…"

"… I read it straight through to the end without putting it down."

For ***A Commission on Murder:***

"… A witty thriller and great summer read…"

"… Strongly recommend adding this selection to your summer reading list."

"… Another great offering in the series…"

For ***Bad Intent:***

"… Suspenseful, funny and tragic and filled with more mysteries than Grace wants or needs, *Bad Intent* is Cheril Thomas's best offering yet."

"…Enjoyable page turner with equal part humor and suspense."

For ***Death and Consequences:***

(from the Advance Reading Copy reviews)

"…Every time I thought I had it figured out - I didn't! Great ending… loved revisiting my favorite characters…"

"…I loved it! One of my favorites in the series!"

DEATH AND CONSEQUENCES

AN EASTERN SHORE MYSTERY

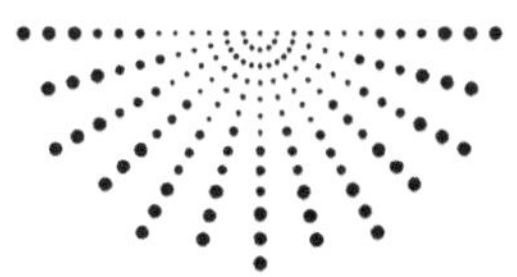

CHERIL THOMAS

TRED AVON PRESS

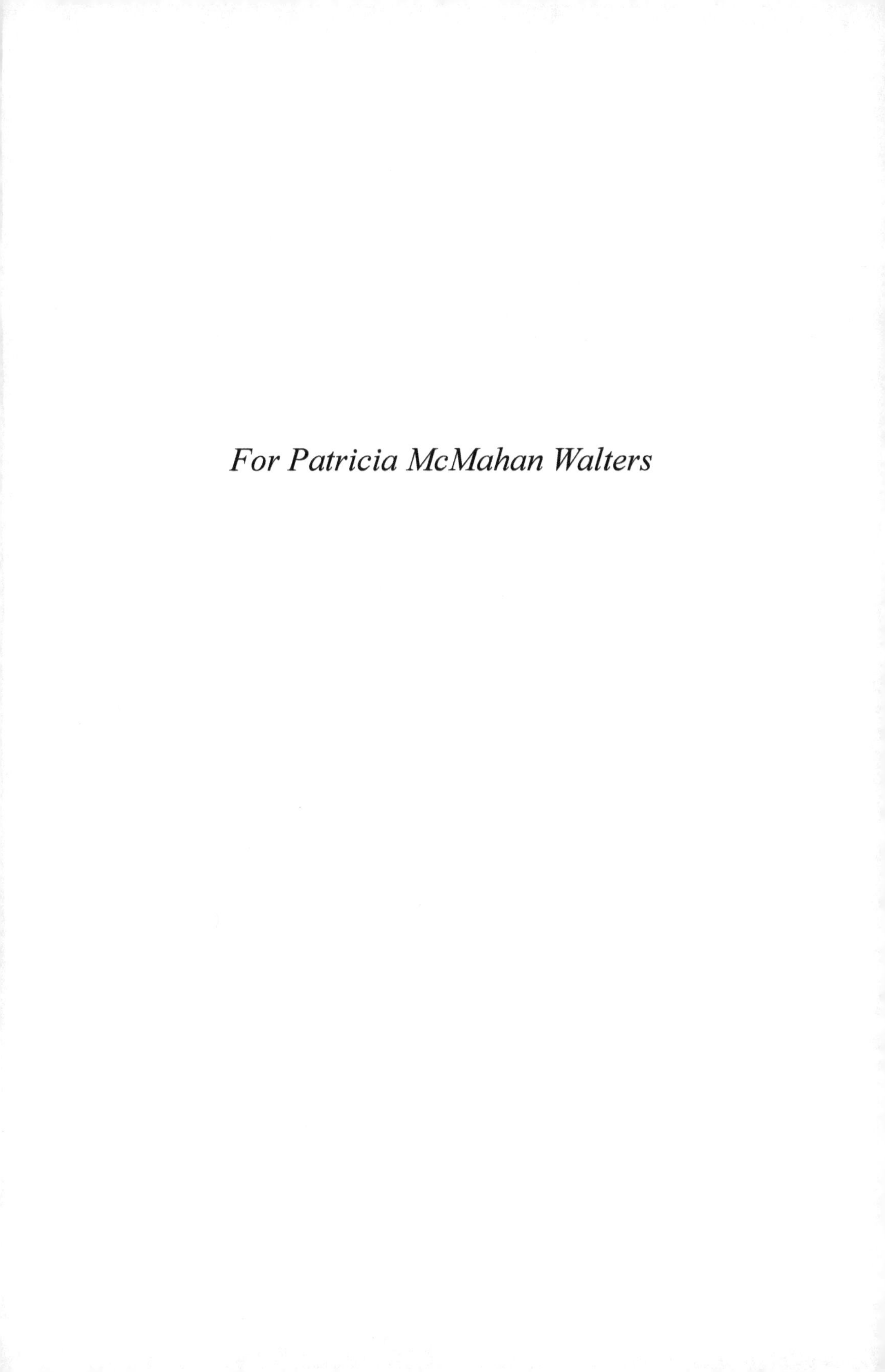

For Patricia McMahan Walters

PROLOGUE

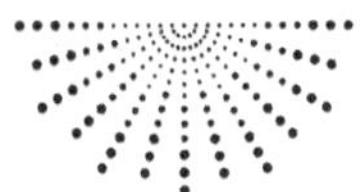

He was ready to go. His feet and hands felt lighter, and soon the rest of his body would be, too. At some point, after all the sirens and lights and people had disappeared, he'd been moved to a quiet place. It might be twilight on the other side of the windows, or just his sight fading. Wherever he was, it was peaceful.

He wasn't afraid, only worried. It wasn't his time. He was supposed to grow old, well, older than he was. If he died now, who would set things right? His most important task was left undone.

"Owen?"

It was a soft voice. One he thought he'd lost. He wasn't alone.

The gray light grew brighter, lit by a golden sun he couldn't see. The room fell away, and he took his last breath.

It wasn't his time, but Owen went, anyway.

CHAPTER ONE

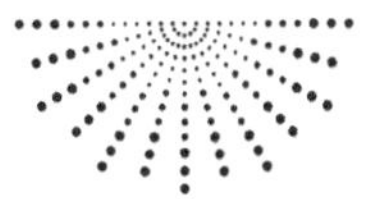

The grandfather clock in the large entry hall of the Inn at Delaney House was striking nine, and Grace Reagan was already in trouble. A bride-to-be and her entourage were demanding breakfast, while the baby in Grace's belly kicked her kidneys. To add to the fun, her ex-fiancé was calling for the third time in ten minutes. She took Bridezilla on first.

A tall blonde in a pink silk robe waved a leather binder. "You're late with our . . ." she yanked the notebook open and jabbed at a menu. "French Bistro Experience. When do you plan to feed us?"

Two pink-robed women leaned over the second-floor bannister to watch the show. Grace didn't want to know how many more caffeine and sugar deprived bridesmaids might be waiting to pounce. She slung her tote over her shoulder and said, "I don't work here. I suggest you look for the innkeeper."

"Look for her?" The woman followed Grace out the front door and down the steps. "She said the housekeeper would be here to serve us. This is not what we paid for!"

Paid. The magic word. Grace reluctantly turned around. She was late for work, but forced herself to smile. "I'm just amazed," she said as she walked back into her home. "Everything is usually right on time. Let me see if I can find someone to help you."

The someone in question was in the kitchen whacking a pineapple with a wicked-looking knife.

"Gracie! Thank goodness. Grab the muffins from the oven, please. No! Wait, get the table set in the dining room. Everything's out on the sideboard."

Grace looked around the food-splattered room and tried to remember why turning her meticulously restored, historic home into an inn had ever seemed like a good idea. Then she remembered—it hadn't.

"Niki, what happened? Those women are furious."

Her cousin continued chopping as she described a no-show catering crew and a malfunctioning alarm. "You've got to help me." She shoved a platter of fruit at Grace.

"You may notice I'm wearing my work clothes, not my bail-Niki-out uniform." Grace set the platter down. They'd had this discussion before. Her half of the business was to provide the premises. Niki's was everything else.

"You're wearing a too-small maternity top and I'm desperate," Niki said. "Kill me later, but get the dining room ready first."

Saying no to Niki was one thing, undermining their struggling business was another. Grace put her briefcase down and picked up the fruit.

She hadn't wanted an inn, but Delaney House had been expensive to renovate. She wouldn't recoup her investment if she sold it now. Some income was better than none, and giving into Niki's plan to add Grace's property to her small B&B business had been expedient and easy. Living with the result was proving to be slow and painful.

Niki was conducting a soft opening to test the new inn's operating plan before the winter hiatus. They'd had staffing problems from the beginning, and this morning was more of the same. It was an hour before Grace escaped from Bridezilla hell.

The ringtone signaling David's fourth call blasted from her phone as she was maneuvering her swollen body into her car. Swallowing curses in her ongoing effort to be a good mother, she answered and tried to sound cheerful. David stayed angry these days, and when she could make herself consider their circumstances objectively, it was hard to blame him. She was nearly eight months pregnant with his child, a frustrating situation that was the best thing that had ever happened to her. She was having the baby she'd always wanted with a man she couldn't stand.

It's a trade-off, she thought, then realized she'd said it out loud.

"What's a trade-off, Grace?" David shouted from his office in Washington. "What else do you want besides the money I'm trying to give you? Are you into outright extortion, now?"

From anyone else, the comment might have been a joke. They were both attorneys, but Grace liked to think she was at the human end of that species, while David was firmly encamped with the litigators. He never made jokes about money.

When she answered the taunt, she kept her voice light and even. "Sorry. I didn't mean it that way. When you yell, I get indigestion and that upsets the baby. I was thinking that my life's a trade-off. I get Sweet Pea, but we have to listen to you yell at us."

Until recently, making the baby real for him had kept things somewhat calm between them. That magic was eroding as she neared her due date. And there was the added complication of a new man in Grace's life. David had plenty of reasons to be upset, and she humored him when she could. It was a difficult goal in the best of times.

"Concentrate," he snapped. "Sign the damned contract and get it back to me before we lose the offer on the house. You know we don't have any other interest in it."

His final play to win Grace had been the surprise gift of a home on the Wye River. The deed was in her name alone, something he now regretted, loudly and often. When she'd finally convinced him their split was permanent, he'd gone along with her proposal to sell the property and put the proceeds in a trust fund for the baby. That was the last time they'd agreed on anything.

She'd received an offer on the house almost immediately, but the buyer's financing had fallen through. Now, she had a second contract, but at a price so low, she couldn't imagine why David wanted her to accept it.

She lowered her voice, hoping he'd have to stop talking to hear her. "It's a ridiculous offer. I don't have to rush into a sale that's three hundred thousand below the list price. I can wait for a better deal."

She let him rant while she concentrated on driving through the narrow streets of Mallard Bay, Maryland. October was beautiful on the Eastern Shore, and tourism was still in full swing. There were enough people wandering around the historic little town to make the short trip challenging. She arrived at work to find the only open parking spot was next to the dumpster.

"Are you listening to me?"

"I am," she lied, and dropped the phone into her tote. When she'd squeezed out of the car and straightened her clothes, she fished it out and made herself listen. She hadn't missed a thing.

"And now you tell me you can wait?" he was saying. "How nice for you. I've spent hours trying to negotiate this deal. How dare you—"

She disconnected and turned the phone off. She had been telling the truth about his yelling upsetting the baby. Or maybe it was her reaction to David's anger that caused the little kicks and pokes to speed up. Whichever, she was grateful to have an off button for the noise. One day, one hour, one argument at a time was the only way to handle her baby's father. Somehow it would all work out.

It had to.

CHAPTER TWO

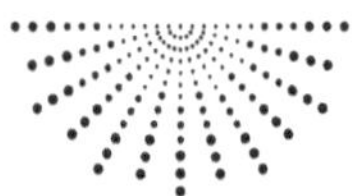

There had been a time when her legal practice had been her pride and joy. At least, that's how she remembered the days when she wore stilettos and tailored suits. She was pretty sure her salon-maintained hair hadn't frizzed back then, either. Now maternity slacks and tunics topped flat shoes, which were sized up to accommodate her swelling feet. The indignities that came with pregnancy in her late thirties should have entitled her to a workplace with helpful and agreeable people, but no. She had a secretary nicknamed "The Bat" for reasons richly deserved, and a third-year law student who needed hand-holding while he prepared to snatch her job out from under her.

"You're late," Marjorie Battsley said in a tone

meant to convey that Grace was also a waste of air and wrong about anything she might be about to say.

"Good morning. You are correct, as usual." Grace nodded agreeably as she passed the reception desk of Cyrus Mosley and Associates.

The Bat wasn't deterred by sarcasm. "Jake needs to see you and he's a busy man."

"A busy man who reports to me," Grace said as she closed her office door. It didn't help. Sweet Pea picked that moment to do gymnastics and nearly dislodged her mother's breakfast. It took a while for both of them to get settled. By the time she buzzed for Jake Briard to join her, she'd counted her blessings and kicked her shoes off under her desk. As long as she stayed seated, the man she was supposed to be training wouldn't see her as barefoot and pregnant.

She was adding "Buy Bigger Pants" to her to-do list when he tapped on her door and opened it with a cheery, "Hi there!"

"Did I say come in?" she snapped, looking up.

He froze mid-smile. Everyone liked handsome, agreeable Jake. Everyone but Grace. Her first impression when they'd met was that he resembled Rob Lowe in his *West Wing* days. As she'd gotten to know him, she'd been impressed with his intelligence and sense of humor, but it was a grudging assessment. Sort of in line with finding out your husband's girlfriend cured cancer in between photo shoots for *Vogue*.

Professionally, Jake was a pain, too. Mallard Bay's former town manager was now an attorney in training and he constantly tried to engage her in discussions on the theory of law. She always shut him down, fast. The firm's principal attorney may have agreed to mentor Mr. Charming, but Grace hadn't. If Jake needed hand-holding, he could get it from Cyrus Mosley, who managed their firm from a golf cart.

"I can call you," Jake said, but she waved him in.

He sat on the edge of the chair in front of her desk, poised to run at any hint of further hostilities. Perhaps because he was perfect, Jake didn't do conflict, which in Grace's mind disqualified him from earning a license to practice law.

She let him sit, then said, "Close the door, please. The Bat will still listen through the keyhole, but let's not make it easy for her." It was petty and satisfying. He was off-balance again and she envisioned Marjorie out in the hallway, turning six shades of purple. He complied, and as he returned to his chair, she picked up a remote control and aimed it at a floor fan that sat beside the desk.

"White noise." He looked at her with admiration. "She said you were having hot flashes."

Grace really didn't want to like him, but she burst out laughing. "That'll happen eventually, but the fan's part of my defense strategy. And it infuriates her. Win, win."

Now he seemed uncomfortable. "Marjorie is very helpful to me. I know you don't care for her, but she's not so bad. Not to me, anyway."

Her amusement evaporated. Of course The Bat helped him; Jake was everything she liked. He was male, gorgeous, and he took all of her "suggestions" as commandments. Grace had decided several months ago that since he was almost as old as she was, he could figure Marjorie out on his own. She asked for the daily office update.

"A new client, Ellender York, came in yesterday after you left. She had two friends with her. Mr. Mosley was here, but she insisted on waiting until you were available." He gave her one of his smiles. Not the melt-anything-in-its-path Jake Special, just an ordinary smile, which was still something. He had the double whammy: perfect pearly whites and dimples.

Ordinarily, Grace was a sucker for dimples,

but his were wasted on her. In addition to weaseling his way into Mosley's good graces and a job he wasn't qualified for, Jake had also dumped Grace's former secretary and friend, Lily Travers. Lily had wanted—and in Grace's opinion, deserved—the job Mosley had given to Jake. Her subsequent move to Annapolis and another firm left a hole in Grace's life, even though their friendship had been on rocky ground when Lily left. Except for a few awkward conversations, not much had changed. It was easy to blame Jake for it all, and some days she wanted to slap him just on principle.

"Ellender York made an appointment and will be here soon."

She realized she'd missed half of what he'd said.

Jake frowned. "I'm guessing from the look on your face that Marjorie didn't tell you any of this."

Grace said, "Correct. You should always assume Marjorie has told me nothing useful. Why is Ms. York coming in?"

"A dispute with a neighbor. As I said, Mr. Mosley tried to help her, but the people who were with her insisted she see you. I know Ellender but she didn't want to talk to me, either."

She wanted to say that sometimes people

prefer to discuss their problems with strangers, but settled for asking who had been with their new client.

"Tyler Forester is Ellender's boyfriend. At least I assume so, because he was holding her hand. The woman with them said she knows you. Cherish Sunsong? She said you met last winter."

"Yep." Grace smiled at the memories the name brought up. "Cherish's chickens had a run-in with a neighbor's boa constrictor."

"Huh. Maybe that's why she's advising Ellender."

Grace raised an eyebrow and waited, refusing to ask for the punch line.

"Ellender says a neighbor is slandering her."

She sighed. "Okay, I give. What's the neighbor saying?"

If there was one thing Jake did better than smiling, it was sympathizing. Worry crinkled the edges of his deep blue eyes, and he doubled-checked the door he'd shut only minutes before. "I'm really glad you'll be representing her. Mr. Mosley's wonderful, but you know how he feels."

"About?"

His crinkles grew crinkles. "It's utter nonsense of course."

The answer he was teasing her with could be

anything, so vast and varied were their employer's opinions on the law. But there was an area that Mosley refused to touch unless Grace roped him into it.

"Who did Ms. York kill?" she asked.

The dimples reappeared. "Oh, nobody yet. But wait until you hear the story."

CHAPTER THREE

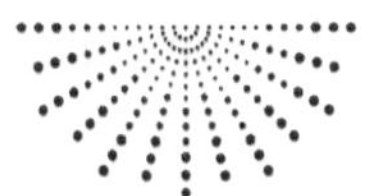

"I told Ellender she could trust you," Cherish Sunsong said as she adjusted the fluffy mohair scarf she wore over a blue silk shirt. The last time Grace had seen the Chicken Lady, she'd been in overalls and was yelling. Today, she looked sophisticated but was still agitated. "Even when all those miserable neighbors of mine got mad at you, you stuck to your position. You didn't pull any punches with me, either, but you were fair. I checked you out after that. I can't imagine why you gave up your practice in Washington, but I'm glad you're here now. What's happening to Ellender isn't right."

"Well, let's talk for a bit and see if I can help,"

Grace said, turning to the young woman who sat beside Cherish. "What is the problem?"

Ellender York wore black leggings and a bulky black sweater, which on her slender frame had the effect of swaddling her. Her features were on the plain side, with one exception. Her fine auburn hair was a sheet of silk, the ends feathering lightly where it brushed her shoulders. Grace wanted to ask which stylist she used, but knew it didn't matter. Only a wig would give her that sleek look.

Perched on the edge of her chair, looking earnest and nervous in equal measures, Ellender said, "I'm running a business out of my home. My neighbor, Natalie Wilkens, doesn't like it. I checked the zoning regulations carefully and I don't see where I'm doing anything wrong, but she complained to the police, and I got this in the mail a few days ago."

Grace took the letter and recognized the return address of an Easton law firm. "Has anything else happened?" she asked as she scanned the meager contents of the envelope. "I was told you were accused of attempted murder."

"What? No! Oh, Jake must have thought Tyler was serious. My friend, Tyler Forester, was with me yesterday. He gets upset and exaggerates sometimes."

Well, there went her exciting case, Grace thought. This was probably a neighbor-versus-neighbor spat with her in the role of hall monitor. She noticed Cherish could barely contain her irritation, so maybe there was more to the story. "How much of an exaggeration did he make?"

Ellender said, "Natalie complains constantly about my use of chemicals on my lawn and garden. I only buy the mildest stuff on the market, but last April when I sprayed the grass with a weed killer, she called the police to say I was trying to kill her."

"She complained again last week, when Ellender put a fungicide on her roses," Cherish broke in. "That's what Tyler heard, and I wish he'd stop repeating it. That kind of story can really make the rounds fast."

"So, to be clear, you haven't assaulted anyone, or been charged with assault?" Grace asked.

"No. Natalie's been complaining about my family for so long, I doubt anyone would take her seriously if we didn't have a new police chief. He's at her house a lot, but eventually, he'll see she's making everything up. The zoning problem is new, though. And that's what I need help with."

"This letter says you're running an illegal business operation out of your home. Is this the only communication you've had from Mr. Steinlen?"

"Me? Yes," Ellender said. "But when my parents were alive, they heard from him often. Our property—I should say my property—and Natalie's share a driveway, and that used to be the biggest problem. Now it's anything I do. Natalie is always unhappy about something."

It sounded like a miserable situation. The kind that, in Grace's experience, usually had fault on both sides. "What type of business do you have?"

Ellender glanced at Cherish, who gave her an encouraging nod. "I do tarot readings." Her features hardened. "Is that going to be a problem?"

"Don't know yet," Grace said, mildly. "Do you charge for the readings?"

"Yes. The going rate."

"Is that your only business?" Grace was relieved to see both women nod. Ellender's attitude concerned her. "Anyone else living in the house?"

After a slight hesitation, Ellender shook her head. "My mother passed away when I was fourteen. My father and sister, Verity, died in a car accident two years ago. I live alone, but Tyler and Cherish are over a lot. Natalie yells at them, too."

"Yeah," Cherish agreed. "Nat's an equal-opportunity hater."

"Which, unfortunately, isn't illegal," Grace said. "What exactly does Mrs. Wilkens object to? Is there much foot traffic in and out of your house? Cars parking on her property or blocking her drive?"

Ellender threw her hands up. "She complains about everything. I limit my readings to two appointments a day, but lots of times, I only have one—or none. If Natalie wasn't glued to her front windows watching me, she wouldn't know anyone was at my house. She isn't even subtle. She'll come out in her yard to see who's coming and going. It freaks me out, not to mention my friends and customers. I've been advised to sue her for harassment, but I prefer not to do that."

Grace thought about calling Jake in. He'd have the background on someone like Natalie Wilkens. Then she remembered he'd gone out to the Country Club with papers for Mosley to sign. Even when he could be useful, he wasn't.

As if reading her mind, Ellender said, "Jake asked if he could help me when we were here yesterday. He's a very nice guy, and I want to keep him out of this. Natalie could make things hard for him. Do you know her?"

"The name's familiar," Grace admitted. "But no, I don't."

This appeared to please Ellender, as well as Cherish, who said, "Told you she'd be impartial. Now tell her all of it."

~

MRS. WILKENS WAS THE TYPE OF CRANKY neighbor kids try to avoid, but her husband, retired Circuit Court Judge Owen Wilkens, had kept her in check and was well liked in Mallard Bay. Things were different after he died. In the four years since she'd become a widow, Mrs. Wilkens had ramped up her feud with the Yorks. Now that Ellender was the only one left, her every move was scrutinized.

"I'm moving to Annapolis as soon as I can manage it. I've told Natalie I'm looking for a new place, but it only makes her angrier. If there was an illegal way to breathe, she'd accuse me of it. She has health issues that she mentions a lot. A weak heart is her usual complaint, although she certainly seems to have enough energy to make my life miserable."

Grace read the letter from Malcolm Steinlen more carefully, not learning anything more. "This says that your business is encroaching on Mrs.

Wilkens's property and causing her emotional distress. You're also accused of devaluing her property. Why would she say that?"

Ellender shrugged. "It's the tarot readings. I used to do them in a bookstore in Chestertown. I only started working from home this summer. One of her best friends is a client of mine and a couple of weeks ago, she stopped by Natalie's house after she left me. I thought I'd catch flak from Natalie, but instead, I got that letter. I guess I shouldn't be surprised, but it worries me that she's getting worse, even as I'm trying to leave. You'd think she'd be happy."

Grace said, "Please don't be offended, but usually there's a core reason when someone behaves that way."

Ellender's head was shaking before Grace finished. "She's always been mean. I don't know what to tell you beyond that. She seems to enjoy it. Sometimes, after one of her tirades, she'll smile and even laugh as she leaves."

"So, she confronts you?"

Ellender nodded. "Believe me, I stay as far away from her as possible. I don't answer the phone if it's her number, and I've kept copies of her most recent messages. Here." She handed

Grace a folded paper. "I have transcribed and recorded copies."

It didn't take long to read through the messages, which were all versions on a theme: Ellender was thoughtless, noisy, careless, and a danger to everyone around her.

"She's clear in her accusations, but short on proof," Grace said. "Unless there's more to your business than I understand, it should be permitted in a residential zone. I can answer her lawyer on your behalf and advise him you're represented by counsel. Sometimes that's all it takes to end these types of conflicts. Paying an attorney to write a letter is one thing, but running up legal fees for a frivolous complaint is another. And you'll note, the wording in this letter is vague. Deliberately so, I'd say."

Cherish finally spoke. "Can't you tell him that Natalie is harassing Ellender? That's illegal, isn't it?"

"No," Ellender said sharply, ending Grace's worry that her client was being manipulated by her friends. "Just the letter, please, Ms. Reagan. I don't want to make things worse; I want to get out of this town. I can't go until I sell my house, though, and I want her to leave me alone in the meantime."

"Got it," Grace said. "Let's try the letter. I'll look into the zoning first, of course, and I'll call if I have any concerns."

"Wonderful." Ellender rose and held her hand out to Grace. When their palms met, the smile dropped from her face. A second later, she was through the office door. Cherish hurried to catch up with her friend while tossing perfunctory thank-you and goodbye noises over her shoulder.

Confused, Grace followed them to the reception area.

"Doesn't look as if that went well," Marjorie said as the front door closed behind the women. "I knew Mr. Mosley should have handled them."

Grace ignored her, but not the uneasy feeling she had. Ellender York's story was odd, and her behavior even more so.

Back in her office, she scanned the local zoning codes, confirmed there was no conflict, and drafted a response to Malcolm Steinlen. It was a necessary first step, but unlikely to put an end to the long-running Wilkens-York feud. She was only responding to the latest development in an argument so old, only one of the original combatants was still alive.

She had a professor in law school who'd said ninety percent of their work would be first aid and the rest would be hand-to-hand combat. She slapped a fresh bandage on Ellender's wound and hoped it would hold for a little while.

CHAPTER FOUR

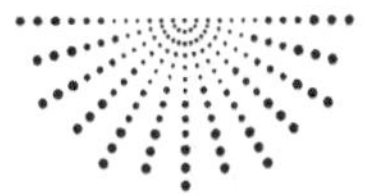

"What happened in there?" Cherish demanded. She was a head taller than Ellender, but was nearly trotting to keep up. "Ellie, *stop*." She grabbed Ellender's arm, breaking her stride. "What's wrong?"

"Get me out of here," Ellender said. "Let's go to your house. *Please*."

The twenty-minute drive from Mallard Bay into the countryside was mostly silent. Ellender closed her eyes, only saying "headache" in response to questions. The women had known each other most of their lives, but in the two years since Verity York's death, her sister and her best friend had become family.

When she couldn't take the silence any longer,

Cherish said, "Are you having the dreams again?" It was a wild guess, one that wasn't answered.

After the car accident that killed Hank and Verity York, Ellender had been emotionally lost for months. When the dreams began, they tormented her, but they also had a cathartic effect. She could function in the daytime and punish herself at night. Cherish thought Ellender used the dreams to stay tied to the past instead of moving on with her life. The memory of her friend's reaction to this analysis was painful. Ellender had exploded.

"I was driving the car, Cherish! I killed my father and sister, and I crippled Tyler. Bad dreams are a small price to pay for what little peace I have now. I don't deserve any at all."

Cherish remembered the scene and remained quiet.

When they reached the long, rutted road to the small farmette that Cherish had recently bought, Ellender sat up and looked around. Color returned to her face, and she smiled as the chickens in the driveway scattered before the slow-moving car. "It must be nice to have this welcoming committee every time you come home."

"What's nice is not having any neighbors. After that mess last winter, I couldn't wait to get out into the real countryside." Cherish stopped abruptly, realizing that with her usual artlessness, she'd brought them to Ellender's problems. "Maybe you should buy a farm," she said, trying for a lighter note.

The farmhouse boasted two wide porches, both with rockers, a cushioned chaise, and a swing. They chose the one overlooking the field at the rear of the property, opting for the shade from the noon sun. In an extraordinary display of restraint, Cherish poured them each a lemonade before demanding answers.

"I wasn't being evasive, not really," Ellender said. "I don't understand what happened. But it scared me and my head still hurts."

"So, what happened when you touched her hand?"

"Brown."

Cherish wanted to understand. She also wanted to shake Ellender until something sensible came out of her mouth. "Brown?"

Ellender nodded. "When I read for someone and they're having a hard time articulating their feelings, I ask them to name the first color that comes to mind. Usually I interpret the answers loosely, as a guide. Blue and pink are cheerful. Greens are focused and sometimes guarded. Reds are intense, and grays I recommend to professionals, obviously."

"Oh, obviously," Cherish said, even though she had no clue what one would do with a gray client.

Ellender went on as if she hadn't been interrupted. "Usually, people who want readings aren't feeling gray. They have hope for a positive outcome, or help."

Ordinarily, Cherish would have found this fascinating and delved into her own feelings, laying everything out for Ellender's opinion, but she tucked the information away, and stayed on point. "Brown?" she prompted.

"Fear. Danger." Ellender stopped, then added, "A brown knows what's wrong, but either they don't know how to fix the problem or they refuse to see it. They are fighting what needs to be corrected in their lives."

"Wow," Cherish said. "I would love to see people the way you do."

"Oh, stop it!" Ellender said. "You always romanticize this stuff. I don't *see* anything. I feel things and I get ideas, that's all. I keep my observations general and sometimes what I say to clients makes them look at their situations differently. I'm sympathetic and a good listener. I have empathy, and that's what most people want when they're in trouble, just someone to listen to them without being judgmental."

"But you said you saw brown for Grace."

"No, you asked what I *felt*. There was nothing special, but I thought about brown with a few pink streaks. It's a hideous color combination, by the way."

Cherish wasn't buying it and said so. "Ugly colors made you run away from her and gave you a headache? Come on, Ellie."

But Ellender got up without answering and went out to talk to the chickens that clustered around her, picking the ground as if she were throwing out handfuls of feed. Cherish remained on the porch, waiting to hear whatever it was her friend was working through.

"I'm not psychic," Ellender finally said. The words were directed to the matriarch of the flock, a plump Buff Orpington named Lady Betty. "And I don't want to be labeled that way."

"Okay," Cherish said. She noticed Ellender's nod of acknowledgment went to the chicken.

"Today with Grace was different."

"How?"

"If I knew that, I wouldn't be scared, would I?" Ellender climbed the steps to the porch, followed by Betty and three of her coop mates. When she sat on the top step, Betty settled in her lap and glared at the others until they retreated to the yard.

"Could you ask her to lay a few eggs?"

"Sorry," Ellender said as she stroked the soft feathers. "Not in my skill set. But I do sense she'd prefer a private apartment and a cute rooster all to herself."

Cherish smiled with relief. She still didn't understand what had happened when Ellender touched Grace Reagan, but she was smiling now, and making chicken jokes, and that was enough for a while.

"I want to throw the cards for her," Ellender said when they went inside to make sandwiches.

"For Lady Betty?" Cherish teased.

"For Grace. Something's wrong and I'm supposed to tell her. Maybe. Or not."

The interior of the farmhouse had been opened up, and light came in from windows on three sides of the first floor. While Cherish made sandwiches and tea, Ellender pulled a small scarf-wrapped bundle from her backpack and sat in front of the fireplace. She laid the cards out on a coffee table and studied the spread before scooping the deck together and repeating the process. She was on the fourth round when Cherish handed her an avocado sandwich and chips.

"I thought you weren't supposed to keep trying until you got an answer you liked."

"I was looking for consistency and clarity," Ellender said with a sigh. "But Grace is a mess. Or her cards are, anyway. She's so close to term, I might be getting thoughts about the baby and not her, but I don't think so. There's a lot around those two right now."

"A lot like?"

"Cher*ish*."

"All right, I know better than to ask, but for the record, if you aren't the real deal, then how can what you feel about somebody be confidential? They're just your thoughts, after all."

"I don't gossip."

Cherish raised her eyebrows, and Ellender smiled.

"Okay. Busted. But talking about Grace doesn't seem right, which usually means whatever's wrong isn't something she'd want known." Ellender thought for a moment, then said, "Maybe that's why I can't sort her out. And if I really was a reader, I could." She took a bite of the sandwich, realized she was famished, and dug in.

Keeping the conversation light, Cherish said,

"We need to find a better word than reader, but 'feeler' sounds creepy. How about 'senser'? Although, that makes me think of a car part. Really, you give good advice. You also go a bit woo-woo sometimes, but that's okay, too. Let's come up with a slogan for that."

"Yeah, that'll sell well. Madam Ellender, Adviser and Feeler of Important Woo-woo Things."

"You're making light of your gift again," Cherish said, gently.

Ellender froze midchew, then slowly finished her sandwich. "You're the one with gifts," she eventually said. "I feel better. You know, I only follow where my instincts lead me. Most people would get more out of a professional counselor."

"Counselor! Perfect." Cherish refilled their teacups and pushed a plate of pecan cookies across the table.

"Maybe when I have my PhD. That's years away."

"And in the meantime, you're still helping people."

Ellender considered this. "I didn't help Grace. But then she didn't ask me to, did she? She's helping me. And speaking of which, I think I should take Tyler with me next time I go to see her. You don't mind, do you? It will be a sensory distraction for me, and if he hears what she has to say for himself, I won't have to argue with him later."

Cherish did mind, but she kept her opinion to herself, for once. Tyler Forester was an argument that she wouldn't win. Lately, there'd been signs that Ellender was growing tired of the manipulative jerk, and Cherish was determined to nurture that trend. But she'd have to be careful. Verity had loved him, and Ellender was bound to him by guilt. Trying to protect either sister had only ever resulted in Cherish being cut out of the picture.

They moved through the afternoon, Ellender slowly recovering from the morning's events while Cherish entertained her with the chickens, then plans for a new greenhouse, and finally a comedy on Netflix. It wasn't enough to make either of them happy, but it kept the bad dreams and bad luck at bay for a little while.

CHAPTER FIVE

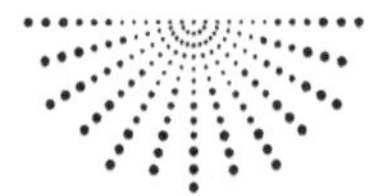

No one except his immediate family called Lee McNamara by his first name. To his colleagues in law enforcement, he was McNamara, Major, or Chief, depending on the rank and agency of the individual addressing him. To the rest of the world, he was just Mac. As he sat across from Grace while she described her morning, he wondered what her baby would call him. He doubted it would be the name he'd choose if he could get the stubborn woman he loved to listen to reason.

"It was bizarre," she said, describing Ellender York's reaction to their handshake.

The late lunch was just what she needed. She wasn't sure what to make of her new client's behavior, but as an orphan herself, she felt pulled to the young woman who'd lost her entire family in a short time frame. As usual, Mac was the perfect sounding board.

He reached across the table and took her hand in his. "Nope," he said after a second. "Don't feel a thing," but he gave her a smile that belied his words.

"That only proves you aren't psychic."

"And neither is Ellender York." He squeezed her fingers gently as she pulled away.

The crab cake sandwich was excellent and deserved her full attention, but that wasn't why she reclaimed her hand. They were eating outside at Morsels Cafe, and while there weren't many people around, Grace wasn't used to being romantic in public. Especially not when she was pregnant with another man's baby. For a woman whose life's work focused on getting her clients out of sticky situations, she seemed to stay mired in social quicksand.

"How did Marjorie react?" he asked.

"I sure you can guess."

As usual, he'd made her laugh, and the tension eased as she finished describing her morning. She'd learned early on in their relationship that Mac had once been married to Marjorie's sister,

Meri. In the years since Meri's death, The Bat had watched over her brother-in-law with a proprietary air. Now, she made it clear to one and all that she did not approve of Grace.

"So, can Ellender run that kind of business out of her home?" Mac asked.

She wasn't surprised to learn that he was familiar with the York family's story. Until two months ago, he'd been Mallard Bay's chief of police and knew almost everyone in Kingston County.

"I think so, but you tell me. Am I missing any salient details? What's the deal with those two families?"

He hesitated, then said, "I can fill you in on some local history, but later, okay?"

She knew he meant when they were alone, and it piqued her curiosity. Maybe he could tell her why Ellender's neighbor had a grudge. Or she could call Avril Oxley, her best friend and keeper of all local gossip. In her eighties and still involved in many civic groups, there wasn't anyone in town who was a stranger to Avril.

He moved on to a more neutral topic. "You haven't asked how I got free for a midweek lunch."

"I thought they changed your class schedule. Didn't we talk about that?"

There were too many bits of important information fighting for the small corner of her brain not occupied with pregnancy hormones, and she'd given up pretending otherwise. Mac's new job as an instructor with the Maryland State Police Academy had started last month, and she hadn't adjusted to having him on the western shore three days a week.

"Yes. Monday was switched for Tuesday, so I'll work three days in a row and have four off over the weekend."

"So, what are you doing here today?"

"I changed a few things around. I was in a rut for a long time, you know."

His eyes twinkled, and she relaxed. "Rut" was how he often described his life before they were together. "Sane" was the other word he used, but that was when they were arguing.

He finished the last of his shrimp salad and looked longingly at her french fries.

She pushed her plate toward him and said, "Eat. Save me from myself. We'll diet together after the baby comes."

"I'm fine." He smiled and added, "And you're perfect."

Pregnancy had her sniffling at every tender moment, as well as at puppies, pre-Christmas commercials, and diaper ads. He handed her an extra napkin and changed the subject by asking what she had planned for the afternoon.

"Shopping for the baby. Want to come with me?"

She had cut her schedule to half days, partly to keep Cyrus from worrying, but mostly because she'd been exhausted during the first months of the pregnancy. Now that her energy level was up, she had a long list of items to accomplish before her due date in December.

"I'd love to," he said with a smile of a man with a good excuse. "But I have another session with the town council. They've selected two candidates to fill the patrol position, but one's a slam dunk. We should be able to wrap things up and hire him today."

"Anybody local?"

"As local as they come. Tremaine Harper, Jeannie Harper's son."

"She's the baker at Three Pigs, right?"

He nodded. "Tremaine's just graduated from Salisbury University. The other candidate is a corporal in Frostburg PD looking for a change of scenery. She's well qualified, but the council members all know Tremaine."

"What does Tate say?" Grace asked. Tate Grassley, Mallard Bay's new chief of police, had served in the Maryland State Police like Mac, but that was the only similarity between the two men. Mac's career with the MSP had been long and successful. Tate's had ended after five years when he moved to Pennsylvania and joined a small county sheriff's office. So far, his transition to the Eastern Shore had been rocky.

When Mac didn't answer her immediately, she said, "Let me guess. He wants to hire the experienced officer who knows Maryland regulations. And I'll bet he'll hand over the foot patrols right away." The chief was a sore spot between them. Grace had taken an instant dislike to Grassley, and Mac refused to humor her.

"I could argue both positions, but I think it's going to be Tremaine."

"Good," she said. "Anybody raised on Jeannie's wonderful food would have to turn out well."

"Well and huge. Kid's six five." Mac asked a passing server for the bill. "I'll be free by four. If you're up for dinner, decide what you want and I'll have it ready when you get back."

"Nope. My turn. I'll surprise you with something marvelous."

"You do that every day." He stood and looked down at her, smiling again.

She grinned back at him, then quickly busied herself looking in her tote for the car keys that were clipped to the inside zipper. He'd kiss her if she gave him half a chance, and they'd already given the other diners enough entertainment.

CHAPTER SIX

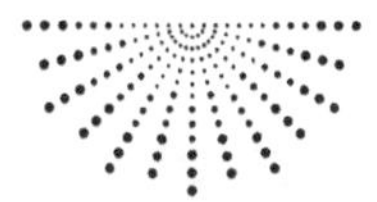

Delaney House was blessedly quiet when Grace returned. She'd intended to run in and change clothes before going shopping, but the temptation to sleep came over her when she reached her apartment on the third floor. This had been happening a lot lately. It seemed her bursts of energy were fueled by noonday naps.

So far, she'd refused all suggestions that she move to a lower floor until after the baby was born. David had even tried to give her an elevator, but when she'd finished laughing, she'd said no to that, too. While she agreed that as the baby's father, he had a right to express his opinions—as if she could stop him—she had no intention of letting him tear out two-hundred-year-old plaster ceilings and wainscoting. On days like this, though, a lift was a nice thought.

She'd just drifted off when someone opened the door to the sitting room. David didn't have a key, and Mac was too polite to come in without knocking. It had to be Niki.

"Oh, you're sleeping. Sorry."

Grace kept her eyes closed, hoping her cousin would leave. She felt the foot of the bed dip as Niki sat down.

"We need to talk."

"You're smarter than this," Grace said.

"Yeah, well, you're going to be mad anyway and it will only be worse if I wait."

The nap was gone, replaced by visions of the many things Niki might have done. Upfront confession wasn't her style, so this should be a doozy. Grace sat up and waited.

"I know you said not to rent this place out after this month, but I had to. Only one weekend, but it's important. It's a wedding. Our first wedding, Grace! And they're taking all of our rooms here and in my inn and the Queen's Brooke house, too. The profit from those three days will carry us until you let me reopen in February."

"The reopening is in April. Don't start."

"Oh, right," Niki agreed. "My mistake, but all

the more reason to make this wedding booking a success. All you have to do is stay with Mac for a few days."

Grace closed her eyes again.

"Or Avril." Niki's voice was taking on a hint of desperation. "That would give you quality time with Leo. You don't see the poor thing enough, anyway."

"We're talking about your deficiencies, not mine, and he's Avril's dog now, you'll recall. He's happier living with her, where no one rents out his bed. Besides, Avril's tied up with renovations to her rental house."

"But I'm sure Leo misses you. It would be fun, wouldn't it? Helping her pick out colors and . . . Please, Grace."

Grace narrowed her eyes. "When's the wedding?"

"Over Thanksgiving weekend." Niki didn't even try a sales pitch on this, but braced herself for the blast.

"A week before my due date? What if the baby's early?"

"You keep saying it's a girl, but you don't know. It might be a boy and they're always late."

Grace stared at the woman who was the closest thing she had to a sibling and wondered for the umpteenth time how they had emerged from the same gene pool.

"Come on, please. Let me do this. At Avril's you'll have Leo and at Mac's you'll have the man you love."

"And David would react so well to visiting his baby at my, my . . ." she stopped, anger and sarcasm coming to a screeching halt in front of embarrassment.

"Your lover's house. Say it, Grace," Niki grinned, apparently unaware how close she was to danger. "You and Mac are—"

"Stop. It."

"Well, what do you call yourselves? He'd call you 'wife' if you'd let him."

This was true, and they both knew it. Mac had made no secret of how he felt about Grace since the first time she'd let him kiss her. She, however, was still adjusting to the changes in her life. Her final breakup with David Farquar had taken two drama-filled years, with one reconciliation lasting just long enough for her to get pregnant. Transitioning from that lunacy to a happy love affair with a stable, kind man still seemed surreal. Each time they woke up in the same bed, she was shocked. Thrilled, but shocked. She hoped she got used to it before there was a bassinet in the room with them.

"Earth to Grace, you're smiling. Does that mean you'll stay with Mac?"

"Why do I have to go anywhere?" Grace demanded, refocusing on Niki. "It's three days. Assuming you don't have a sincere death wish and that's the only event you've booked, I'll lie low up here and let you handle the business downstairs."

"That won't work." Niki scooted back against the footboard, her nonchalant expression slipping. "They're taking all the rooms. Up here, too. This is going to be a bridal suite. You won't believe what they're paying for it."

"What? It's not enough you have the rest of my house, you've taken my apartment, too?" Grace could see Niki was on the brink of tears. What had happened while she wasn't paying attention? Not that she should have to pay attention. Delaney Inns, LLC, was Niki's operation; Grace was only a silent partner. A silent partner, major investor, and landlord who did not work in the business. And who never, ever, had her apartment rented out from under her. She waited, arms crossed over her suddenly very active baby.

"I didn't have a choice," Niki wailed. "I've spent their deposit and I can't give them a refund.

They were booked for April, but had to change the date. I don't have a choice."

"Sure you do. Tell them they lose their deposit. The language is clear in the rental agreement. I should know, I wrote it."

"No, I can't! I had to agree to the new date because I defaulted first, and this was the only way I could make it up to the bride. I struck the change penalty and agreed to have the wedding here over Thanksgiving. I tried to rent a room for you at the Egret, but they're full. Nobody has vacancies in Easton, Oxford, or St. Michaels, either."

"How did you default?" Grace asked, refusing to be sidetracked by Niki's feeble attempt to compensate her.

"Well, you know about the little snafu this morning. It was an expensive breakfast, and I screwed it up."

Grace groaned. "The witch who took my head off is the Thanksgiving bride?"

Niki only nodded, but her point was made.

After a moment, Grace said, "Call and tell her that the new date has caused a problem, but you have a solution. At least three of the rooms are set up for double occupancies. Have two of the bridesmaids share and give the bride the large room for free. Tell her it comes with Champagne and a chocolate basket."

"But Grace, if you have the baby early—I can't have a crying baby in the house."

"Oh, don't worry," Grace said as she got up and eased her swollen feet into a pair of flip-flops. "I'll just cross my legs and refuse to deliver until December. Simple."

"But, Grace—"

"And my child will be perfect and never cry." She stopped at the doorway and looked back at Niki, who flung herself across the bed and put a pillow over her head. "I should have tried this sooner. It's so freeing, living in La La Land."

She knew she'd have to come to terms with living in an inn eventually, but she didn't have to do it now.

CHAPTER SEVEN

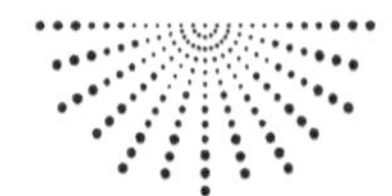

Thinking if she couldn't sleep, she may as well be productive, Grace ran a few errands, then stopped at Baldy's Market for dinner ingredients. She'd decided on sautéed rockfish, new potatoes, and a salad, then killed time picking out a pot of geraniums for Mac's kitchen window. It would be her first stamp on his home, and small as it was, the gesture seemed momentous.

Fifteen minutes later, she stood on his front porch, fingering the key he'd given her months ago. She'd never used it, and now she felt ridiculous.

Put it in the lock. Open the door. Go in and cook dinner.

Cross your legs and refuse to give birth until your due date.

One goal was as impossible as the other.

She'd promised him dinner. She shouldn't be late with it because she couldn't make herself open his door. But the key in her hand could unlock permanency. It could be a commitment on training wheels, taking her down the path to forever. Forever in another woman's house. If she unlocked the door and cooked in his kitchen, she'd be stepping into Meri McNamara's place and she wouldn't measure up.

Go in or go home.

The sound of tires on the oyster-shell driveway saved her from deciding, and she said a prayer of thanks that Mac would never know she had almost run away.

"You brought the food and flowers. Let me cook," he said as he unloaded the groceries.

"No," she insisted as she looked for the perfect spot for the geraniums. Why hadn't she remembered that a monster-sized aloe plant took up the entire window? She put the pot on the kitchen table and said, "Have a drink and relax. My cooking is every bit as good as yours." They both knew that wasn't true. "And don't open that." She snatched a white bakery box from him. "I have a surprise for you."

The slow smile that lit his face made her flush.

He said, "There was a time when those words would have had us eating at midnight."

"We'll be able to go back to that before long." She tried not to panic and hoped he still thought the wait for a post-pregnancy love life was worth it. After the baby arrived, midnight dinners would be for three and probably noisy. What *did* he see in her?

Before she could come up with something else to worry about, he wrapped her up in his arms and whispered, "Please. Please say yes." His warm breath tickled her ear and made her shiver.

This was her biggest fear of all—that he'd propose, and her life would go from stressful to impossible. She was on a tightrope as it was. Adding a new marriage to the turmoil was un-thinkable. "Mac." She tried to push away.

He tightened his hold and whispered again, "Please . . ."

"Mac—"

"Please let me cook dinner."

The surprise, a chocolate cake, was excellent,

as was the dinner he prepared. They ate out on the patio, relishing one of the last warm evenings of the year. The swing glider was comfortable and the clear night sky was lit with stars and a sliver of a rising moon. Grace thought if she could stay right here, just as they were, she could spend forever with this man.

He was the only person she knew who loved a companionable silence as much as she did, but eventually the mood slipped away. He told her about the interviews, and the council's decision to hire the local rookie instead of the experienced officer the new chief wanted. She told him about Niki's booking disaster.

"Stay over tonight," he said, pulling her closer and kissing her hair. "Call it a trial run for Thanksgiving."

Panic threatened again. This was a frequent conversation. She said, "I can't."

"Grace. Honey, I'll be good, I promise. No more cooking jokes, either."

She wanted to focus on the positive. She'd never felt less attractive and here he was, obviously in love with her, and all he wanted was for her to spend the night.

"I can't stay. I don't have anything with me."

"You don't need anything," he replied, and the matter was settled.

~

DAYBREAK CAME WITH THE REALITY OF RUMPLED clothes, teeth brushed with her finger and his toothpaste, and no makeup. He brought her coffee and told her she was beautiful.

"You're blind," she said and kissed him.

"Still lucky, though." He looked at his watch. "But that'll end soon. I promised to go in and talk Tate off a ledge. He's taking the rejection of his hiring plan pretty hard."

She pushed aside her dislike for Tate Grassley and said, "Did the council treat you that way? Overrule you on staff and management of the department, I mean."

"The town didn't have a police force when they hired me. Mallard Bay used to be the sheriff's jurisdiction."

"I didn't know that."

"And to answer your question, no, they never overturned any decisions of mine that I can recall, but they did insist I hire Aidan. Same deal, local boy who wanted to be a police officer and needed a job."

"I was thinking about him yesterday. Do you miss him?"

Mac's smile turned thoughtful. "Surprisingly, yes, I do. He was a thorn in my side, but I was used to him. I think he made the right decision to leave. Law enforcement wasn't the job for him, and I'm glad he found something that he likes. Has Niki seen him?"

Aidan Banks and Niki had been a couple since junior high, but the relationship ended last spring at the same time Aidan turned in his badge and left the department.

"No," she said. "Not that she's told me, anyway. She did say she's heard through friends that he's doing well in his new job and has a place over in Towson. Who'd have thought he had the training to be an IT tech?"

"I did, and I should have encouraged it. We talk every week or so, usually by text. He seems happy enough. He's not complaining at any rate."

"That in itself is a miracle. Speaking of local kids, you were going to tell me about Ellender York. It would help to have some background on her and the neighbor."

His smile faded. "I knew her parents pretty well. Nice folks. Both raised here, went off to school and careers, then came back, maybe twenty-five years or so ago. The mother, Ellen, died of breast cancer, the same type as Meri's."

They were in the kitchen — Meri's kitchen — and Grace thought the room shrank a little at his mention of his wife's name. She tried desperately to think of something appropriate to say, but settled for a murmur of sympathy, hoping he'd take it as a blanket expression for both women. Meri Mc-Namara was a saint in her husband's eyes and was remembered fondly throughout the community. Since Grace and Mac had become a couple in the juiciest romantic scandal to hit Mallard Bay in years, it seemed everyone liked to reminisce about Meri within Grace's hearing.

"Did you know about the father and older daughter dying, too?" she asked, shamelessly redirecting him.

Mac, who seemed oblivious to her insecurities, said, "Yes, a car accident. Ellender was driving."

"That's awful," Grace gasped.

Mac nodded. "That's just the headline. The details are worse. I was the first responder at the scene."

"Oh, Mac."

He let her hug him and kissed the top of her head before continuing. "It happened out at Fulton

Road and Route 23. A deer ran out in front of them and she swerved. Hit a tree. Verity York was thrown from the car and killed. Their father, Hank, was strapped in, but the impact was on his side and he died instantly. Verity's boyfriend was seriously injured." He paused, then added, "It was gruesome, as you might expect, and Ellender saw it all. She had only minor injuries and recovered physically, but I've heard she has problems."

She nodded. "And some people aren't helping."

"That would be the lovely Mrs. Judge Wilkens," Mac said dryly. He picked up his keys and jacket. "And before you tell me not to be sexist, she insists on being called that."

"Good grief! How old is she?"

"It's not her age, it's the entitlement. If you wanted a happy client, you took the wrong case."

She wanted details, but he was out the door, and she had to get home. The rest of the story on Mrs. Judge and Ellender would have to wait.

CHAPTER EIGHT

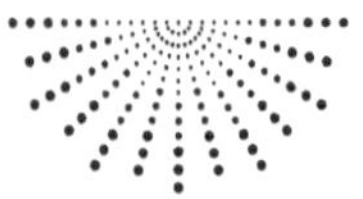

Evenings with Grace always put a smile on Mac's face and took decades off his heart. When it was right, it was perfect, and when it wasn't, he wanted her, anyway. When he was angry and she was contrary, there was still a part of him that was happy. Happy to be alive again.

There was a price to pay for his new life, though, and it was steep. On the professional side, giving up the job of chief of police was harder than he'd expected. He could handle that, but the personal complications were more troubling. It was becoming clear to him that Grace had a problem with his house. It was hard not to bring it up. Every time she was there, she looked miserable.

A McNamara from one branch of the family or other had lived on the high side of the Wye River in the same general location for almost three hundred years. Their houses rose and fell over the centuries, shifting as the river itself changed. The current sturdy waterman's cottage had come to him through his parents' estate, and since the morning he and Meri walked through the front door as its owners, he'd never wanted to leave. Living with Grace would make him happy, but leaving his house would be hard. Maybe impossible.

When he thought about renting it out, his mind went right to a list of instructions for the tenants. Then five minutes later, he would decide that anyone who agreed to the level of care he wanted would have to have a maintenance firm on speed dial. The idea of strangers in his home didn't sit well, and wouldn't solve the real problem, anyway.

Grace didn't like his house, but would moving help? At what point would she stop wondering which things had been Meri's, and just be happy to live with him? He wouldn't erase his memories of a twenty-year marriage, even if it was possible. His life with Meri had shaped him and would always be in his heart. If

Grace loved him, she'd have to accept him and his past.

If she loved him.

No new answers presented themselves, so he turned his thoughts to the unpleasant task ahead. His problems could wait until he'd sorted Tate Grassley.

He didn't want to intercede, but Ruby Blanchard, Mallard Bay's mayor, had asked him to talk to the unhappy police chief. Mac liked Ruby. She and the other two council members worked well together, and with the small town staff of two police officers and a part-time town manager. At least, that's how it was during his tenure. Mac had advised the council against hiring Grassley. He'd kept up with his former classmate and knew that despite the charismatic glad-handing, Grassley had never been on anyone's team but his own. Nonetheless, the retired deputy sheriff talked his way into the job. As Ruby put it, the town had lost its entire police force when he and Aidan Banks resigned. They couldn't pass up the chance to have an experienced officer step into the chief's position.

Mac pointed out that a lackluster career in Pennsylvania didn't indicate experience that would be useful in Mallard Bay, but the council was unanimous after Grassley's first interview. He had done his homework and sailed through the process without exposing his less desirable character traits. The new chief was in place before Mac had cleared out his office.

And now he was on his way to mediate an impasse between the town council and his replacement. He'd known he'd be in this position eventually, but he'd thought Grassley's snow job would take longer to melt.

~

THEIR BREAKFAST MEETING WAS INFORMAL. MAC brought a box of Jeannie Harper's still-warm donuts from Three Pigs Deli and tried to ignore the clutter that had taken over his old office in the short time he'd been gone.

Around a mouthful of sugar glaze, Grassley said, "They wanted me for my experience, Mac. They need to trust me, but I can't even hire my own people? What the hell?"

So, it was a power struggle, Mac thought. That persistent part of Grassley's personality hadn't taken long to emerge. He surveyed the donuts as he said, "Tremaine Harper's a local kid, Tate. The council knows him and his family. He's got a degree in Criminal Justice—"

"Which will do me no good whatsoever. I need someone trained and with skills. Maria Doren is perfect. She'd hit the ground running and I like her. She's a hard worker. But the important thing is, she's my pick. I'm not here to play teacher for a kid who doesn't know his ass from his elbow."

Mac decided his donut ruse was a failure and closed the box. "I've told you this isn't the same as the MSP or a sheriff's department. Here, you do what your oath requires, and you also do what the council asks. If the two conflict, then you take a stand on the oath. But in ten years, that never happened to me."

"So, you just jumped at whatever stupid idea the elected officials came up with?"

Mac refused to take the bait. "I didn't go into it thinking they would have stupid ideas." The office was a small space, and it was heating up fast, but he resisted the temptation to open the door.

"Okay, I get it." Grassley leaned back in his chair so far that the frame squeaked in protest.

Mac tried not to wince. The chair was practically new. He'd supplemented the department budget with his own funds to buy it when the one he'd used for years had finally fallen apart.

Grassley grinned and pushed back another squeaky inch. "No way you took crap from them, so tell me how you did it. Ruby's the key, isn't she?"

Mac sighed. There was no use pretending he didn't understand what Grassley meant, they'd known each other too long. But he ignored the comment, anyway. "The mayor has no more power than the others, Tate. They're a team, she's the titular head, only." He immediately regretted his choice of words as Grassley's laughter bounced off the walls. "You work for all three of them," he added, louder than necessary.

"Got it. Thanks, man. This has been a blast, but I gotta go on patrol." Grassley rolled his eyes and stood. "Some of us are still real cops." His cell chimed, and he answered the call with a hearty, "Hey, pretty lady. What a nice surprise. I'm on my way. Be there in a sec."

Mac, smarting from the "real cop" jab, nearly missed the woman's last words before she disconnected the call.

"Just so you know, I've got friends here, too," Grassley said. "I'll be fine and the council will come around. But I sure appreciate all your help."

He turned the phone to display the screen where the caller's name was visible. Natalie Wilkens.

"You always did work fast." Mac stood and put out his hand, adding, "No hard feelings."

"Sure thing," Grassley agreed. And for the first time since they'd met more than thirty years before, he didn't try to crush Mac's hand with a viselike grip.

The restraint bothered Mac more than their conversation. An opponent who could change tactics midfight was far more dangerous than one you could read. He left his former office with two new bits of information. Grassley had a well-planned agenda, and whatever his endgame was, it sounded like he'd already picked up a powerful ally.

To Mac's knowledge, Mrs. Judge Wilkens never socialized without an agenda of her own. He couldn't imagine what Tate and Natalie had in common, but her last words had been, "You're late!"

Late for what?

CHAPTER NINE

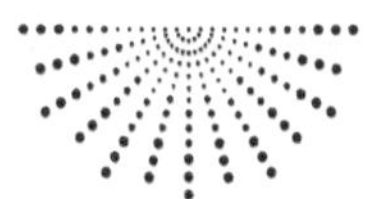

A shower and shampoo in her own bathroom set things to right, but now Grace felt guilty for wanting to escape Meri McNamara's home. Mac had done absolutely nothing to make her feel this way, which made it worse.

Attacking her wet hair with a towel, she blotted and rubbed as if she could scrub away her negative thinking. Then, faced with a tangled mess, she overdid the leave-in conditioner and ended up on the verge of needing another wash. Twenty minutes with the dryer, ten more twisting and pinning a chignon that required half a can of hair spray, and she was officially late. All because she'd fiddled around worrying about a nice woman who'd been dead for years.

It was in this fine mood that she discovered none of her maternity tunics were clean and only her least favorite slacks were back from the cleaner. She had to settle for a belly-hugging tank top and a linen jacket that showcased rather than covered her middle. She told Sweet Pea to look sharp and tried to be grateful that her black flats still fit.

Unfortunately, the shoes were the last good thing to happen for a while. At the office she had to deal with an irate Marjorie, a missing Jake, and a cranky boss.

Grace ignored The Bat and couldn't do anything about Jake staying home with a sick child, but she was ready to square off with Mosley.

"I'm taking the York case," he said. "You stay on the Stedman contract." He was calling her from the golf course, and geese were squawking in the background. "I need to go. Can't hear a thing."

"Don't hang up!" Grace raised her voice. "I finished Stedman last week. It's all signed and processed. York won't take any time. I'm just going to look into a couple of things and write a letter to Malcolm Steinlen."

"Not a good idea. Mal Steinlen is no light-weight, Grace—"

"Neither am I," she interrupted, patience exhausted. He couldn't agree or disagree with that statement without insulting her, and she mentally dared him to respond.

But Mosley had been dealing with the women in Grace's family for over fifty years, and he had some skills of his own.

"I know you could take him out with one hand tied behind your back," he said. "What I was about to say was that Mal won't stop until his client is satisfied. Now, I've had a long acquaintance with Mrs. Judge Wilkens—she prefers to be called that, you know. Anyway, she won't stop until she gets her way. You'd do well to remember that small towns have long memories, and from one source or another, I know about most of Natalie Wilkens's grudges. I will handle this. Now, I must go, m'dear, I'm up."

Squawking and honking burst out of the phone before the line went dead, leaving Grace fuming and determined that she wouldn't give Ellender over to a lawyer who wasn't even working.

She picked up a stack of documents Marjorie had left on her desk, put them on Jake's, then stopped. She rarely came into the cramped room that had once been Lily's office, but even if she had, she wouldn't have noticed the photograph angled so that only Jake, sitting at the desk, could see it. Lily's face beamed from the plain gold frame. Why would Jake keep it? She pushed the uncomfortable thought away with a mental vow to check in with Lily. It had been too long.

She told Marjorie she would be out for a while and left. Ellender's house was only a half mile away, and she wanted to check out the neighborhood where her client was causing such a stir. It was a beautiful sunny day, and she enjoyed the autumn sunshine, relaxing as she walked.

Americus Street ran parallel to the northern end of the harbor. Number 303 sat in the middle of a block lined with nineteenth-century homes, most with water views. She strolled along the park side of the street, hoping to look like an admiring tourist, but she saw a lace panel being pulled aside in the window of 301. Someone in the Wilkens house was watching her.

She walked slowly, but soon passed the two properties. At the next corner, she turned, and then turned again when she reached the alley that ran behind the houses. She studied the rear of the York property, but saw nothing remarkable. A car started up and a black Suburban emerged from the gravel parking area behind the Wilkens house. The tinted windows hid the driver's face, but Mallard Bay was a small town. Grace knew who was at the wheel.

~

Malcolm Steinlen took her call and sounded genuinely sympathetic to Ellender's situation. He did not, however, hold out any hope of a compromise with his client. Instead, he described a long-running feud between the Yorks and Natalie Wilkens that even the deaths of Ellender's family hadn't ended.

"An Eastern Shore replay of the Hatfields and McCoys, Ms. Reagan," he said. "Only very polite in public."

Grace was surprised at the off-hand remark. Steinlen admitted that his client's motive was a vendetta, something he'd undoubtedly deny in court, but which was useful to her, nonetheless.

"How does Ms. York's business affect Mrs. Wilkens or her property?" she asked.

"My client is a widow who lives alone. She has chronic health issues that are exacerbated by the stress caused by Ms. York's actions. They share a driveway that spans both property lines. Ms. York's friends, and presumably, clients, frequently block Mrs. Wilkens's car, and the noise from the York house disturbs her."

"Noisy cards?" Grace kept her voice light while making her point. "My client's version of events is quite different, Mr. Steinlen."

"I'm sure it is. I've been down this road with these two families before. Sometimes we win, sometimes we lose, but Mrs. Wilkens never backs down. Occasionally, she gets bored and drops an issue, but this time, she's especially determined. She doesn't want a business activity taking place in the house next to her. Public persona is very important to her, and she believes the, shall we say, *mystical* aspect of Ellender's business is offensive."

"The mystical aspect?"

"The fortune-telling enterprise Ms. York is conducting."

"Anything else?"

"Mrs. Wilkens has been intimidated by a gentleman who is a frequent visitor at the York home."

Tyler Forester. Grace asked for details and wasn't surprised to hear that he and Natalie Wilkens frequently clashed.

"I can certainly talk to my client about Mr.

Forester," she said. "And about keeping the driveway clear."

Steinlen chuckled, then said, "I appreciate your optimism. However, you're relatively new to the area and you are definitely new to this situation. Please understand, I say that not to be disrespectful or dismissive, it's just a statement of fact."

"It is also a fact that Ms. York is acting within her rights."

"I'll talk to Mrs. Wilkens," Steinlen said in an amiable tone, "but I don't expect her to agree to drop her complaints."

And she didn't. A brief letter appeared in Grace's email two hours later. Mrs. Wilkens wanted the fortune-telling business to stop, and she would continue legal action until it did.

An hour's worth of research and a call to the zoning office gave her the answers she expected.

CHAPTER TEN

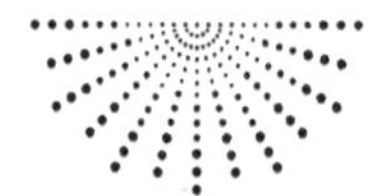

"But I'm not violating the zoning for our neighborhood," Ellender York insisted.

Cherish was missing today, and in her place was Tyler Forester. Grace could see why Jake had assumed the fidgety Tyler was Ellender's boyfriend. From holding her hand as he limped into the office, to draping his arm around the back of her chair, the slender young man with tousled hair maintained a consistent hold on her.

Grace broke the news that Natalie Wilkens's attorney was now referring to Ellender's business as a fortune-telling enterprise. Tyler argued each point, even though no one was disagreeing with him.

"You're getting all worked up," Ellender said.

She reached out and tapped Forester's knee to still the foot he'd been jiggling for the last five minutes. "Take a breath, dude."

"How did you start the business?" Grace asked.

"Both my mother and her mother read cards for the family and friends. So, I grew up with it. Since college, I've worked in a shop called Spice and Spirits over in Chestertown. It's just what it sounds like, all kinds of tea and spices and other items related to spiritual healing and manifestation. When I told the owners I knew tarot, they offered me a chance to do readings in the store. I soon had a lot of repeat clients, and I made enough money to give up the sales job. They still send me referrals. That's why I don't advertise. And because I don't, I'm in compliance with the zoning."

"Advertising isn't necessary because you're that good," Tyler said. To Grace he added, "Don't call her a psychic, she doesn't like it, but it's the best way to describe her."

"No, it isn't, and I've asked you not to say that." There was a warning tone in Ellender's voice. "No wonder Natalie calls me a fortune-teller."

"How would you describe what you do?" Grace asked.

"I took a course in college on personality types, and a subsection was about empathic traits. That resonated with me, so that's how I label my work. I sense things and I enjoy helping clients unravel their problems. Most people only want someone to listen to them. What I do isn't unusual, or new. A hundred years ago it was nothing to have your cards, or tea leaves, or palm read."

"You're special. You see things other people don't," Tyler insisted. "You have a gift."

"What I have," Ellender said, "is an active imagination and the ability to read people. I'm not psychic."

Grace thought Tyler would drag Ellender into his lap if they were alone. Ellender apparently felt the same way because she gave him a not-so-subtle poke with her elbow before continuing to explain herself.

"I don't want to do it forever, just a few more months. On my birthday in February, I'll receive the rest of the money from my father's will. I have an allowance now because I'm in graduate school, but it isn't enough to cover my expenses. If I could stay in my house and do readings until I inherit, it would be perfect. After that, I can move without having to worry about money."

"You wouldn't want to move at all if Natalie would shut up." Tyler picked up her hand and intertwined their fingers. "We've talked about this. Your parents wouldn't give in to that old bitch. They always stood up to her. She'd never bother you if your mom and dad were still alive."

"Well, they aren't." Ellender yanked her hand back.

Grace wanted to applaud, but her client wasn't finished.

"They're all dead, Tyler, and I'm the only one left. I'm doing what I believe is right, and you aren't helping."

He finally moved away, folding his arms with a petulant sigh. "Fine. I get it. I'm not your family. You don't want me."

"Again. Not helping."

"If I may?" Grace interrupted, regaining Ellender's attention.

Tyler's left foot resumed jiggling as if dislodging fire ants.

"Your property and that of Mrs. Wilkens have a special condition tied to the deeds, an easement that allows you to share a driveway. If you directed your clients to park in the alley behind your house, that would be one problem solved."

"I can do that." Ellender sent Tyler a sideways look that said, *Don't start.*

Grace repeated the neighbor's objections, cutting Tyler off when he began to argue. "Her societal prejudices don't carry any legal weight, but I believe you both have plenty of experience with her intractable nature? According to her attorney, she will not change her mind or compromise. And Mrs. Wilkens says she feels threatened by you, Tyler."

Ellender seemed to deflate, but Tyler reared back as if he'd been slapped.

"Me threaten her? I should sue her! She's the one—"

"Stop it," Ellender said. "This is my consultation, and I want you to wait outside for me."

Grace noticed the limp was more pronounced as Tyler huffed his way out of the office.

Once the door closed behind him, Ellender continued. "I'm afraid Mr. Steinlen is right. Natalie hates Tyler and me. She hated my whole family."

"Do you know why?"

"No. My mother always brushed it off, and my father never seemed to care. He worked a lot and wasn't home most of the time. Besides, the judge was nice. Natalie's such an unhappy person. I wish I could help her as a gift to him. That's how I try to use whatever talent I have. I like to help people be happy. None of us have as much time left as we think we do. I'd give anything to talk to Mom and Dad about this."

Grace knew what it was to need parents you would never see again. "I can argue that you're free to invite anyone you like into your home, and that you aren't breaking any laws with the readings."

"Good!" Ellender said. "Let's go with that. It can't hurt to try, and it'll give me some time to figure out what to do."

"You can see clients in a professional sense," Grace said, easing into the bad news. "But you can't run a commercial operation out of your house. You don't have a business license and you don't advertise, so it will be hard for her to prove you're in violation. But it's a fine line because the law was written for accountants and insurance agents and other licensed professionals. The wording is vague enough, in my opinion, to cover what you do. Obviously, Mrs. Wilkens disagrees and a sympathetic judge might side with her."

Ellender's face fell. "You believe I should stop, don't you?"

Grace nodded. "You'll save yourself legal fees and headaches if you do. You're moving soon, anyway."

"I only want to go on as I am for another four months," Ellender said. "Until my birthday."

Grace tried to refocus the conversation. "How old do you think Mrs. Wilkens is?"

"Old." Ellender shrugged. "I don't know exactly."

"Well, I do. She's sixty. She's been in that house for twenty years and is unlikely to move anytime soon. She's willing to fund a legal battle, and she has influence and support in the community. And, for whatever reason, she really dislikes you and Tyler."

Ellender mumbled something that might have been, "Who doesn't?"

"I sorry I can't be more positive, but if she has been hounding your family for years, won't she pick another fight even if you stop the readings? We can fight if you insist, but do you really want to keep doing this?"

"I agree with Tyler," Ellender said with a sigh. "It isn't fair, and the idea of just rolling over and giving in makes me sick. I don't want to move for any reason other than to get away from her. She's made me hate my home. Hate this town. Knowing she has friends of any kind, let alone ones who are influenced by her, is infuriating. She was so mean to Verity and Mom and me."

Grace said, "I'll write the letter to Malcolm Steinlen, but you'll need to decide what you want me to say."

Ellender would not be rushed, but eventually she said, "Tell Natalie she wins. I won't do tarot readings from my house. I'll go back to working out of the store and clients' homes until the will is settled."

It felt awkward to advise her client not to pursue her rights, but Grace knew she'd given the best advice under the odd circumstances. Natalie Wilkens had no incentive to drop her crusade.

And there was the added complication Grace had discovered on her walk. The black Suburban she'd seen leaving the secluded parking area behind the Wilkens house was the personal car of the chief of police. She didn't know how Tate Grassley fit into the picture, but she didn't think he'd be on Ellender's side.

CHAPTER ELEVEN

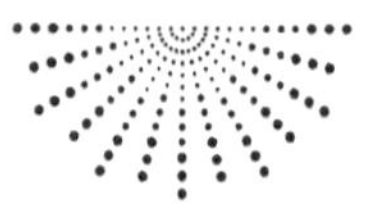

Ellender's decision had immediate repercussions. Her first reading in a client's home was nerve racking, even though Gemma Garfield was happy to have the personalized service. They were alone in Gemma's bright town house, but photographs, paintings and sculptures of cats were everywhere, and Ellender imagined she heard an occasional mewling from the ornate china urns on the fireplace. Ordinarily, she could block such distractions, but she was tired and so stressed it was difficult to concentrate. Cherish had been right when she asked about the dreams. Ellender was in the middle of a cycle of particularly bad ones, and they made her thinking scattered and dark.

"I told myself I'd know when it was time to sell," Gemma said, twisting a tissue in her hands and showering her dark slacks with bits of lint. "But this offer came out of the blue. I don't think these people understand anything about running a restaurant and they aren't local. They're offering more than the business is worth. I should accept it and give them the keys today, but that place has been my life since . . ." she stopped and looked embarrassed.

"It's fine," Ellender said, reaching over to pat Gemma's hand. She maintained contact for a few seconds longer than necessary, but felt nothing. *Idiot*, she chastised herself. There was no spark. The incident with Grace Reagan was a one-off, she decided. Just her always active imagination on overdrive with nervous energy.

She realized Gemma was waiting for her to finish her sentence. "It's okay to say it. You've owned the restaurant since my father died."

Gemma gave her a sad smile. "Well, I was going to say, since I bought it from you. I've put everything I own into it, including my heart. Handing it over to strangers after only two years is hard. I don't feel like I've finished with it, but I am tired. And it's a lot of money."

"Let's see what the cards say." Ellender shuffled the oversized colorful deck, then offered it to Gemma to cut before laying the top four cards out in a row.

"Well?" Gemma prompted. She'd scooted to the edge of her chair and was leaning over the cards on her dining room table.

Ellender glanced at a painting of a slightly cross-eyed tabby and lost the faint train of thought she'd gotten when laying the cards down. She made herself focus. "Actually, this is pretty clear," she said, trying not to sound relieved. "The Ten of Cups signifies your satisfaction with the outcome of your decision. The Two of Pentacles indicates it will be a favorable financial transaction, and I usually see the Eight of Cups when there's going to be a change or move."

"And this one? The Queen of Pentacles? Is it bad that she's upside down?"

"No, but it is curious. The other three cards point to a successful outcome for a sale, but the woman you're dealing with might cause some problems or delays. Or she may only be someone you don't feel at ease with. Still, the reading overall is positive."

Gemma frowned. "Positive, how? Are you saying I shouldn't sell, or that the wife will be hard to deal with, but I should do it, anyway?"

Ellender was irritated with herself for not having Gemma rephrase the question into a specific scenario with a yes or no answer. She really was off-stride today. Scooping up the cards, she said, "Let's try this again. You shuffle and deal, but this time ask if you should go through with the sale."

She watched the woman awkwardly handle the cards and helped her interpret the spread. She was sure the restaurant would be sold, and that pleased her. The business her parents built would benefit from the sale, and so would Gemma; but it wasn't Ellender's decision. She relaxed and let her client talk, becoming animated as new ideas occurred to her.

Some days, she loved her work. And she didn't dream in the daytime.

"I don't understand why you didn't tell the lawyer to sue her."

Tyler had been on the same topic since she'd come home to find him unloading the ingredients for tikka masala onto her kitchen table. She should take back the key Verity had given him, or change the locks. She winced, thinking of the scene that would ensue with either move.

She said, "Did you just come over to yell at me, or to ask me to make curry for you?" When she took the key back, she'd work on cutting out their dinners. Lately, she'd thought Natalie wasn't the only bully in her life.

"I can cook, El," he said, the bluster instantly gone, a lopsided smile in its place. "You tell me what to do and I'll give it a go. It'll be fun."

This was the cute boy her sister loved. Had loved. The one who always included Ellender, making her laugh and treating her as an equal when she was twelve and impossibly awkward. Sticking beside her even now, when what she wanted most was to be free from him and the sadness he wore like a second skin.

She pretended it was all a joke. "Don't be silly. Masala sounds great. Open that wine while I get things started."

It didn't take him long to return to the subject of Natalie Wilkens. By the time the curry was ready to be ladled over fragrant basmati rice, he'd replayed every unpleasant thing her neighbor had done recently. Everything he knew about, anyway.

She didn't tell him that Natalie had caught up to her earlier in the day. Furious about an oil stain on the driveway, she'd followed Ellender to her car, yelling, "You have to take responsibility, Ellen!" It wasn't the first time the hateful woman had called Ellender by her mother's name.

"Are you dumping me?"

It took her a moment to respond. She was so used to blocking Tyler out, she sometimes forgot he was there. "Of course not," she said, giving him a smile and telling herself it wasn't a lie. Yet. "But I'm moving to Annapolis, and I'm leaving all this angst behind, so let's drop it, okay?"

"Angst, meaning me, right? I can tell that you're angry with me, because you're eating too much and that's your third glass of wine."

"Don't. Start."

This was their routine. All disagreements devolved into his disappointment in her. The first time he'd done it, she remembered the comments he'd had made about Verity's weight. Her beautiful sister had been tall and model thin, and he had discussed her assets as if she'd been a show dog. Teenage Ellender had thought it was romantic. She knew better now.

The rest of the meal passed quietly, Tyler pouting and Ellender finishing the bottle of wine. He left her with the dishes, which was unusual, and her immediate relief turned to worry when there was a delay before she heard his car engine start. She imagined him standing in the shared driveway, glaring at the Wilkens house. She hoped that was all he was doing.

She had to get away from him, and she had to do it without abandoning him. It was a loop that wouldn't close—the end wiping out the beginning, and the beginning rendering the end impossible. She didn't know what to do, and Tyler was getting worse.

CHAPTER TWELVE

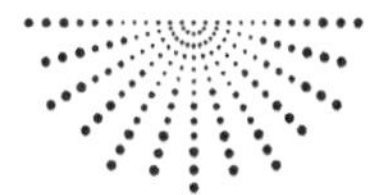

Tired of work and life in general, Grace wrapped up her half-day at the office and went to visit her dog. She still referred to the Chihuahua wannabe as hers, but the nervous and digestively challenged Leo wasn't a good fit for Niki's busy inn.

Leo and his best friend, a small German shepherd named Louise, met her at Avril's front door. For a few minutes, Grace let herself be ambushed by the only happy souls she'd seen since she'd left Mac that morning.

"What are you doing here?" Avril asked.

Grace found it difficult to get up from the floor after playing with the dogs. Her balance wasn't helped by Avril's bony fingers digging into her elbow. She said "Ow!" just as Avril asked if she was carrying twins.

When everyone was settled on the sunporch, the women in rockers and the dogs on their pillows, Avril repeated her questions.

"Yes, I'm sure it's only one big baby, and I didn't realize I had to have a reason to visit you," Grace said, then took a couple of deep breaths and reminded herself that Avril was only a little younger than Cyrus Mosley. The two old friends seemed to be in a race to see who could get crankier, faster.

"You know you don't," Avril said in a grudging tone.

Grace decided not to explore the reasons for Avril's bad mood, for fear she'd be expected to do something about it. "I missed you," she said. It was true. Hard to explain, but true.

Avril looked thoughtful. Eventually, she said, "It's not so bad here, is it?"

The rambling house needed a complete overhaul and a thorough cleaning. Avril hated polite lies, and Grace struggled for an answer. "I love this place," she said, neatly sidestepping the issue altogether.

"Exactly," Avril agreed, and fell quiet.

As Grace tried to work out what they'd been discussing, she watched Louise and Leo sleeping in the sunshine and felt peaceful for the first time all day. Her eyes grew heavy, and when she opened them again, the light had shifted away from the porch. She was alone, covered with an afghan, a small pillow tucked behind her head. Even Sweet Pea had cooperated, leaving her to sleep undisturbed.

She followed the mouthwatering smell of chicken soup and found Avril in the kitchen.

"Sit. Eat," Avril ordered, placing soup and a plate of warm corn bread in front of her suddenly ravenous guest.

"You cooked?"

"Of course not. I picked everything up at Three Pigs this morning."

A dish of sweet pickles and cheddar cheese cubes rounded out the feast. Grace ate and waited for whatever was coming. Avril was nervous, and that didn't happen often.

"I ran into Niki today," Avril said when the corn bread she'd been toying with had been reduced to mush.

Grace tried and failed to connect the dots, so

she didn't respond, helping herself to another bite of pickle and cheese instead. The wall clock, a plastic black cat whose tail served as a pendulum, said she was eating either a late lunch or early dinner.

"She told me about the Thanksgiving wedding," Avril continued, "and was actually wringing her hands. I gave her a piece of my mind."

"I knew something like that could happen when I agreed to let her open the inn," Grace said. "We'll figure it out." She finished eating and sighed with contentment.

"Well, she's messed up my plans. I wanted to have more done before I showed you Sweet Pea's gift, but I guess my surprise can't wait. Come with me."

They went down a short hallway to the rear of the house. The only time Grace had been in this section, it had been packed with cast-off furniture.

Avril opened a door to the first of three rooms and switched on the overhead light. "I hope you like it because it's a bribe."

Grace stepped inside and turned slowly, taking it all in. Freshly painted white walls were accented with yellow linen drapes and a creamy, thick carpet. A four-poster bed sat against the far wall, and next to it was a bassinet. A dresser topped with a changing station, a paddle-arm rocker, and an overstuffed armchair and ottoman finished the room. A large oil painting of yellow irises looked as if it had been commissioned just for this setting.

"But . . ." Grace stared at Avril. "Why . . ." She stopped again. "Why did you do this?" would sound ungrateful, especially when she wanted to cry with happiness. She'd been missing her mother more than usual, and this room was like a visit from Julia. It was exactly the decor she would have picked for her grandchild.

"You approve, then?"

Grace nodded, not trusting her voice.

"Now, I did all of this for me, so don't get all emotional." Avril pushed Grace's hug away, alarmed as she always was at any display of affection.

"You wanted a new bedroom with a bassinet?" Grace asked when she could talk.

"I certainly did. And an updated bathroom and the rest of this wing overhauled. These were rooms were Dad's office, and then Glenda's studio and gallery. They've both been gone a long time. I'm ready for someone else to have fun in here.

I'm hoping it will be Sweet Pea—and you, of course."

Grace choked up again. Avril rarely mentioned her father or the woman who had been the love of her life. Clearing out this space would have been hard.

"Knock that off," Avril said. "This is a happy place. The bassinet is temporary. The baby won't need it forever, but she'll always have a home here. You can stay, too, when you want, as long as you don't cramp our style."

"So that's your game." Grace laughed and wiped her eyes. "You have my dog and now you want my baby?"

"That child will need me for stability. And I need someone to pass my wisdom down to. Lord knows, you ignore everything I say." Avril fluffed an already plump pillow. "I modeled it on your nursery at Delaney House. The one Julia and Emma designed. The rooms are different sizes, but I think they have the same feel. The painting was done for that room, by the way."

That's why she'd felt her mother nearby, Grace thought. She inspected the signature in the lower right corner of the painting. "It's one of Glenda's! It's perfect. Beautiful and perfect, just like this room."

"Emma gave it back to us after Julia took you and left," Avril said. "We understood. Well, Glenda understood, and she explained it to me. Emma closed off the whole third floor, but she didn't want to lock the irises away."

"This room won't change," Grace said as she looked around. "Not like my nursery."

"No, it won't. It will always belong to your daughter."

"I might have a boy, you know."

"Not a chance. Now, let me show you what else I've done." An adjacent room had also been repainted and had new carpeting. Another had been cleared and awaited its transformation. "Whenever you need a place, or just want to get away, these are yours. You and Sweet Pea can come and go as you please."

A home, Grace thought. And not just one. She had Delaney House and now this suite, and Mac's cottage. She wasn't losing anything; she was being propelled forward. She only had to choose the direction.

"Well, don't stand there gawking," Avril barked and turned to leave. "Some of us have work to do."

With a start, Grace realized she was right.

"Give me ten more minutes," she said. "I want to talk to you about Judge Wilkens's widow."

~

AVRIL KNEW ELLENDER'S NEIGHBOR, BUT SHE didn't call her Mrs. Judge Wilkens. "Natalie's a hard worker for many of our community action committees, but she wants to be in charge and can go overboard unless somebody keeps a tight rein on her." She dug around in a bed of hostas that had been nervy enough to sprout weeds.

Grace sat on the front porch steps, throwing a ball for the dogs. "Have you ever heard her talk about the York family?"

"Her neighbors? Those poor people." Avril sat back on her heels and sighed, which immediately brought Louise to her side for ear scratches. "I knew the grandmother, Ellen's mother, Addy, very well. And, by extension, Ellen and her husband and girls. Little Ellender is the only one left. Her whole family gone within a few years."

"And how did Natalie get on with the Yorks?" Grace asked.

"They were friends in the years when Owen and Natalie were first married. Then something changed. Overnight, it seemed, Natalie was telling everyone that Ellen was rude and her girls were out of control. Addy refused to discuss the rift and told me not to mention it to Ellen. I tried to reason with Natalie, but it didn't help. It was a big blowup. Probably Natalie's true nature coming out after pretending to be nice for so long."

"How was it resolved?"

"It wasn't. Ellen was diagnosed with cancer, then passed away. A few months after that, Addy had a stroke, and she was gone. Natalie stopped the sniping during that horrible year, and for a good while afterward. Then, about four years ago, Owen had a heart attack and died, and she started up again, only worse. Still, Owen was a very popular and respected judge, so most people who knew him make allowances for her behavior." Avril's expression said she was not "most people."

"But?" Grace prompted.

"Natalie is prissy and pissy, and without Owen to reign her in, she can be unbearable. But she has a heart condition, or says she does, so nobody pushes her too far. And she donates money to all the town's fundraisers. Lots of money. People try to stay on her good side, but eventually, everyone seems to tick her off."

Avril pushed herself up on the handles of her kneeling bench and picked up the basket of weeds.

"I'm assuming if you're asking about the Wilkens-York feud, one of them has hired you to go after the other?"

Grace explained Ellender's tarot reading, curious to know what Avril, who involved herself in anything to do with Mallard Bay's historic district, would say.

"Everyone knows that." Avril said. "I have her read for me every other Tuesday."

"You?"

Avril glared at her. "Yes, *me*. The child needs money, and she likes my company. She's also quite insightful. Then there's the bonus of seeing Natalie's outraged face peeking out from behind those pretentious lace curtains when I leave. I usually race the engine before I pull out of the driveway just to make her jump."

"I thought you said she had a weak heart?"

"She claims she does, but who knows? She doesn't believe in doctors." Avril gave Grace an appraising look. "You are representing Ellender, aren't you?"

"Didn't she read that in your cards?" Grace asked as she got to her feet and brushed off her slacks.

"She asked me for a reference." Avril grinned at Grace's reaction. "I said you're a little slow to catch on sometimes, but once you do, you get with the program. I also told her you and Cy don't tolerate bullies. That was good enough for her."

Grace wondered how Avril would react when she learned Ellender wouldn't be seeing clients in her home anymore. It had been the right advice, the prudent thing to do, but it felt wrong. The bully had won.

CHAPTER THIRTEEN

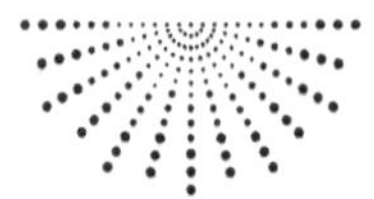

The sight of Mac's truck in her driveway made her smile. Then she saw David's Porsche sitting behind it, and any chance of a happy evening evaporated. Her lover and her baby's father were probably squared off in her house. She told Sweet Pea to cover her ears and went to see how close the men were to a fistfight.

She found them drinking beer and studying the ceiling in a corner of the front parlor. David was waving his phone around and talking about a six thousand pound load capacity. Mac was nodding and looking amused.

"There you are," Mac said when he saw her. "Niki let us in, but we haven't been here long."

Sometimes it seemed she'd known him forever. Her blood pressure eased back a bit. He'd let her know he didn't use his house key in front of David and that nothing of importance had happened between them. As if the beer hadn't been a clue.

"Hey, Babe," David said. He came to meet her and kissed her cheek.

Behind David's back, Mac grinned at her and tipped his bottle in a mock toast.

She smirked at him over David's shoulder. "Hi, yourself," she said when she pulled away. "I didn't know you were coming today."

It wasn't as if he lived across the street. His downtown DC condo was a solid two-hour drive on a Friday afternoon. And that was if the Bay Bridge traffic backup was moving. Grace had told him more than once that he was no longer welcome to show up without calling, but he'd absorbed her objections about as well as he accepted any information he didn't like. He'd ignored her. But he was also ignoring how she'd cut off their last conversation, so she let it go with the mild rebuke.

True to form, he didn't answer, telling her instead about a new type of elevator that would require only minor modifications to the floors and ceilings.

"No elevator, David."

"Look." He held his phone up to her and pointed to a series of measurements superimposed over a photo of the parlor. "See how small the footprint is? And your guests can use it to send their luggage upstairs. Even Niki loves the idea."

"Is she here?" Grace asked Mac, who seemed to find the question funny.

He said, "It's the oddest thing. She suddenly remembered an appointment in Easton. She gave us beer, though, and told us to help ourselves to the food in the fridge. She's been testing recipes again."

"And I'm starved," David said, and headed down the hall to the kitchen.

"Stop encouraging him!" Grace hissed at Mac as he stole a kiss.

"Just being polite." He winked, got another kiss, and added, "Besides, I'm hungry."

The men ate quiche and brioche and made a significant dent in the tray of mini-cheesecake squares. Grace sipped tea and tried to be patient as they discussed the Washington Football Team's chances for the playoffs, and David's latest win in court. When they showed no signs of winding down, she got a plate for herself.

"I had another reason for coming," David said when they'd polished off most of the food.

"Please, I don't want to argue anymore about the offer." She was tired, and even if he had been nice until now, he could change without warning.

David shook his head, as if amazed at her assumption. "No arguing, Babe. The buyers backed out. Want to guess why I'm not stressed?"

She wanted him gone, not a guessing game, but she knew the fastest way to get rid of him was to play along. "An offer came in that I don't know about?"

"Possibly. I told you the market will be down until spring at the least. Fortunately, I have a client who wants a getaway for his family. A place big enough that he can host corporate retreats, too, and write the expense off. He won't pay what we're asking, but it's time to move on. That's what you've been saying, right?"

Grace was sure there was more to it. She also knew details would be light while Mac was with them. She was so tired of arguing; she was ready to agree until he told her his client's budget.

"Are you kidding? We can't take that! It's five hundred thousand less than you paid for it."

"And I'll eat the loss," he said, as if they were discussing the eclair in his hand. "I want to move on, Grace." With a brief glance at Mac, he added, "Just like you have."

The words flew out before she could stop them. "You won't be the one eating a loss. It's a half-million less in the baby's trust fund." She knew she should be grateful that there would be a trust of any size, but none of this made sense.

He surprised her by not exploding. "I didn't do my homework when I bought it, okay? I overpaid, and there's no point in denying it. I can grab some goodwill from my client with this deal and you'll still get over three million in the bank. It's a direct sale, no agent, so we also save a bundle there."

She knew there was more to the deal, but he was throwing her own argument back at her. It was time to move on. She said, "If that's what you want to do, I'll accept the offer."

The smile on his face was one she hadn't seen in a very long time. But, being David, he couldn't stop with a single victory. He brought the elevator up again as he was leaving. "I had to take the measurements and check the second and third floor to make sure," he said as he pulled on his jacket. "But it should work. It's a straight shot from the front parlor to the landings for the upper staircases. Just think about it. I'll pay for every-thing and it should seriously up the value of this place. Who knows? It might attract a buyer, unless you intend to let Niki play innkeeper forever?"

It took ten more minutes of conversation, in which David continued to smile, cajole, and tease her before he cleared the driveway.

"What was that?" Mac asked when they were finally alone. "Or maybe I should say, *who* was that?"

"He is actually human," Grace said as she cleared away the plates. "But, you're right. He was putting on an act, so don't get used to it. He doesn't like either of us, no matter what he says. Although, I have to say, when he's genuinely happy, it looks the same as tonight's performance. David doesn't have a second gear."

"Would he really buy an elevator to keep you off the stairs?" He put food away as she loaded the dishwasher. "It would cost a fortune, and I can't imagine he could get it installed before the baby comes."

"Just shy of a hundred thousand," she said, then laughed at his expression. "I checked when he started talking about it. First, he offered to pay to convert the rear parlor into a bedroom and en suite. I said no to that, and he came up with the elevator idea."

"Is he printing money in the basement of that

law firm he runs? A hundred thousand here, a few million there?"

She'd thought a lot about David's motives for insisting on the elevator, but wasn't ready to share them. She could be wrong, and she didn't want to malign him unnecessarily. She and Mac would be dealing with David for the rest of their lives. The next few years would be especially rocky as they worked out co-parenting and visitation. She had grown up without a father and wanted more for her child. She had known, and once loved, David's rarely displayed tender side, and that gave her hope for his relationship with the baby.

"What are you smiling about?" Mac asked, handing her the last of the dishes. "Is he printing money?"

"I wouldn't be surprised." She leaned into his arms and kissed him. "I was thinking about Sweet Pea giving her dear old dad a run for his money."

"If it's a girl, he's a goner," he agreed.

"Well, boy or girl, this child can hold its own," Grace said, and rubbed her side. She'd thought "girl" from the first ultrasound, even though there wasn't much detail that early on. "I'll be thrilled with a boy, too. It's just . . ." She stopped, not wanting to voice her worries that a boy would have a harder time pleasing his demanding father.

For some reason, she felt sure a daughter could handle David. Instead, she said, "I'm hoping that not knowing the gender now will ease him into fatherhood. But, if he knew what to plan for, he'd have a head start on directing Sweet Pea's life."

Then she pushed David, and the problems that came with him, aside, and hugged Mac. She had enough worries without imagining sad phantom children.

"Want to help me up that long, dangerous staircase?" she asked.

"No guests on the second floor tonight?"

"Nope." She took his hand and pulled him along. "Niki has a full house tomorrow, though."

He stopped and reined her back into a kiss. "Stay the weekend with me, then?"

"I don't think—"

"It's going to be fine, Grace," he whispered, cuddling her closer. "You'll see."

She tried not to cringe. He couldn't know those were David's words—her consolation prize for giving in to his demands.

Only this was her Mac.

"Of course it will," she said, and hoped they were right.

CHAPTER FOURTEEN

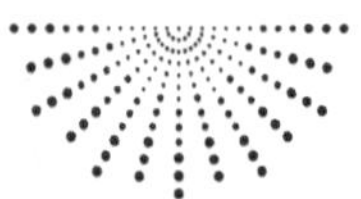

Saturday morning was a blur of bed making, dusting, and baking as Grace helped Niki ready Delaney House for its big weekend. Months ago, when Niki had explained how she would run two inns and a vacation rental home, Grace had missed the part about being the unpaid assistant in the grand production. Still, she had to admit that the inn was slowly making money, and eventually, she might see a return on her renovation investment. Niki promised to hire a housekeeper as soon as she was solvent.

Guests were checking in before Grace was free to slip out the kitchen door. She sat for a minute in the quiet of her car, luxuriating in the silence.

Sweet Pea gave her a thump as if to say, *You'll never be alone again.*

"Me and thee, lovie," she laughed and rubbed a sore spot under her ribs where a persistent little foot was trying to poke its way out.

She wasn't ready to start her weekend at Mac's house, and she didn't want to go into the office. It was another glorious fall day, and she drove out of town, taking one turn, then another, deeper into the countryside. Kingston County had four hundred miles of shoreline, much of it wooded, and all of it zigzagging like the torn edges of a pleated skirt. A lucky person with a boat and a lazy day to spend on the water would only see a fraction of the small coves and harbors as they wound their way along the inlets of the Wye River and Chesapeake Bay. A daydreaming woman in a car could wander for hours before re-alizing she was going in circles. Grace had done that often enough to become familiar with the area around Mallard Bay. Mostly. She could still get lost a mile from home.

As she drove, farms replaced houses and woods replaced farms until she reached the end of a gravel road, facing a broad expanse of water. She'd happened on this spot a few weeks ago and was pleased to have found it again so easily. As she had the first time, she found herself smiling as she studied the scenery. It was a peaceful place.

Exploring had become a hobby that somewhat appeased her travel lust. Her twenties and most of her thirties had been spent first in school and then in a high-pressure law firm, with the goal of seeing the world one fabulous trip at a time. She still had the travel dream, but whenever she pulled out a suitcase, either fate, bad timing, or her own ill-considered decisions derailed her. Now, any future trips would involve a baby pack. She was still determined to go, but it was getting harder to work out the details.

A storm had come through overnight, leaving the river water muddy and fast flowing. She let her thoughts roam and her body relax. The morning's activity and the warm sunshine made her sleepy. She wasn't far from Mac's house. He wouldn't be home yet, but she could let herself in and take a nap. There was nothing remotely feminine about his bedroom, and she could stay out of the kitchen until he arrived.

"Time to use his key," she said out loud, as if that would make it easier.

She might have done it, too, if her phone hadn't buzzed. Marjorie's strident voice woke her up, fast. Their conversation was short and followed by another call, this one from a hysterical Cherish. Naps and lazy daydreams vanished as Grace raced back to Mallard Bay.

Ellender York had been arrested.

WHEN MAC HAD BEEN MALLARD BAY'S CHIEF OF police, the two-room station had a comfortable, no-nonsense feel. Grace thought Tate Grassley and his new PFC dwarfed the small space. Her client looked childlike and scared in the crowded room that smelled of overheated men and fear.

After identifying herself as Ellender's attorney, Grace said, "First things first, gentlemen. Can we get some air in here?"

"Okay," Grassley said, dragging the word out to let her know what he thought of the request. "But the AC went off October first. New budget priorities." He nodded at Harper, who hurried to open a window and set up a box fan.

Grace had heard that Grassley had been critical of the department he'd inherited from Mac. Since she had a client who needed his goodwill, she pushed those thoughts aside and thanked Tremaine.

"What's my client charged with?" Grace asked

when the air was moving and she could breathe again.

"Resisting arrest and assault." Grassley didn't waste words. "We responded to a noise complaint, observed apparent illegal drug use, and arrested Ms. York after she refused to cooperate and became combative."

"None of that is true!" Ellender cried.

There were no interview rooms, so Grace had to agree to be locked in a narrow cell with her client in order to talk to her without the officers looming over them. When the front door shut behind the men, Ellender burst into tears. Through sobs and hiccups, she described how Grassley had pushed his way into her house, disrupting a small gathering of friends. Once inside, he yelled at everyone before walking through each room. When she protested, he arrested her.

"I was holding sage when I answered the door," Ellender sobbed. "I swear to you, I don't use marijuana and I didn't have any. I had a bundle of dried sage that I was using for blessings. It didn't look anything like a cigarette! The other people who were there will confirm it. They all tried to tell Chief Grassley what it was, but he was awful. Looking back, I'm surprised that I was the only one he arrested."

"But marijuana? Why would he say you had it if you didn't?"

"One of my friends had picked up a pound of dried sage for me at Trader Joe's. I make smudge bundles and give them to my clients when I read for them. A pound looks like a lot, and that's what the chief and Tremaine saw on the coffee table. He eventually admitted he was wrong, but only after he threatened my friends and broke up the meeting. What he said about us making noise is completely bogus. The loudest thing we did was recite a prayer for peace and understanding. It's that kind of group."

The idea of police officers breaking up a prayer group was appalling. Grace asked what else had happened, sure she was missing an important detail. Ellender insisted the group had only been talking, and just before Grassley and Harper showed up, they were praying.

"Did you resist arrest?" Grace asked.

"No." Ellender straightened and wiped her eyes. "That man is harassing me on Natalie Wilkens's instructions and I want you to make them stop."

It took the remaining few minutes she had to persuade Ellender to stop arguing with Grassley. It could only make things worse. Once he and

Harper returned, both women were released from the cell. Grace took this as a hopeful sign and asked him to remove the handcuffs on Ellender.

"Sorry," Grassley said. "It's protocol unless she's in the cell. Would you prefer that?"

Grace didn't bother to hide her surprise at the antagonism in his voice. "Chief, my client was leading a prayer group—"

He rolled his eyes and cut her off. "We received a tip that she was having a loud party. When we arrived, she was holding what appeared to be a smoldering marijuana cigarette. We could see a large amount of what we believed to be marijuana on a table in the room behind her. After ascertaining that she owned the house, we asked to search the premises. She refused."

"Because we weren't doing anything wrong!" Ellender broke in.

Grassley continued as if she hadn't spoken. "She became belligerent when PFC Harper attempted to arrest her."

"All I did is ask you to leave!"

"Not how I remember it." Grassley remained unfazed.

Grace put a hand on Ellender's shoulder to stop the exchange. To Grassley, she said, "I find it hard to believe an officer of your experience couldn't tell the difference between marijuana and a bundle of cooking herbs." She reined herself in when she saw how much he was enjoying the argument. "You admitted to Ms. York that you knew it wasn't marijuana she was holding, yet you insisted on searching the house? Why?"

"I think she's confused about the way it all happened. I walked through the house—a visual search only, mind you, before I examined the material that looked like marijuana. I immediately admitted I was wrong."

"Where does the assault charge come in?" Grace asked.

He smiled and shook his head. "Oh, did I forget to explain that? Miss York was very unhappy there for a while and behaved rather badly. Then she resisted arrest for the disorderly conduct charge. Now, I would have let all that go, but she nearly broke Harper's arm when he had to restrain her. So now, she's also charged with assaulting a police officer. A felony, as I'm sure you know."

Tremaine Harper's shoes suddenly required his full attention.

"PFC," Grassley snapped. "Foot patrol, remember?" He turned to Grace, his smile gone. "Things have changed, Ms. Reagan. The good time you and Lee McNamara enjoyed in this office are over. We do real police work these days. Your client will be arraigned in District Court, and since it's late and a Saturday, she'll probably be held over until Monday. As long as she behaves herself, you might be able to bail her out then. Now, visitation is over, so you need to leave."

And nothing she said made any difference.

CHAPTER FIFTEEN

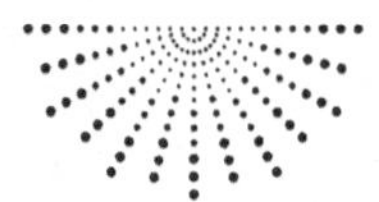

This wasn't the evening Mac had planned. The sensible thing to do would be to keep his mouth shut, but he was rarely sensible where Grace was concerned. He tried another version of "You did the best you could" and watched her continue to pace around the room as if he hadn't spoken.

They were in his den, supposedly enjoying the first fire of the season, but even the Monkey Shoulder he was drinking couldn't distract him from Grace's pent-up energy. An oak fire and excellent Scotch whisky were no match for a large, angry pregnant woman who wouldn't sit still.

"You don't have a nursery set up yet," he said, effectively drawing her full attention. Too late, he decided he could have lived with the pacing and silence. "Come, sit down and have your tea. Let junior rest."

She didn't sit, but she stopped moving. And glared at him. Giving in to the inevitable argument they were going to have, he said, "I get it, Grace. Grassley's a strutting ass. He's always been one, and he'll never change. I don't like him and it's mutual."

That wiped the scowl off her face. But now she regarded him with a more dangerous expression. One that said he was going to tell her everything.

"Why didn't you say something sooner, instead of defending him?" she demanded "You had to know he couldn't do your job. You've always stressed community policing, working with people, helping. This guy is the antithesis of your work ethic."

It was a conversation he'd known they'd have at some point. It was his turn to stand and pace. And since the den was small, she finally sat down.

"I don't like controversy," he said when he stopped by the fire to put his glass on the mantel. "I don't run from it. I just look for ways to fix whatever's causing the strife. Sometimes I can, sometimes I can't. When I can't, I have to decide if I can live with the situation the way it is and if the answer is no, I move on. I don't bang my head against brick walls."

He thought Grace had gone a bit pale. Against his better judgment, he kept talking. "People like Grassley are bent. There's something broken, or missing in them, and they're constantly looking for someone or something to blame. In Tate's case, I think it was his childhood, but that's neither here nor there. By all accounts, things worked out for him at a sheriff's department in upstate Pennsylvania. And he had good technical skills when he was in the MSP. He's smart, understands the criminal justice world, and is likable when he wants to be. He's well spoken and thinks fast on his feet. He and I were at the top of our MSP training class. I was number two. That's one reason why I know so much about him."

"That's quite a list of compliments for someone you don't like," Grace said, when he paused for a sip of scotch. "I read his resume. It doesn't match yours. Not even close."

Mac nodded and said, "I know. His career plans were derailed early on."

Grace gave up on her tea and settled into the corner of the couch. "Tell me."

Another finger of the Monkey Shoulder and

another log on the fire, then he joined her. Pulling her feet into his lap, he rubbed them gently and picked up the story.

"We'd been out of the academy for about five years and were following parallel paths. Tate was assigned to Hagerstown, and I was at Princess Anne. We were both at a conference in Ocean City and staying over a few days for training. The last night, a group of us went out for a drink at a bar on the boardwalk. Tate drank too much, made a pass at a woman, insulted her date, and nearly got himself killed. Some of us broke it up, but not fast enough to avoid the local cops. We might have been able to smooth things over, but Tate kept running his mouth. He wasn't arrested, but there was a police report and there were consequences. It set him back, mainly because it showed his supervisors that the jerk they had at work could become violent in his private life."

"Violent?" She frowned. "That's a strong word."

"It's the right word. No one who was there that night stood up for him with the brass. Which, especially in those days, was rare. I gave my statement in the investigation, but said as little as possible. I didn't want to be vindictive, but I couldn't lie, either. Others had no problem letting it all out.

Tate started the fight and was verbally abusive to the local officers. He was lucky to find a position in Pennsylvania and resign before he was kicked out of the MSP. We didn't see each other much after that, but I heard he made out okay in Singleton County."

"How much of this did you tell the council?"

As usual, she'd gone right to the point he didn't want to discuss.

"When Grassley applied here, there weren't a lot of candidates. I argued against hiring him, and I didn't mince words. But he can be a charmer, and he aced the interview. So, now he's here, and he's making friends, believe it or not."

"Not," Grace said firmly. "You didn't tell the council about the fight in Ocean City, did you?"

"It was a long time ago. People change."

"He's rude and crude, Mac, and the charges against Ellender are ridiculous bordering on misconduct. Couldn't you beat your head just a little on this particular brick wall?"

"Well, some things are worth the effort." He leaned over to kiss her, making sure she knew exactly what he was talking about. Then, straightening, he added, "Until now, Grassley wasn't one of them."

"Does that mean you'll help her?"

"I'll make a few calls."

~

MAC'S CALLS RESULTED IN ELLENDER'S RELEASE early on Sunday morning. The charges were still in place, but Grace was confident they wouldn't hold up, and went into the office to make sure of it. To her surprise, she found Mosley was already there.

"Tate Grassley is a piece of work," he said when she asked why he was working on a perfect golf day.

"Apparently his fan club is dwindling," Grace said. "What's he done to you?"

"I didn't say he was stupid. Not to be a braggart, but I don't think he'll attack someone of my position."

Grace couldn't remember a single time she'd ever heard him use the word *stupid,* or refer to his own social standing. "Okay then, who has he hurt? I mean besides Ellender."

Mosley didn't deny her assumption. "Jeannie Harper is a friend of mine, a fine person. She's raised a good young man. I encouraged Tremaine to look at the police academy, thinking he might be chief here one day. Now his career could be scarred by association with Grassley."

Grace sat back and studied her boss. He looked healthy enough, but was agitated. She never knew what would set the old guy off, so there was no point in guessing. "What happened, Cyrus?"

"Jeannie is worried because Tremaine is talking about leaving. The job and Mallard Bay. He says police work isn't what he thought it was and isn't for him. They're still paying for his undergraduate degree in criminal justice, and he's considering becoming a paramedic."

Grace thought about the dismissive way Grassley had spoken to the PFC. She was counting on Tremaine's testimony if they went to court. He'd known Ellender since nursery school, and had apologized to her during a brief period when Grassley was out of earshot.

"So," Mosley said, rocking back on his heels, thumbs hooked in the waistband of his khakis in Legal Warrior Pose, "first I'll get Miss York straight, then I'll handle Mr. Grassley."

Grace argued that Ellender was her client, but common sense told her that Mosley, who'd been practicing law and running local politics since her mother was a child, was the right person to take on the council and their new chief of police. She reminded herself that part of being a good attorney was knowing where to find the best resources. She wouldn't capitulate, but in her client's interests, she could share.

"I'll set up a meeting with Ellender," she said.

"Thank you, m'dear. Of course, you're welcome to assist as you feel able."

The Warrior left her office while she was looking for something to throw at him.

THEY WENT TO THE YORK HOME TO MEET WITH Ellender after she was released. The three of them sat in her dining room, while Tyler bobbed up and down, fetching a pitcher of tea and glasses, adjusting the thermostat, and getting a sweater for Ellender that she hadn't asked for and didn't want. Grace noticed he wasn't limping as he trotted around. When he tried to bring Ellender food, she snapped at him. This ended the irritating parade, but then they had a pouting Tyler at the end of the table.

Grace could see by Mosley's expression he didn't like Tyler's presence any better than she did.

And while Tyler was terse with Grace, he openly objected to the appearance of a second lawyer. Ellender ignored him and immediately agreed to adding Mosley to her legal team. She enquired after Grace's health, then latched on to her new lawyer and seemed relieved. Grace reminded herself it had been Cherish who'd made the initial appointment. Maybe Ellender was more comfortable with Mosley than a pregnant woman who looked as if she could pop any time.

Ellender's statement was essentially the same as the one she'd tearfully given Grace the day before. It took her longer to tell this time, because Tyler frequently interrupted her to give his opinion of the events, even though he hadn't been present when she was arrested.

"Nobody could believe she hurt that cop," he said. "I told the police I've found the Wilkens woman snooping around our property. I'm determined to keep Ellender safe, so I'll be staying here until this farce is over. No one will hassle her again."

"Tyler." Ellender drew his name out in a warning tone. "It's my property, and I live here alone. We've discussed this. I am fine."

"You call *that* fine?" He reached over and yanked the sleeve of her t-shirt up to reveal multiple fingerprint-shaped bruises on her upper arm. "I won't leave you and that's final."

Ellender pulled her sleeve down and said, "May I speak to you in the other room?" After excusing herself to Grace and Mosley, she left, trailed by a red-faced Tyler. Moments later, the kitchen door slammed with a force that likely brought Mrs. Judge Wilkens running to her window.

"There now," Ellender said as she reentered the room. "Where were we?" Her eyes were wet, but she seemed calmer.

"The bruises," Mosley said, as if nothing had happened. "How did you get them, m'dear?"

CHAPTER SIXTEEN

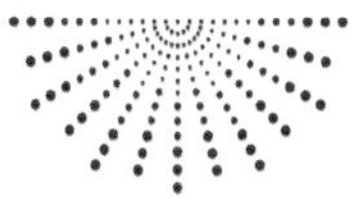

"I can't say for sure," Ellender began, then backed up. "I would tell you if I knew. The problem is, I bruise easily. The curse of a red-head's complexion, you know. I was out on Tyler's boat on Friday and I tripped and he caught my arm, but I don't remember which one. I also banged into the side of the boat when I was climbing out. I can be pretty clumsy. Some bruising might be from that. But Chief Grassley also held my arm really tight when he was putting me in the patrol car and getting me out. I told him he was hurting me, but he yelled at me to shut up." Her eyes welled again. "He actually said, 'Shut up.' No one's done that to me since forever."

"May I photograph the injury?" Grace asked, holding up her phone. She had to bite her tongue when Ellender checked with Mosley, who nodded his approval.

"I already took pictures, last night," Ellender said, then pulled up both sleeves to reveal rainbows of bruises.

Grace snapped a few shots and asked if there were any more.

After a second's hesitation, she said, "Only from the boat," and pulled her sleeves down.

"Why doesn't Mr. Forester want you to be here alone?" Mosley asked.

"Isn't that obvious? He thinks Grassley might come back. Plus, he doesn't always think clearly. He's not well."

"Is he a relative?"

They were getting off the topic of the arrest, and Grace expected her to balk at answering the question. But once again, their client surprised her.

Ellender shook her head. "Do you know about the car accident that killed my father and sister?"

Mosley's eyebrows rose, but he only said, "Why don't you tell us why that sad event is relevant?"

Ellender looked like she regretted raising the

subject, but after a moment, she got on with it. "Tyler and my sister, Verity, dated for years. That night was supposed to be special. Dad was treating Verity, Tyler, and me to dinner up on Kent Island. He'd gotten an offer for our restaurant—that's Adelaide's Garden, the restaurant he and Mom started. He wanted us to eat out and celebrate without having to work. I was the designated driver. Dad had way too much to drink, which was par for the course for him after Mom died. Verity kept him company. Matched him drink for drink. Tyler wanted to sit in back with her, so I drove. I should have stayed on Route 50, but I took the back roads to save time. We weren't far from here when a deer ran out in front of us. I tried to miss it, but I clipped it and lost control of the car. I hit a tree."

Grace and Mosley waited silently for Ellender to gather the rest of her story. When she began again, she was steady.

"They died. Dad and Verity. She was thrown out of the car. Tyler had a concussion, and a broken leg, but he still reached Verity and she died in his arms. When I say I owe Tyler, I mean it, but I need to move on with my life. We're having a hard time with that."

Mosley topped off their glasses of tea, giving

them all a chance to breathe. They still had to deal with the arrest, but Ellender went on with her story.

"Tyler's had two surgeries on his leg, but there's only so much they can do. His limp might be permanent and whenever I see it, I feel terrible."

"It was an accident," Grace said.

"Yes," Ellender agreed. "It was. But, one I could have avoided. I should have insisted on leaving earlier so we wouldn't be in that area at dusk, or refused to start the car until Verity buckled up. I could have paid attention to the road instead of arguing with Dad about getting drunk. I can't undo any of it, but I can look after Tyler."

"Look after him? How?" Mosley asked.

"He can't leave the accident behind us. He's on a lot of medication and sometimes I think it makes him worse, not better. I couldn't function for nearly a year. I just gave up. But even with all of his injuries, Tyler tried to take care of me. My father's attorney handled all the legal stuff and there were plenty of people around for a while, but then only Tyler and Cherish, and she was living in Belgium at that time. She flew home for the funerals and stayed with me for a few weeks, but eventually she had to leave. I was an adult, legally, but I was a mess and for a while, I let Tyler take over."

"Does he handle your money?"

Grace looked at Mosley in surprise. His abrupt question was past inappropriate and well into patronizing, but Ellender didn't seem to mind.

"No. My father made sure I could do that, myself. He insisted that Verity and I work in the family business and taught us how to handle our money. So, to answer your question, Tyler doesn't have access to my accounts. Every penny I've given him has been my decision, and it helped me sleep at night. A little, anyway."

Grace thought for a moment Mosley would ask how much Ellender had given Tyler, but he only frowned and leaned in when she continued.

"I didn't care about anything and he wanted to make all the decisions. It kept him busy and let me sit and vegetate. Which, I'm ashamed to say, is what I did for months. Then I began to get better. I'm not sure why, but one day, I got dressed and went to the grocery store. A week after that, I returned to work. Then, I started reading cards and helping other people, and that's saving me."

"And Mr. Forester?" Mosley prompted.

"My therapist says part of recovering is recognizing that we can't be fixed—not back to our old selves. We have to learn to live with what's here, now. I slip. A lot. Tyler doesn't even try anymore. He's still fighting reality, I guess. I don't know how else to describe him. Look, Mr. Mosley . . ." Ellender looked embarrassed, then plunged on. "I understand this conversation is confidential, so I'm okay with telling you whatever you want to know, but what does any of this have to do with my arrest? I'm strapped for money at the moment and I have two lawyers at my house on a Sunday. That's got to be expensive."

Grace was surprised to see Mosley smile.

"I'm sorry, m'dear. I should have put your mind at ease when we started. We're waiving our fees for this situation. Your arrest is an outrage and Chief Grassley's behavior will not go un-challenged."

Grace kept her face straight, but it was hard. What was going on? Her boss was waiving fees and going after the police? She'd never seen him so eager to climb on his white horse and ride into battle. Usually, she had to drag him, protesting every step of the way.

She interrupted Ellender's "I couldn't possibly" protest by asking, "Is it possible that Tyler's the one causing problems with Mrs. Wilkens?"

"He doesn't miss an opportunity to take a dig

at her," Ellender said. "But cause all this? No. He's only defending me."

"And you defend him," Mosley said.

"You don't understand what I did to him. His medical bills are handled by the insurance company, and he got a cash settlement, too. But none of it makes up for the pain and the limp, or the chunk of time he lost. And nothing will ever take Verity's place. He loved her and I ruined his life." Ellender waved away their sympathetic responses. "I'm handling it." She gave them a wan smile and added, "Except in the middle of the night, and what can you do about that?"

"Not much, m'dear," Mosley said. "Bad things happen, and sometimes we may feel like the one at fault, when we're only the catalyst. Your Mr. Forester needs to carry his own burdens."

"I've just made him whole financially, at least to the best of my ability. And I've let him believe he's like a brother to me, but that's gotten out of hand. Now, I'm trying to distance myself as gently as I can and I'm starting over in Annapolis."

"And that upsets him," Mosley prompted.

"It's why he's so angry with Natalie Wilkens. He knows she's one reason I'm leaving Mallard Bay. Not the only one, of course. I want a do-over on life. I guess Natalie is my catalyst." She nodded at Mosley. "If you can make this arrest disappear and keep Chief Grassley off my back, I'll manage everything else. In fact, I've already started."

Grace thought about this new information while Mosley asked for details on the party. Ellender gave them names of everyone present at the meeting on Saturday and assured them that all ten guests had already offered to give statements on her behalf. Tyler wasn't on the list.

"I invited him a couple of times," Ellender said, "but you may have noticed he gets bored easily. Quiet talk, sharing feelings, and praying aren't Tyler's idea of fun. Everyone in the group is a client of mine, and we mostly talked about my move to Annapolis and how to set up my readings there."

"When do you think you'll move?" Grace asked.

"The first of December." She smiled at their surprise. "Your advice made a big impact on me, Grace. When you asked me if I wanted to defeat Natalie at the expense of my own happiness, it gave me a new perspective. Natalie and Tyler are part of my past. They've impacted my life since I was a child and I want that to change. I'm tired of being sad."

Mosley shot Grace a look she couldn't interpret, and said, "That was a fast decision. Are you sure you'll be ready to leave your home in just a few weeks?"

"No," Ellender said. "I'll never be ready, but I have to do it, anyway. I'll start graduate school at UMD in College Park in the spring, but most of the classes are online and Annapolis is as close to the DC area as I want to get. I put in an application yesterday morning for an apartment that has a view of the Severn River. When the leasing agent called to tell me I got it, I was in jail. In jail! Me! I can't believe any of it happened. Natalie's worse than ever, and now she has the police helping her."

"I knew Judge Wilkens well," Mosley said. "And I've successfully dealt with his widow, although I don't believe she's very fond of me. Does she mention her husband, other than to trade on his status and good name?"

Grace said, "Cy, I think—" then stopped when he gave her a sharp glance, communicating his message without a word: *Be quiet.*

Ellender hesitated, then answered. "Not specifically, no. I've tried to make peace with her, but I shouldn't have bothered. She hates me, and everything I do makes it worse."

Mosley ended the session, telling Ellender he would take care of everything and not to worry. Grace thought they should all worry until they figured out what made Natalie Wilkens tick, but she kept her thoughts to herself. She wouldn't challenge him in front of a client, but she couldn't wait to hear his plan.

CHAPTER SEVENTEEN

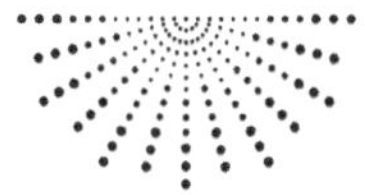

By midmorning on Monday, Mosley had effectively reversed the effects of Ellender's arrest. In the short time since they'd left their client, he'd talked to the Kingston County state's attorney and Mallard Bay's mayor. According to Mosley, the last interaction did the trick because Mayor Blanchard called Natalie Wilkens directly, then met with Chief Grassley.

"What is it with Mrs. Judge?" Grace asked. "How does one little widow . . ."

Mosley's laughter cut her off. "Careful. Your prejudices are showing. I also made the mistake of underestimating Natalie when I met her. She was quite a bit younger than Owen, but she propped up every area of his life, dragging him out into public and up the social ladder. He loved it. Most folks around here still view her as an extension of Owen, and he was well liked. When his health started deteriorating, she was very attentive and kept him on a healthy eating regimen. I'd take him out to get a steak when her back was turned." He looked nostalgic for a moment.

"I didn't realize you and Judge Wilkens were so close," Grace said. "Do you think Natalie could have a valid grievance with Ellender?"

But Mosley's attention had been diverted by an incoming call, which turned out to be a summons to the golf course for his Monday morning game. He was gone before she had her answer. She told herself it didn't matter, their client was exonerated, and that was the important thing. However, there was still the not-so-small matter of Tate Grassley. She wondered how he was reacting to Mosley's interference and felt sure they'd know before long.

GRACE HAD GROWN TO LIKE THE HALF DAY schedule at the office. Afternoons off and second breakfasts had crept into her routine when she wasn't looking. Ordinarily, such a loss of structure and discipline would bother her, but her life was different now. She recognized and welcomed her situation for what it was. Fate, Mother Nature, God—any or all of these had given her a gift, and she was determined to appreciate and enjoy it. Soon Sweet Pea would be a toddler, then a teenager, and then gone. But today they were together, and second breakfast was a warm lemon scone. She smiled, imagining the baby enjoying it as much as she was.

She reviewed her goals for the rest of the day. Another hour of work, and then she'd make a quick trip to Annapolis, get the stroller, take a look around Nordstrom's children's department, and be home before three. Plan set, she started in on the pile of paperwork Marjorie had placed in the middle of her desk.

Almost immediately, everything went awry. The extra-long buzz of the intercom told her Marjorie was upset. When she picked up the handset, she could hear voices in the background. A moment later, Ellender York was in her office holding out a small crystal vase with yellow roses.

"I wanted to thank you," Ellender said, but she seemed apprehensive.

"They're beautiful." Grace admired the flowers, but inwardly groaned as Ellender sat down.

There went her schedule. Which, she reminded herself, didn't matter as much in her new world order.

"I left some chocolates at the reception desk for Mr. Mosley," Ellender said. "Could you make sure he gets them?" She looked over her shoulder at the open door, then added, "I don't think Ms. Battsley likes me."

"I'll make sure," Grace said. "Thank you for the flowers, but—"

"There's more, it won't take long."

Grace tried not to let her irritation show.

Ellender reached out across Grace's desk. "May I hold your hands?"

"Why?" Grace asked.

"Please," Ellender said. "It's important."

As soon as they touched, the baby kicked. Hard. Grace yanked her hands away. "Stop it!"

Color flooded Ellender's cheeks. "I'm so sorry!"

"It's all right," Grace called out in a shaky voice. They'd come to an understanding about The Bat charging in at the first hint of raised voices, but she knew Marjorie was in the hallway, probably poised to call 911. Or wielding a pickax. She did enjoy a good fight.

"Oh, please listen to me," Ellender begged. "I

can explain. Well, not explain, exactly, but I have to tell you something." She looked sick. "I'm so sorry. I didn't know that would happen. I swear. But I think it's a warning."

"A warning." Grace cradled her abdomen. The baby was back to gentle thumps and stretches. "Let me see your hands."

Ellender complied, pushing her sleeves up and turning her hands over. "No buzzers or anything. It was just me. I've had little jolts once or twice when readings were intense, but nothing like that. What did you feel?"

Grace found it hard to speak civilly. "I suggest you stay away from pregnant women. That hurt." Her side ached where Sweet Pea had kicked out in response to Ellender's touch. Surely, such a thing wasn't possible?

"What I told you when we met is true. I'm not psychic and I'm not a con artist. I read people, and I can't describe it any other way. But what I experienced when I touched you the other day is new. And this," she gestured to Grace's side. "I've read for lots of pregnant women and I've never caused a baby to kick that way."

Grace felt a chill. "I didn't say the baby kicked. I said you hurt me." She remembered it had happened, to a lesser degree, when Ellender touched her hand for the first time. Sweet Pea had been so active that day, she hadn't noticed, but today the reaction was undeniable.

"I understand. I'm not trying to scare you, and I feel awful. But if I didn't warn you, I'd feel worse."

"Well, we can't have that, can we?" Grace snapped. Then, because Ellender looked so miserable, she added, "I'm not angry."

"Yes, you are. And not only with me. You're pushing your healthy emotions away, and allowing your anger to blind you to danger."

Grace's small reserve of patience evaporated. "This is ridiculous and we should end things right here. Mr. Mosley will handle anything you need from here on out."

"Yes, it is ridiculous," Ellender agreed. "I tell myself that all the time. But it happened. If I could take it back, I would."

"What are you talking about?" Grace asked uneasily.

"The connection we have. I had to be sure. I don't make this stuff up. I find myself worrying about you at odd times, and I'm positive it has to do with your baby. You should be careful. Your children will take care of you one day, but you're the only one who can handle the threat to them now."

"What threat?" Grace demanded. "You sound like a bad movie. And I'm only having one baby." She was angered in equal parts by the unsolicited psychic reading and the insinuation that she was big enough to deliver triplets. The gap she'd just noticed between the bottom two buttons of her tunic didn't help her mood.

"I'm not explaining this well," Ellender said. "I sense things sometimes and you've been on my mind. A lot. I like you and I'm worried about you."

Grace stood. It took all the self-control she had not to throw the melodramatic, baby-jolting, non-psychic out of her office. Taking care not to use the words *fraud* and *crap*, she thanked Ellender for her concern and crossed the room to the door. She wanted the freak show to end.

"I've upset you, and I'm sorry," Ellender said. "I usually make people feel better. All of this intensity is new to me, too. Please consider what I've said, even if you don't believe me. Be careful."

When she was alone in her office again, Grace tried to decide what Ellender York was after.

"Obviously, I don't know how to be careful,"

she said to no one, "or, I'd be in France right now."

~

"YOU SAID YOU WERE TAKING HER FLOWERS," Cherish said as she hugged Ellender. "I got here as quickly as I could. You sounded upset on the phone."

"I was." Ellender waved Cherish to a seat at the kitchen table. "I've made coffee. Can you deal, or do you want tea?"

"Lots of milk and sugar and I'll pretend it's a latte. Now what happened?"

"I screwed up, big-time." Ellender put a carton of cream on the table next to the sugar bowl. "I took her some of Mom's roses in that little Waterford vase that was Gran's, but I never got the chance to explain why they were special. I didn't finesse the situation at all. I asked to hold her hand, and the baby kicked her really hard. It scared both of us."

"You saw something was wrong? With the baby or with Grace?"

"I don't know! I only pay attention when I need to, Cherish. I listen, I'm observant, and I have a good memory and imagination. That's it.

That's why this business of zapping pregnant women is so upsetting. I *hurt* her. I might have hurt the baby. It's a wonder she didn't throw me out."

"It sounds as if she did."

"Not the way I would have if she'd done it to me. This is scary, Cherish. I think Grace is in trouble, but she doesn't believe me. I feel like such a faker sometimes. I try to be honest about what I do, but everyone wants more. And now that I actually am having some kind of sixth-sense experience, the person I need to help won't listen."

"You and Grace are a lot alike," Cherish said in a tentative tone. She didn't want Ellender to go off again. "You're both good at fixing other people, but you don't want anyone to help you."

Ellender started to argue, then stopped. Maybe she and Grace were alike. Readers and attorneys both helped solve problems, although she doubted Grace would agree with the comparison. Was this why she'd been worrying about a woman she'd known less than a week?

"This is lame," Cherish said, pushing her faux latte away.

"How about a Bloody Mary?" Ellender suggested. "Doesn't have to be five o'clock for that."

Cherish laughed, but Ellender didn't join in.

She fixed the drinks with a grim intensity she didn't bother to hide from her friend. Earlier, she'd wanted Cherish's company. Now she wanted to be alone.

She added another ounce of vodka to her glass. It was the only thing that helped.

CHAPTER EIGHTEEN

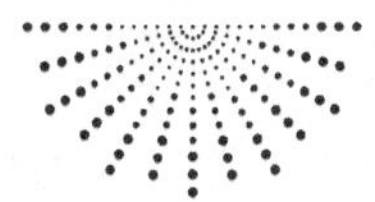

I t was a bad day when a call from David was a bright spot, but Grace thought anything that distracted her from Ellender York's visit was a blessing.

"I got it, Babe!" he said, excitement in his voice. "The offer I told you about. I just sent it to you."

Her email showed a message from "DFarquar" with an attachment. She felt her spirits lift. Selling the house would mean financial security for Sweet Pea and one less tie to David.

He said, "All I need is for you to sign the contract and we can settle next week. It's a cash deal and the title company will rush everything for me."

"What about the trust fund?"

He'd insisted on doing the paperwork and, although she could have handled it herself, she'd agreed to let him. After all, the house was in her name; she was selling it; the proceeds were hers; and she'd be the one to put the money in the account. To the extent possible, she was determined to limit his opportunities to manipulate either her or their child. In David's world, money was the best leverage there was.

"Way ahead of you," he said. "All done, just waiting for the sale."

"Wonderful. Shoot me a copy of that paperwork, too, and I can sign off on it today."

"It's all handled." His hearty facade was gone.

"But, I'm the trustee."

"Are you going to second-guess me every step of the way? I gave you the damned house."

So that was it. Whatever he wanted to keep from her was in the terms of the trust. From his reaction, she guessed he'd named himself as a trustee. Maybe the only trustee. She said, "I'm going home. I'll call you later."

When she got him off the phone, she opened the email with the purchase offer and gasped. The price had dropped another five hundred thousand. One million less than he'd paid.

Her first thought was he'd arranged a kickback. Two million to the trust and the balance of the purchase price to David. She discarded that idea immediately. He might lie to her, but he'd never violate his professional ethics. Which didn't mean he wasn't working a deal. She read through the entire document, looking for nonstandard language, or any way the contract's provisions could be manipulated, but found nothing. The agreement of sale was between Third Street Development, LLC, and Grace F. Reagan. Cash, no contingencies. The buyer didn't even ask for a home inspection.

Knowing she would set off a firestorm, she sent David a text. *What happened to the price?* She had to know.

His answer pinged back seconds later. *You blew the last offer. This is more than you have now.*

She sent everything to her home computer and packed up. There wouldn't be a nap today, and she wouldn't get to Annapolis. She had work to do.

Setting up the trust wasn't complicated. She soon had the basics in place, and she'd established the bank account with a transfer from her savings. There was only one trustee, and she was it. The low price for the waterfront property still bothered her, though, and she hadn't accepted the offer, despite several texts and calls from David—all of which she ignored.

"Why haven't you signed the contract?" he demanded, when she finally answered.

Mac had arrived a few minutes earlier. They were in the sitting room of her apartment and she'd been telling him about the trust and her dilemma over the price. David's voice was loud and sharp, and she knew Mac was hearing every word.

She said, "It's a big decision. The new offer was a shock and I've reconsidered." She wanted to hear how he'd argue his position. David never walked away from money without a very compelling reason.

He didn't respond.

"David? Are you there?"

"Yes, but not for much longer. I can't believe you're so greedy."

Mac straightened up. Grace tightened her grip on the phone, willing herself to listen to David's words, not his anger. She had to figure out what he was doing.

"I gave you a house," he shouted. "An *estate*! Three million, eight hundred thousand dollars delivered into your hands, and I didn't ask for anything in return. I suppose I should be grateful you gave the engagement ring back. Don't you want that to auction off to the highest bidder? You've made an interesting choice, Babe. Your police officer doesn't have the kind of money you like. I know because I've checked, and I'm guessing you have, too. Is that why you don't care if I lose a client?"

This was going nowhere. She said, "I don't understand why you want to give away a million dollars that belongs to our child."

"Because this is the client who will be a major source of the child support, which you'll no doubt be happy to take, so sign the contract, Grace!"

She disconnected. It was all she could do to face Mac and apologize for what he'd heard.

He looked as upset as she felt. "I'm not surprised," he said. I'll never understand what you saw in him."

She hated apologizing for David and said so. Loudly.

Mac didn't argue, and he didn't stay. She had a long evening to consider her future with the man she loved, and the other man she'd never be rid of.

As she moved around the apartment, randomly cleaning and rearranging the small space, Ellender York's warning wouldn't leave her alone. Was she allowing her anger to keep her from seeing some danger to the baby? Danger from whom? David? And what healthy emotions was she ignoring?

She tried to look at the warnings with a dispassionate eye. Why would Ellender make up such an outlandish story and scare a pregnant woman? The practical part of her brain said if her client would do that, she might also torment her paranoid neighbor. But no matter how she turned the pieces of her mental puzzle, nothing fit except her gut feeling that Ellender was the caring, kind person she appeared to be.

Which meant nothing good for Grace.

You're the only one who can handle the threat.

Maybe it was time she stopped obsessing over David's house, over David in general, and paid attention to what was important. "Let's go to bed and read that book on how not to be a neurotic mommy," she said to Sweet Pea. She didn't have to solve everything right now.

Soon, though.

~

GRASSLEY'S FAKE-HEARTY "HEY, BUDDY!" MADE Mac groan. He was already angry at himself for being so blunt with Grace, and he wanted to punch David Farquar. He didn't need to add to the heartburn blooming in his chest. None of this showed as he answered with equal insincerity. A minute later, he was turning his truck around and heading back toward town. He was tired and stressed, but curiosity still pushed him to hear what Grassley wanted to say face to face. If it was about his interference in Ellender York's arrest, they had to have it out sometime, and sooner was probably better than letting it fester like the fiasco in Ocean City. They would never be friends by any definition of the word, but they should come to an understanding.

Grassley had rented a small house near the southern edge of town. Porch lights and nearby streetlight bathed the plain facade of the run down rancher in harsh tones. He stood on the front steps, arms crossed, watching as Mac parked at the curb and walked across a scraggly lawn to join him.

"Glad you could make it." In worn, baggy jeans and a wrinkled shirt, Grassley didn't look like someone who wanted a social visit. Didn't smell like one, either.

Mac followed him into the nearly empty

house, regretting his decision to come. "I see you're settling in," he said when they reached the kitchen. At least this room was furnished.

Grassley pointed to a chair jammed between the table and refrigerator, and said, "Have a seat. I can get you water, bourbon, or both."

"Nothing, thanks."

"Not very sociable." Grassley added bourbon to a half-full glass sitting on the cracked tile counter and then peeled foil off a paper plate on the table. "Maybe a cookie's more your style these days. These are the worst damned things I've ever tasted, so please, be my guest."

"What's up?" Mac asked, already tired of the bad small talk. "Why'd you want to meet?"

Grassley took a cookie, bit into it, and made a face. "Natalie keeps practicing and I keep suffering. Can't hurt her feelings, though. She's all into that vegan, no taste, live miserable forever crap." He took one more bite and dumped the plate into the trash. Malice shone from his eyes.

It was a look Mac remembered from decades before. Grassley wanted a fight, and he was standing in front of the only exit from the room. Mac was caught in a corner, literally and figuratively. "You had something to tell me. I'm listening."

"Right. I'd give you a tour of the house, but it's a crap place. I won't be here long, though. No sense in unpacking. And don't get your hopes up. You're not getting your job back."

Mac decided to play along. "Moving?"

"Getting married soon. Natalie and me. That shocks you all to hell, doesn't it?"

"Not at all," Mac said. It was true. The notion of two of the nastiest people he knew in a romantic relationship didn't surprise him, but he couldn't wait to see Grace's reaction.

"Whatever. Nat's not well, Mac, and this crap with the girl next door isn't helping. Maybe I did jump the gun with her arrest. That's what the mayor says, anyway, and she got it on good authority."

Mac sighed. There was no avoiding it now. Maybe he should have accepted the bourbon. If he got drunk, too, Grassley might start to make sense. "I called you first, Tate, and tried to reason with you, remember? There was still time to turn it around, but you wouldn't listen. Hell, man, you broke up a prayer meeting in a private home. Over dried sage. In front of ten witnesses. Did you think no one was going to complain?"

Laughter was the last thing he expected.

"You should have seen her face," Grassley

said when he stopped and wiped his eyes. "I'm telling you, the little witch had it coming. And I mean witch. The kid's weird. Horror movie material. Talks to the dead, casts spells, she does it all. Natalie's afraid to come out of her house. I'll admit I enjoyed giving Miss York a taste of her own medicine."

Mac didn't believe Mrs. Judge Wilkens was afraid of anything. He could, however, easily understand someone trying to put a curse on her. Grassley's attitude was worrying, but not surprising. He hadn't changed much in thirty years.

"There's more," Grassley said, laughter gone and his features hard again. "The boyfriend threatens Nat whenever he sees her alone. She doesn't want me to do anything. Says the punk's spreading rumors about her and I'll only make it worse. But if you have any influence with him, you'd better use it. I won't let him hurt her."

Mac nodded and got to his feet. "I'm not sure what you want from me, but if I hear anything helpful, I'll let you know." He crossed the kitchen. "Right now, I need to get home."

"Nah, c'mon, man. A few more minutes. We've got real stuff to talk about."

"Not tonight." Then, thinking it couldn't hurt

to show some civility, he added, "I hope you and Natalie will be happy."

"We almost were, once. Remember Ocean City?"

So, they were going to do it all tonight.

"Well, well," Grassley said. "I can see you do. Here's the part you don't know. Nat and I were engaged back then, too, but after that weekend, she cut me off and went for a guy with better prospects. If you'd stood up for me, taken my side with the disciplinary board, it all would have gone away. She'd have never known what happened, and we'd be married today."

Mac weighed his words. The bourbon fumes that came with Grassley's speech reminded him of the futility in arguing with a drunk, especially one who's nursed a grudge for decades. He gave up trying to put the right spin on his words and just told the truth. "Nothing I could have said would have fixed what you did in the bar that night. I'm sorry things turned out the way they did for you, and I wish we'd cleared the air before this."

For the next ten minutes, he listened without interrupting while Grassley spewed a miserable tale of missed opportunities and thwarted love, all of which he claimed stemmed from the night in Ocean City when his friends had abandoned him.

Alcohol slurred the words, but his meaning was clear. He'd been cheated, and it was payback time.

"Here's what we're going to get straight, buddy. I had Natalie's problems all fixed up until you screwed things up. You made me look bad, and I won't let you ruin me again, understand? Keep your girlfriend and her client quiet. Think you can manage that? Let all the gossip die down so Nat and I can move on. It's the least you can do."

Mac judged the short distance to the door and his odds of getting out without answering. It wasn't happening. "I'm leaving," he started, then stopped when Grassley's mouth tightened. "Look, you're overestimating my influence in this town and with Grace. I don't tell her what to do."

Grassley stepped aside just enough to clear the doorway, but the space between them was thick with his animosity. "Then it's a good time to start. Tell her to leave Nat alone. They'd all better leave her alone."

It was a long walk to the front door.

CHAPTER NINETEEN

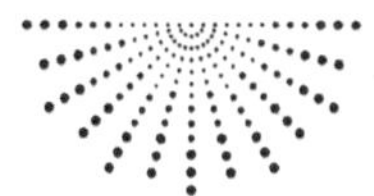

"They say if you eavesdrop, you never hear anything good about yourself. I'm sorry about how things ended yesterday. That was a conversation between the two of you. I shouldn't have listened."

Grace hoped Mac couldn't hear her sigh of relief. His call woke her on Tuesday morning, and that was a relief, too. It had been a long, restless night.

"You'd be surprised," she said, sitting up in bed and brushing her hair out of her eyes. "Sweet Pea says the nicest things about you when you aren't around."

His chuckle made her smile. "I'm on my way

to Reisterstown. I didn't want to leave for three days without talking to you."

That was Mac. Kind, but to the point.

"About last night?" she asked.

"We're not always going to agree, or be polite to each other, you know. And we'll be angry from time to time. We're humans, even if we're in love."

Her heart did something funny. She wanted to ask him to turn around and come home. She wanted to tell him she loved him, and that not seeing him would be awful, but he had moved on and was offering to meet her at the Annapolis Mall on Thursday evening to shop for the stroller and have dinner.

She agreed. Then, since he had time to get over it if she made him mad, she said, "Are you comfortable talking about the contract David wants me to accept?"

"Not my first choice of topics, but sure."

Relieved, she jumped into the questions that had worried her all night, or at least during the moments when she'd been able to forget Mac's hurt expression. "He says he overpaid for the house because inventory was low. But I've checked, and the list price is in line with comparable properties. I can't figure it out. Accepting a million dollars less makes no sense."

"You're looking at other houses for sale, but how long have they been on the market?"

"A while," she admitted. "I tried to set a lower price at the beginning, and he nearly took my head off. Now, he's done an about-face."

"You've always said he's all about money. Think about the lowest amount you'd be comfortable with. If you got that much, then paid the closing costs and agent's fees, how far off his client's net offer will you be?"

"Close to a half million, and it's Sweet Pea's money I'm giving away."

"If you're right about David working a deal, you might be returning his money to him," Mac said. "It could make things easier for you down the road."

"Then you wouldn't think I was enabling his awful behavior if I did what he wanted?"

"I believe you've made it clear that his behavior is not your fault. You're right. You spent years looking past his antics to maintain the peace, what's different this time?"

"It feels wrong. Expedient, but wrong. It feels like a mistake."

"Like a mistake, or like letting him win?"

She sighed. "If I knew that, I'd know what to do."

They discussed weekend plans and the knot in her stomach eased until he said, "I had a talk with Tate last night, at his insistence, actually. I need to fill you in, but it will take some time. Are you expecting to see him or Ellender York today?"

"No."

"Good. I'll call you tonight."

After they disconnected, she stayed in bed, her thoughts hopping between Mac and David, and then to her break with Ellender. She felt bad about her unprofessional behavior in the office, but over-sharing it all with Mac bothered her more.

"How much is the man supposed to put up with?" she asked the empty room.

WHILE SHE SAT IN THE OB-GYN'S WAITING ROOM with a half dozen other women in varying stages of pregnancy, Grace tried not to obsess over either Ellender's warning or David's demands. The doctor wiped away her concerns, assuring her that what she'd experienced when Ellender touched her wasn't so unusual.

"Some people just can't help themselves. They

feel compelled to give advice and warnings to pregnant women. I could write a book about it." Dr. Allyson laughed. "Baby may have picked that moment to shift around, or your emotions may have shaken things up in the nest. No harm done. And by the way, Baby's shifted. It's head down now, did you notice?"

"Is that good?" Grace asked anxiously.

Dr. Allyson smiled. "Depends on how you feel about more bathroom breaks."

"Oh, wow. I was afraid ten a day was all I'd get."

"It means you're getting ready to have the baby in a few weeks and we don't have to be concerned about a breech delivery. Are you sure you don't want to know the gender?"

Grace groaned as the nurse helped her sit up. "Let me guess. David called you again."

"Twice, but I don't return his calls anymore." Dr. Allyson waved off Grace's apology. "I've had to handle worse than him. Anyway, everything looks fine."

One worry off the list.

Take that, Ellender.

AN UNEVENTFUL DAY LET HER EMOTIONS SETTLE. Niki was out, and the house was empty when Mac rang that evening. She was glad they'd waited to have a video call so she could see him. She curled up on the love seat in her apartment and listened to him describe his day with the current class of State Police recruits. The best part was just watching him. The screen showed a calm, satisfied man describing work that pleased him. Everything about him made her feel good. When he turned the conversation to Tate Grassley and their meeting the night before, he became guarded. She knew he was omitting a lot of the details.

"I can't believe it," she said when he finished. "Tate and Natalie Wilkens."

"I knew you'd get a kick out of that. Can you imagine two more disagreeable people?"

"I'd rather not. I'm a mother now, you know."

"He insists they've been in love for years. Nearly got married once, but she backed out. Tate moved on and had a number of relationships."

"Relationships," Grace said. "Is that what he called them?"

"No," Mac admitted. "But that's not the point. He said he married twice, but was divorced both times because Natalie never let him go. They had an affair throughout most of her marriage to her first husband. When he died, Tate thought their time had come, but Natalie turned him down. Next thing he knew, she'd snared Owen Wilkens."

"And became Mrs. Judge."

"Exactly. When the council advertised my job, he decided to try again."

"For Natalie Wilkens," Grace repeated, surprise still in her voice. "But she's so . . ."

"Old?" Mac laughed. "She's only a couple of years older than Tate. And me."

"Not possible."

"She hasn't had a happy life."

"People with her kind of disposition usually do."

"According to Tate," Mac continued as if she hadn't interrupted, "she's got a good side. She loves him and even cooks for him. He says her food's terrible, though. Maybe that's why she always looks like she's just bitten into something sour."

Grace tried to adjust the mental image she'd held of Ellender's troublesome neighbor. "Well, I'm not looking forward to seeing them team up publicly."

"They already are a team of sorts. He says Ellender and her boyfriend intimidate Natalie. He also accused Ellender of using witchcraft." He waited through Grace's outraged protest then added, "And he claims the boyfriend threatens Natalie when he can catch her alone."

Grace thought about Tyler. Tate could be right about him.

"Here's the thing, Sweetheart. Tate's got a bad temper. He thinks you can control Ellender, and he has the really absurd idea that I can influence you."

"Wow, he is off base, isn't he?" She laughed, then thought about what Mac said. "You think he's after me, too?"

"I'm checking around, calling in some favors. He was drunk and blowing off steam last night, but I'm not taking any chances. If I hear anything to make me think he's a danger to you, we can decide how to handle it. In the meantime, could you humor me and stay away from him?"

She wanted to argue, but instead said, "I don't suppose you've told Cy all this, have you?"

"No. Should I?"

"He's insisting on being Ellender's sole attorney. I couldn't figure out why, but he might have the same concerns you do."

"I'll call him. I know it goes against your nature, and having Cy and me hover is probably irritating, but right now—"

She cut him off with a laugh. "I'll be careful and I'll avoid Tate. You talk with Cy. I've already agreed to give Ellender over to him, anyway. Just don't get used to this. I'm doing it for Sweet Pea."

They discussed dinner plans for Thursday. Then he asked if she'd decided what to do about David's house.

"Yes. But I want to sleep on it one more night."

He didn't ask what her decision was—yet another reason to love him. He trusted her to do the right thing, and he usually kept his opinions to himself until they were asked for. He was unlike any man she'd ever known and she often felt out of step.

Sometimes she thought she was learning how to be happy.

SHE'D LEFT ELLENDER'S FLOWERS OUT IN reception the day before, but when she arrived at the office, a huge vase of blue irises and pink roses sat in the same spot on her desk. She didn't have to open the card to know they were from David.

"Well, m'dear, whom have you bewitched to-day?" Mosley said as he walked in behind her.

"David's pulling a fast one and I don't know what he's up to," she said, as she read the card. *I'm sorry. Take your time.*

"Do you need to?" Mosley asked.

She looked up, startled. "Have you talked to Mac?"

"About David?" Mosley asked. "No. Why would I?"

Was the answer that obvious to everyone but her? Was she as blind as Ellen*d*er said? David had given her the house, and now he was asking for a favor. She'd been too suspicious to consider that simple point of view.

"That's better!" Mosley said. "I'll take that smile as a sign of an epiphany. Glad to be of help."

After he left for the golf course, she pulled up the contract offer for the house and read through it twice. "A bird in the hand," she said with a sigh and signed off on the sale. There would still be a generous trust fund, David would have a happy client, and Sweet Pea would have a happy father. Grace was sure one day she'd find out all the details, but today it wasn't worth the stress.

David's secretary emailed information for the

wire transfer of the sale proceeds into a bank account he had set up. Grace thanked her and deleted the message. There was no need to start that argument before she had to. They wouldn't go to settlement for another ten days.

She worked for three more hours, then went home, took a nap, and had dinner with Avril and Niki. By the end of an evening of laughter and dogs, she was tired in a good way and ready for bed. No histrionics, no threats, no warnings. Also, no men.

She didn't look at that last one too closely.

David was a no show over the next week. At first it made her nervous, but then other areas of her life filled the vacuum and for a little while, her ex-fiancé and his schemes slipped into the background.

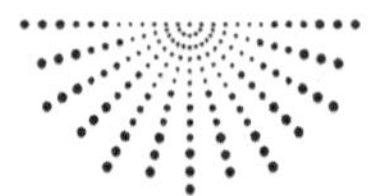

CHAPTER TWENTY

Grace could never be sure what she'd find at work from one morning to the next. With her half-day schedule and Jake ascending the throne as heir apparent of the firm, she was often left out of the loop. Wednesday morning's surprise was the chief of police, whom she found in the conference room that connected her office to Mosley's.

"Ah, Ms. Reagan." Tate Grassley rose and extended a hand, smiling as if their last meeting had never happened. "Nice to see you."

Grace was sure Marjorie had deliberately set her up. "What can I do for you?" she said as her entire hand disappeared into his grasp.

"Since you asked, we've gotten off to a poor

start. I need friends in this community and lately, all I've made are enemies. I'd like to apologize to you."

She studied him for a moment, remembering Mac's warning, but seeing no graceful way out of the situation. She motioned for him to sit and took a chair on the opposite side of the table. He looked pleased with her mild reaction. And that wouldn't do at all. When they were settled, she said, "Is your apology for how you treated Ellender York, or for insulting me?"

He continued to smile, as if she'd said something amusing. "Both, if you like. But, with all due respect, you weren't present at the arrest. It was the right call to make at the moment and I stand by it. However, although I acted within the boundaries of my authority, I could have been more flexible in dealing with Ms. York afterwards."

He did the insincere apology routine well. Grace suspected he got a lot of practice. Her promise to Mac forgotten, she said, "How would it work, this do-over? Will you leave Ellender York alone, or continue to do what Natalie Wilkens tells you to?"

His smile slipped. "That's not—"

"And will you still broadcast your opinion of

Lee McNamara and me, or will you be more flexible in dealing with us, too?"

"Well, now." He braced his arms on the table and leaned closer. The gilt on his badge caught the light, adding to his aura of power. "It was worth a try," he said, drawing each word out. "Now, I'll be blunt. I don't like you. I don't like your morals and I don't enjoy seeing a man I used to call my friend being used by you. But I'm willing to keep those feelings to myself. I should never have let emotions get the better of me when I dealt with your client. "

As if on cue, Marjorie appeared bearing a single mug of coffee and a plate of muffins. Without missing a beat, Grassley smiled up at her and said, "Aren't you an angel."

"I'm sorry it took so long." She was so cheerful, Grace knew she'd heard everything.

Without acknowledging Grace, let alone offering her any of the refreshments that now covered the table in front of Grassley, Marjorie aimed another huge smile in his direction and left.

"There, you've made a friend," Grace said as she got up and shut the door. Marjorie's performance had given her time to collect herself. And to put his words where they belonged—in the category of painful, but unimportant, things.

But he wasn't finished. "The York girl is terrorizing and maligning a fine woman, and so are you when you defend her. She and that Forester punk need to stay away from Mrs. Wilkens and keep their mouths shut. Is that clear enough, or do I have to be more specific?"

Seconds ticked by as they glared at each other over Marjorie's muffins and the fragrant coffee.

"You strike me as a practical woman," he finally said. "Practical and smart. We'll be better allies than adversaries, Ms. Reagan." He picked up a muffin. "How about you act like a professional and try to do what's best for the community."

"Sorry, I'm late." Mosley came in from his office. He nodded to Grace, then said, "Thank you for coming, Mr. Grassley."

The smirk on the chief's face disappeared. He hastily replaced the half-eaten muffin and brushed crumbs from his fingers. "Very pleased to see you, sir," he said as he rose to shake Mosley's hand. "It's been awhile."

Mosley waved toward Grassley's chair and said, "Sit. I'll wait for you to finish your food." His tone conveyed a command, not an invitation. He moved to sit next to Grace.

Grassley, who'd been left reaching awkwardly into space, said, "Well, sir—"

"Ms. Reagan will join us," Mosley said, cutting Grassley off as he turned to Grace. "Assuming, of course, that you have time before your conference call?"

She wanted to hug him. He'd put Grassley in his place, and she'd enjoyed every second. She made a show of checking her watch, then nodded.

"Good," Mosley said. "I asked him"—Grassley got a dismissive nod—"here today to clear the air regarding a few matters."

She kept a poker face, but was surprised. Cyrus had set up the meeting? Then she remembered he'd been the head of the citizens' interview committee who recommended Grassley's hiring. This was going to be fun.

Off balance, Grassley bobbed his head in agreement. "All right, I've apologized to Ms. Reagan, sir, and—"

"Apologized?" Mosley's tone was mild, with just the right note of confusion. "For what, exactly?"

Grassley looked at Grace, who only shrugged. She wanted to hear how he'd describe what he'd done. He couldn't know how much she'd told Mosley about their past encounter.

He said, "As I explained to Ms. Reagan, I want to have a productive working relationship with her and I'm afraid the Ellender York matter has set us off on the wrong foot. We all want what's right for Mallard Bay, so I'm hoping we can start over."

Mosley responded with a "That's it?" look, then said, "A word of advice. You should reconsider your methods of gathering allies."

"I'm afraid you'll need to explain that, sir."

"Do I? This is awkward, isn't it? If you're going to lose your temper, you should remember that your voice carries. I heard what you said to my partner a few minutes ago."

"Oh. Well—" Grassley stopped.

Grace thought he didn't know whether to apologize again, and if so, to whom.

"And," Mosley said, "while your behavior this morning won't be forgotten, we should move on to the purpose of this meeting. I'm distressed to find I must remind you of the town's commitment to community policing, something that we spent a good bit of time discussing during the interview process, if you recall."

"Of course," Grassley said, cautiously.

Mosley nodded, as if this had been a matter of great concern to him. "I'm glad to see that you remember. Short-term memory loss would be a problem for someone your age. But, perhaps you don't understand what the term means in this town. We require respect and fair treatment for everyone. Citizens, visitors, everyone."

"Of course," Grassley repeated. This time, though, his tone was harsh. The "memory loss" shot had hit its mark.

Mosley was only getting started. "Gossiping about police activity for your friends' entertainment is not acceptable. And before you ask me what I mean, you should know that I received several calls yesterday from people who were present when you were talking in public about Ellender York. Two of those citizens heard you giving details of her arrest, complete with unflattering imitations of her and her friends. Three other people called me to say they were at the town office last night, where you similarly entertained a group after the council meeting. Your performance there was slightly more sedate, but still unacceptable. I have made my displeasure known to the mayor and council, but I wanted to tell you, face to face, that I object strongly to your behavior. That sort of thing might be tolerated in Pennsylvania, but not here."

"If what I said was misunderstood—"

"It was not." Mosley stood.

"With all due respect, sir, I don't work for you." Now Grassley stood, stretching his tall frame out to tower over the old lawyer.

Mosley said, "You use that phrase often, yet you display no respect at all." He rose and crossed to open the door. "And therein lies our problem, because you do, in fact, work for every citizen of this town, including me. If you can't accept that, you won't stay here long. And one more thing. Ms. York is my client. Should you decide to slander her again, direct your comments to me, but I don't recommend that course of action."

It was a standoff, Mosley holding the door and Grassley assessing his options. In the end, the chief gave Mosley a curt nod, ignored Grace, and left, taking most of the oxygen in the room with him.

Mosley helped himself to a muffin and said, "That went well, don't you think, m'dear?"

Grace laughed with him, but she knew the problems with Grassley had only escalated. "Did you really eavesdrop on us?" she asked.

Raising his voice, he said, "I've been trained by the best."

They heard a snort of laughter from the hallway. A moment later, the door to reception closed with a bang.

"What do we do about him threatening Ellender?" Grace asked. "Do you think we need to warn her?"

Mosley looked thoughtful, then shook his head. "He didn't actually make a threat, but he certainly has it in for her. She's special. Always has been. Her strength is that she likes herself the way she is and tries to make use of her unusual talents. People like Grassley tear the Ellenders of the world apart, or they try to. You may have noticed she has spunk."

"You know her pretty well to have just met her."

"Whatever gave you that idea?" Mosley hooked his thumbs in his pants pockets and rocked back on his heels. Only the smile tugging at the corner of his mouth told her it was all an act. "You may have introduced me to Ellender, but I've known that child her whole life."

"How?"

"Through her father."

She knew there was more, but Mosley shut her out again.

"We've done what we can for her, for now," he said. "I've warned Grassley, and he seems to be the self-serving type who knows when he's stepped in something he should've avoided. His heavy-handed use of what I'm sure he would say is a warning is his style of policing. Upon reflection, I see no point in upsetting Ellender by telling her what he's been doing. After all, she's moving and that should put an end to things here."

"But—"

"She's my client, Grace. We've both made an enemy today, possibly a dangerous one. Leave me to handle it and please try not to make things worse than they already are."

She didn't argue, but she couldn't stop thinking about Ellender and Natalie. She had a feeling that sooner or later they were going to come back to her.

CHAPTER TWENTY-ONE

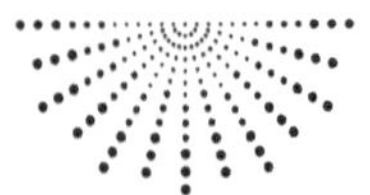

Niki had three rooms booked for the night, and the guests had asked for dinner, too. After breaking the news that Grace would need to avoid the first and second floors until tomorrow, she was only too happy to change the subject and discuss the office drama.

"Tate did *not* say that to you!" They were unpacking groceries in the downstairs kitchen, and Niki abandoned a bag of avocados to stare at her cousin.

"He did. According to him, I've corrupted Mac's morals and I'm using him for my own nefarious purposes." Grace tried to smile, but knew it wasn't convincing.

"That's not how Mac tells it. Hey! Stop that!"

Niki took a head of Bibb lettuce from Grace. "You've bruised it. Go sit down and let me finish."

Grace didn't have to be told twice.

Niki returned to the groceries, falling silent for a moment before saying, "Gossip is flying around, and most of it is from Tate, himself." As she started dinner preparations, Niki relayed Grassley's report of how Grace, Mac, and Mosley had interfered with official police actions, and caused a dangerous criminal to be freed.

Grace didn't want to think about how he would describe this morning's events. "Do you think anyone believes him?"

"Are you sure you want to know?" A corner of Niki's mouth twitched, then blossomed into a wicked grin. "You usually hate this kind of gossip."

"What kind?"

"Sordid. And probably exaggerated beyond all resemblance to the truth."

"Will I have images I don't want cluttering up my motherly mind?"

"Most def."

"Dish. Now."

"I'm warning you, it's stupid, so no comments about me being superficial." Niki started salad preparations as she talked about the Tate Grassley that the average citizen saw. "He's very convincing, I'm afraid. He's all big and commanding and he's good-looking, too, for an older guy. And likable, I mean, he's kinda scary, but it's scary like a roller coaster, you know?"

Grace remembered Grassley's angry red face. "No. I can't imagine what you mean."

"If you weren't wound up in drama with two men and a baby, you could."

Well, she had been warned. "Okay, so I've been out of it—deaf, dumb, and blind to the world outside of my little bubble. Now explain it to me. Slowly. Do people believe what he's saying?"

Niki didn't need further encouragement, but got down to the dirt. "Right now, they probably think some of it's true. I mean, he's new and exciting. I'll just say it. The Tater's a hunk." She had to wait while Grace laughed so hard, she had to run to the bathroom.

"That name will never leave me. Thanks so much," she said when she returned, still giggling. "How am I going to explain laughing the next time I run into him?"

"Do you want to know what he's doing, or not?" Niki asked. When Grace promised to be quiet, she continued. "There's an energy about him that pulls you in, and it isn't sex. Well, not just that. Remember, I go to the council meetings with some other business owners? You should see how he works the room. He comes in early before the meeting starts, but after most of the crowd's there, and everyone sort of flocks to him. He changes with each conversation he has. There's no other way to describe it, but people like it. At least for a while. The night he was talking about Ellender, he went too far. I wasn't there, but I heard about it the next day. I also heard he promised Natalie Wilkens that he could get rid of Ellender, and Natalie's repeating that to everyone who'll listen. Of course it makes sense if they're having an affair. Are you sure about that?"

"According to Tate, they are. I just can't see those two together."

"Yeah. But if you think about it, both of them get what they want, don't they? She gets an attentive Tater. He gets status, and he's hooked up with all the right people." Niki reeled off names from Mallard Bay's current society elites.

Grace was dismayed to hear that the town was gearing up for a turf war between the people who liked Grassley and those who had experienced his temper.

"So, picture it." Niki continued, in full hand-waving, character-impersonating, storytelling mode. "A couple of weeks ago, the chief was working the council room before a meeting, shaking hands and making small talk until he gets around to the back. I think he likes the last row the best. That's the group that attends the meetings to get the latest and greatest, and to critique everything in real time."

"You mean you and your friends?"

"Exactly," Niki said, not breaking stride. "He flirts with us like you wouldn't believe, especially the ones who aren't likely to get much male attention otherwise."

Grace tried to picture Niki's girlfriends.

"Ainsley Bynch? Nina Fahl?" Niki prompted.

"They're both married," Grace said. "Are you saying he's inappropriate?"

"Oh, yeah! And they love it. Ainsley and Nina joined the mom jeans, no-makeup brigade a decade ago." Niki waved her hands, disassociating herself from such foolishness. "That look only works on natural beauties. Well, not the mom jeans. Those can ruin anybody. But seriously. If you were at the shallow end of the gene pool to begin with, would you refuse any help you could get from the cosmetic industry? Sometimes I think those two girls try to outdo each other with their naturalness, if you know what I mean. Even you wouldn't go out in public completely bare-faced."

"*Even* me?"

"I keep telling you, I can show you a few tricks with contouring cream—"

"Get back to Tater," Grace said, enjoying Niki's nickname.

Niki said the contour cream discussion was only being postponed, but she obediently returned to Grassley. "He makes people feel good, except, there's something under the surface. So, there he was, yakking it up with us, teasing Nina about her new haircut. She got all giggly and called him 'Tater'—I can't claim credit for the tag. That was Nina, but it's perfect, isn't it? Anyway, you should have seen his face."

"He wasn't happy?" Grace guessed.

"Bowed up like he'd been sucker punched. He didn't say anything, but we had frostbite from his exit."

"That's the man I'm dealing with," Grace said. "And I think if Cyrus wants to handle all the baggage that comes with Tater, he's welcome to it."

"Good call," Niki said, "but I'll bet that won't be easy."

She was right.

CHAPTER TWENTY-TWO

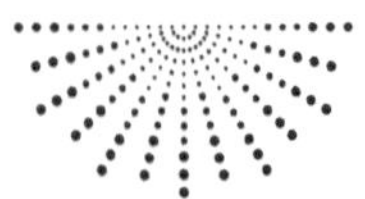

Mac did not take the news of Grassley's behavior well.

Grace was used to David's tantrums, but Mac's silent fury unnerved her. In retrospect, she realized that telling him over dinner in Annapolis was a poor choice, but it was the first time they'd talked during the long day. After extracting every detail of the confrontation from her, he was non-committal until they reached the parking lot with the new stroller.

"You can put it in my trunk," Grace said. "I promise not to lift it out."

"You won't be able to resist." He unlocked his truck and heaved the big box in. "I'll drop it by tomorrow."

Their parting felt awkward. He didn't ask her to stay over at his place, and turned off Route 50 at his exit, leaving her to go home alone and worried. Situations like this were rare with him, but when they occurred, her mind always raced over her years with David, searching for some correlation. The men couldn't be less alike, but she had no other experiences to guide her except for high school boyfriends and brief relationships in college.

Her mother's advice on romance had been short and to the point. She had summed up all of her objections to David in a single sentence: *Never tie yourself to a man unless he loves you more than you love him.*

Grace knew it had been her love for David that had kept them together during their tumultuous relationship. She wasn't sure if he'd ever loved her, or if she had just made it easy for him to stay.

She wanted Mac, but when he pulled back like this, it scared her. Some of their magic slipped away, and she didn't know how to catch it. What if she was making the same mistake—loving a man more than he loved her? Was she ever going to get this right?

∼

OVER THE NEXT WEEK, GRASSLEY STAYED OUT OF sight and, according to Jake, was taking the night shift and letting Tremaine Harper handle day duty. It may have been an end to hostilities, or the eye of a storm, but Grace was grateful for the respite.

The office chugged along with Jake oozing enthusiasm and getting into everything, and Mosley phoning his work in from the golf course. On the home front, she stayed in her apartment, trying to ignore the activity buzzing through the floors below her. The Inn at Delaney House was looking like a success as Niki adjusted to her role as an innkeeper. Most guests were pleased, and their positive energy made the old house a happy place.

She was relieved to see money coming into, instead of flowing out of, her bank account, but as guests came and went, and Niki catered her first dinner in the renovated dining room, she had to agree that the inn was no place for an infant. Before operations resumed after the winter break, she would have to find somewhere else to live, at least until the baby was older and sleeping through the night.

Avril continued to talk as if the matter was settled, but as lovely as her new guest suite was, her life with the dogs was regimented. Babies weren't.

Grace needed a long-term solution, but so far, Avril's house and Mac's cottage were her only ready options. One came with Avril twenty-four seven, the other with a different commitment.

Interaction with David was the way she liked it, nonexistent, except for emails from his accountant regarding the sale of the "river house," as he continued to call the property he'd given her.

On the day before settlement, Grace and Mac took a picnic out to the house for a last visit. Mac had balked when she asked him.

"I haven't been out there in weeks," she told him. "I need to make sure there are no problems before the buyer does the walk-through tomorrow." She sweetened the offer with the promise of barbecue sandwiches and Smith Island cake. When she said that she was going with or without him, he gave in.

It was a beautiful day to eat by the water, but try as she might to make the picnic celebratory, there was a chill between them. When she ran out of chatter without coaxing him out of his funk, the silence was painful. Unable to stand it any longer, she said, "Can't you be happy for me? Or at least relieved that I don't have to deal with this situation anymore?"

The look he gave her was speculative, but

after a minute, he said, "I don't enjoy being here and I'm irritated that I gave into you about it. The best thing about selling this pile of concrete is I won't be reminded of David when I'm on my beach."

He'd never mentioned it, but they both knew that David had chosen this specific property because of its proximity to Mac's land on the opposite shore. His beachfront was in full view from where they stood.

"I get it," she said. "I'm sorry I nagged you into coming today, okay? But the closing is tomorrow. It's almost over."

His jaw tightened and she saw a side of him she didn't know. He was angry. At her.

"No," he said. "Not okay. And it's never going to be over with that guy. Why would he buy this place unless you let him think you'd live with him?"

"What?" As his words hit her, she was too surprised to answer. She'd been positive they were past this. Too late, she realized he considered her silence to be from guilt.

"I don't love him," she said, quietly. "It took me a long time to end it with him, because it wasn't only David I left, it was my old life. I'm not the same person now. Everything changed for me when I came here and things are changing again. Work will come and go, other people will come and go, but none of it matters. You are what matters to me. You and this baby."

He watched her as she spoke, but said nothing.

With a theatrical sigh, she threw her hands up and said, "All right, get your notebook out, Mr. Policeman, and write down my answer to your question. David bought me a house so he could control where I lived. So we would be on his turf, not mine. That's how he thinks and he never learns. He doesn't learn because he doesn't listen, and he doesn't listen because he doesn't care about me. Not really. I never once considered living here with him, because I don't love him. I love you."

Mac crossed his arms, maintaining his distance. "You agreed to marry him, but you loved me?"

"Yes! Well, no."

"Pick one, Grace."

"Stop it," she said, and sat on the low brick wall that edged the patio. "We've already been over this, and you're supposed to be the sane one in this relationship. I can't believe I have to explain this to you. *Again.*"

A smile pulled at one corner of his mouth, but

his arms were still crossed and his gaze steady. He said, "Even I need help now and then. I think I'm okay with it, and then you do something I don't understand, and I'm reminded of how much I don't know about you. Mostly, it's your history with David. It makes no sense to me at all."

His tone hit a nerve with her. He was struggling as much as she was. She focused on his troubled face and tried to put everything she felt into her words. "I never said I'd marry him, Mac. I was awful to him and unfair to myself and all because I was a coward."

His frown deepened. "Don't go overboard. The man's an ass."

"Yes, he is, but he wasn't always, not when we were younger, and never to me. Not when we started out, anyway. I was a coward last winter, because I didn't refuse when he proposed. I just pretended it hadn't happened, even when I was dragging that huge ring around. I was still recovering from Garrett Bishop's murder and the fire, which is no excuse at all. But by the time I was back to my normal, suspicious, David-proof self, he was off and running."

"And you didn't stop him."

"He went home to Washington, and it was easier to wait him out. It was a terrible thing for me to do, but it was also a pattern for us. I was sure he'd get bored and lose interest, and then I could end things without hard feelings."

She had said more than she'd intended. Mac looked frozen, and she desperately wanted to know if he was only sorry he'd asked, or so disgusted that he would leave her and never look back. When he spoke, she wished he'd left instead.

"Where did getting pregnant fall in that plan?"

She stood and backed away from him, unconsciously hugging herself. She knew he deserved an answer, but she couldn't believe he had finally asked. Not after all this time. She forced herself to look him in the eyes.

"I loved him once. It was years ago, but I loved him. When I nearly died in that fire, it rocked both of us. He said he'd always loved me. It was too late for me, but it was easy to lean on him. That's why this child is here." Suddenly, having to explain her baby's existence made her furious. "If that's not good enough for you, it's your loss, but don't ever bring it up to me again."

He came to her and took her hand, pulling her down to sit beside him on the wall. For a while they just watched the river and let their words settle. After a time, he said, "I'd like to believe I didn't mean to hurt you, but I think maybe I did. I love you, Grace, and I'm sorry."

She put her head on his shoulder and tried to believe it would all work out. She had one more thing to tell him, but she waited as long as she could before she spoke. Straightening to watch his face, she said, "I'd give anything if Sweet Pea were yours."

He put his arms around her and whispered, "She already is, sweetheart."

The picnic stretched through the afternoon. When they drove away from the house, they were different. Not better, or worse, but new.

CHAPTER TWENTY-THREE

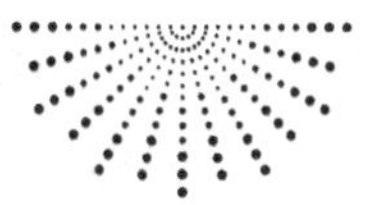

Ellender was tired. It had been a long morning of moving things into the storage unit, and a long week of avoiding her neighbor. Each time Ellender stepped outside, a lace curtain was pulled back in the Wilkens house. Natalie wasn't subtle in the least.

And she wasn't the only problem.

Tyler grew increasingly agitated as Ellender packed up her family home. The apartment in Annapolis seemed like heaven beckoning to her. Unfortunately, she had a few more weeks in her current uncomfortable surroundings before she could leave.

The old wall phone was ringing when she

walked into the kitchen. She answered it without thinking and immediately regretted it.

"So, you're answering the phone, again." Natalie's strident voice blasted through the earpiece.

"Hello. What can I do for you?"

Natalie called daily, and Ellender usually avoided answering. She steeled herself for a lecture about the grass, driveway, trash cans, or the hour she'd gotten home last night from dinner out with Cherish.

"I've received a bill that belongs to you."

Ellender was stumped. It was usually best to let Natalie run down and end the call—but what was she going on about? She'd left several messages about Ellender owing her money, but that wasn't new. Her favorite grudge was the enormous sum she'd paid to have the rear property line landscaped to block her view of the Yorks' backyard. Far from being insulted, Ellender's father had thanked her profusely for the "gift," which resulted in Natalie demanding reimbursement. Ten years later, she was still angry.

"You owe me a hundred and sixty dollars."

The landscaping had cost considerably more than that. Ellender broke her nonengagement rule and said, "I don't know what you're talking about and I'm in the middle of—"

"Well, you'd know if you'd listened to any of my messages."

This was true. Ellender waited for the rest of the tirade.

"You have some nerve contacting a lawyer about *me*. How dare you? After what you and your family have done to me, you're trying to intimidate me with the threat of a lawsuit?"

Against her better judgment, Ellender said, "I didn't do that. I only wanted to find out what my options were."

"So, you saw a lawyer who called my lawyer, who billed *me* for taking the call. A bill you're going to pay."

"At least I don't lie to the police! But I guess that's the only way you can get visits from Chief Grassley." Ellender stopped. Her mother would be so upset to hear her talk like this. The silence from the other end of the line stretched out. She started to hang up, then heard Natalie's shaky voice say, "You'll be sorry."

Ellender hung up. Her heart was thudding and for a moment, the walls seemed to close in on her.

"Baby?"

She screamed, then saw Tyler reaching for her. On reflex, she shoved him, then stumbled backward, slamming into the counter. "Get away!" She bent over, hugging herself.

He hovered nearby, spewing a stream of questions and apologies. She shut him out and tried to stop the shaking that rattled her body. She was overreacting. It was only Tyler, not her father. But Tyler had never called her "Baby" before, and her father had never called her anything else.

When she could stand and breathe without gasping, she said, "Give me your key."

No argument, plea, or insult he came up with changed her mind. She promised herself he'd never be in her house without an invitation again, and once she moved, she'd end the relationship for good.

"I wanted to surprise you," he said, sullen.

"Mission accomplished." She snatched the key from him.

"Is it because I called you 'Baby'? I'm sorry, but I could hear what that old bitch was yelling at you, and I had to make it better. I would have told you I was here, but you answered the phone as soon as you came in."

"Yes, I did. Because it's my house. Mine. Not yours. You don't live here, Tyler. I don't know why you're here, but you need to go."

He smiled and shook his head. "No way, little

sister. You need me. I handled the old lady for you earlier. Guess I'll have to talk to her again and tell her to stay off the phone, too."

Her mind raced over the potential problems she'd have to clean up in the wake of Tyler's help.

"She called before you got home," he said. "Good thing I was here to answer."

Ellender clenched her teeth. If she didn't get out of this situation soon, she'd need dental implants. The smug look on his face made her want to slap him.

"Know why she called? To borrow some flour. Can you believe it? I took it over to her and she actually thanked me like a normal person would. I realized today that she likes me. It's you she has the problem with, El. I told her not to upset you, and she said she'd do her best to fix things. That didn't last long, did it? She's irrational, but she likes me, so I'll handle her for you."

She thought the possibility of Natalie calling to borrow flour was slim to none, as was any chance that she suddenly liked Tyler. What was he doing? "I'm going to change," she said, unable to stand the sight of him a moment longer. "I'm tired and grubby and I want you to leave."

He grabbed her arm when she passed him. "Okay! I really am sorry."

"Let. Go." Pain shot up to her shoulder as she wrenched away from him. "Don't be here when I get back."

"Sure, El. Promise."

But, of course, he was.

Fifteen minutes later, she emerged from her bedroom, wet hair in a towel, barefoot and in sweats, and heard him talking in the kitchen.

"You can't do it, because I won't let you." His voice was low, but harsh. "Tell that greedy little friend of yours to back off."

Ellender padded silently down the hall and stood next to the kitchen doorway. Her arm still hurt, and she didn't want another fight.

"For my own good?" Tyler asked. "That's not even close. You want the money, but you aren't calling the shots. I'm fine. Better than I have been in years. If you had faith in me, I wouldn't have any trouble at all. Leave us alone, understand?"

She wanted to turn around and go back to her room. To lock the door behind her and stay put until it was time to move. She knew Tyler was talking with his mother, and she knew what they were arguing about.

"Little sister?"

He had disconnected and was coming toward her.

"I asked you to leave." She straightened up and tried to look stern instead of sick at heart.

"I had to call Mom and my phone's dead. You heard, I suppose? Don't worry. She won't do anything."

"She's going to sue me, Tyler, and you can't stop her."

"She can try, but when I testify about how wonderful you are, she'll lose. Then we can sue her for our legal fees and emotional distress. We'll come out fine."

"I can't do it!" Ellender felt a crack growing in the walls of the dam that kept her fear contained. "Not one more thing. You and your mother and all your problems have to get out of my life!" She'd said it before, but nothing ever changed. Once again they argued over the same issues, using the same words, and it all ended the same way.

Later, after she'd gotten a still ranting Tyler out of the house and finished a bottle of wine, Natalie, Tyler, and his mother wound through her thoughts. Over and over, she heard Tyler saying, *Baby?*

How long had he been alone in here, and what had he been doing? This house had always been a comfort to her. She'd been safe here.

Until now.

CHAPTER TWENTY-FOUR

The sale of the river house was anticlimactic. Electronic signatures were clicked onto electronic documents, including one from Grace directing proceeds into the account she'd set up for the trust. She was betting that David wouldn't be at the ten o'clock settlement. He had people to handle such things. People who wouldn't be interested in the seller submitting a new bank routing number for the payment.

All the authorizations for the transfer were in place, but she still paced around the office until her bank called to confirm receipt. The baby's trust fund had grown from one thousand dollars to two million, eight hundred and one thousand.

Her relief was short-lived. At two thirty, as she

was packing up to leave, David's name appeared on her phone. The temptation to send him to voicemail was strong, but she answered on the fifth ring.

"What are you doing with my money?"

"Hello, David," she said. "The proceeds from the sale of my house are in the baby's trust fund." She took a breath. "The one I set up."

"You expect me to believe that? What have you done?"

She'd expected the yelling, but this was worse. He was so angry his voice shook. She said, "I did what I said I would. I've encumbered the money, all of it, in a trust account. I'll send you a copy of the bank transaction."

"You do that."

The line beeped, and he was gone.

After months of anxiety, the house was sold, the baby's financial future was secured, and David was, at least for the moment, neutralized.

Suddenly, she was starved. Grabbing her wallet, she slipped out the back door of the office and across the parking lot to the bakery at Three Pigs Deli. Chocolate croissants and strawberry tarts had her full attention when a woman stepped up next to her.

"Do you know who I am?"

Reluctantly, Grace turned to the paper-thin woman who was glaring at her. "Sorry, no. Have we met?"

"I'm Natalie Wilkens. Mrs. Judge Wilkens."

Grace didn't bother to hide her surprise as she held out her hand. "I've heard how active you are in the community. Very pleased to meet you."

It was true. Grace had been dying to see the infamous Mrs. Judge in person, but Natalie was a surprise. The vintage Lilly Pulitzer dress screamed old money, but her thick gold bracelet and Fendi bag were trendy. Even with her face wrinkled in anger, she was attractive. So, this was the woman Tate Grassley had followed to Mallard Bay.

The Widow Wilkens ignored Grace's greeting and got right down to business.

"You should be ashamed of yourself, meddling in local issues you know nothing about."

Nerves still taut from David's call, Grace snapped back. "And you're as rude as people say you are." She had plenty of unspent anxiety and was ready to unload it. She ordered a croissant *and* a tart, and resolved to eat both as soon as she was alone.

Jeannie Harper kept her head down and grinned as she bagged the pastries. "On the house," she said as she handed Grace the fragrant package. "For the little one."

Ignoring the outraged woman beside her, Grace thanked the baker and left.

Natalie, pale and panting, caught up to her on the sidewalk. The short dash out of Three Pigs hadn't shifted a hair of her precision-cut bob, but there was a sheen of perspiration on her face.

Glancing around, Grace said, "We don't have an audience now, so let's have it. I'm busy."

"How dare you!"

Grace remembered Cyrus and his "Small towns have long memories" advice. He was right, and she wanted to know more about Ellender's nemesis. "I could point out that you started it, but I'd rather not argue. If you have something to tell me, I'll listen." She tried to look caring and interested, despite the delectable smells coming from the bakery bag.

Natalie wagged a long, thin forefinger. "You and that little—"

"No." Grace interrupted. "Finger down and no name-calling. I didn't say you could lecture me. I said I would listen to your concerns."

"I'm Mrs.—"

"I don't care who you are." So much for getting the judge's widow to spill confidences.

They stood, squared off, Natalie taking deep breaths and Grace calculating the location of the nearest restroom. Sweet Pea really didn't like confrontation.

"She hurt me," Natalie said, leaning in and hissing the words.

Grace hadn't expected that. "Who?"

"They're all the same, those Yorks, and Ellen is the worst."

Grace put out her arm to keep the angry woman from getting any closer. She didn't want the baby between herself and the rage Natalie projected. "Ellen York is dead, Mrs. Wilkens. You're talking about Ellender, aren't you? What's she done to you?"

Natalie took a step back, but Grace was still leery. And nearly out of time. Dr. Allyson hadn't been kidding about the extra bathroom breaks. "I'm sorry," she said, and was relieved to see Natalie nod. "I have to get to my office. To the restroom, actually." She gestured to her middle in a shameless play for sympathy. "I'd be happy to talk to you further if you will walk along with me, but I have to leave now."

"I believe I've made my point," Natalie said. "You should be careful. It isn't safe to be around her, especially when she's with that nasty man. He had the nerve to threaten me the other night. Said if I didn't stop upsetting his girlfriend, he'd make me pay. Me! Upsetting her? Well, I called the police, of course. And I'll do worse if they don't leave me alone."

Grace hurried away, but she was more determined than ever to find out what was going on. Her promise to Mac wasn't exactly forgotten, just pushed to the side. Could Natalie Wilkens really be afraid of Ellender? Something had to be behind her bizarre behavior.

Later, when Mac called to ask if she would help him pick out a new sofa before they went out to dinner, she agreed. She could tap into his institutional knowledge of Mallard Bay and the Wilkenses, and he could give her his take on Natalie's strange warning.

Things didn't quite turn out the way she planned.

～

THEY WERE STANDING IN THE MIDDLE OF Mallard Bay's only home furnishings store, when Grace realized Mac thought she was moving in with him. They'd been admiring a leather chesterfield sofa when he asked if she would prefer the dark brown model, since it would be best for hiding stains and scratches.

"Well," she said, floundering helplessly. Children and leather of any color didn't mix, and the sofa was expensive. What would a bottle of apple juice do to it, and did it matter? She and Sweet Pea wouldn't be living with him, so why would he ask? But then she'd let David think she would marry him because she didn't speak up. Had she made the same mistake with Mac?

"Would you be more comfortable with a larger sectional instead of the traditional model?" he asked, looking at her quizzically. "I mean, it won't just be the two of us, will it? Down the road, it could get crowded."

His tone was wistful, and another thought jumped into her panicked brain. *Down the road?* Did he want them to have a baby together? Had she missed that, too? He'd insist on getting married, of course. Then she'd have to move into Meri's house. Her mouth went dry and air seemed to be in short supply.

"What is it?" he asked, finally shifting his attention from the array of not-suitable-for-children sofas. "Are you okay?"

"Fine." She tried to smile, but was pretty sure

it didn't look right. "I'm going to step out for a minute. It's warm in here."

"You could take off your coat," he said, but she was already on the move.

He was right after her. "What's wrong?" he demanded when they reached the sidewalk.

"Oh, Mac, I'm so sorry!"

"For what?" He put his arms around her without seeming to notice that they were blocking the entrance to the store.

Grace pulled away, saying, "In the car."

"No. Here. Tell me quick and the group headed this way won't hear." He didn't let go.

"All right! I'm not ready to move in with you, and I don't know if I'll be able to have another baby. Now can we go to the car?"

"I need to buy a sofa first," he said, grinning from ear to ear.

Grace reran their conversation. "That wasn't what you meant about the sofa getting crowded and needing to hide stains?"

"You and the baby are always welcome, for as long as you want, or forever. But sweetheart, I was actually hoping to get a dog. I've mentioned it several times."

He had? Now she really was embarrassed. He

tugged her arm gently to move her aside so the new shoppers could get in the store.

"A dog," she repeated.

"Yes. Sooner rather than later. My last one's been gone awhile and I'm ready. The three of us, a dog or two—we'll need a big sofa."

"Two dogs."

"And maybe a cat." Now he was laughing.

"Oh, go buy your damned sofa," she snapped and stomped off to wait in the truck.

By the time he'd returned, she'd recovered her composure, but he kept teasing her as they drove to the restaurant. "Maybe a budgie for the cats to play with? And Sweet Pea could have hamsters."

"Stop it," she said when she couldn't take it anymore. "I'm worried that I'll disappoint you. And don't you dare think I'm fishing for a compliment!"

"Okay?" he said, hesitantly.

She was sure he was still smiling, but she refused to look over to see. "I haven't been able to find a way to tell you I can't live with you, Mac. It's too much all at once, I'm sorry."

"I don't want you to be sorry, and I don't want to set you off again, but do you realize I've never asked you? I just needed a sofa. You've seen the state of the one in the den."

She couldn't decide if she felt better or worse, and was glad when he kept talking.

"I never want you to have to worry about telling me anything. If I get mad, I'll get over it. I love you."

Better. She felt much better. "Which sofa did you buy?"

"The leather. They had a sectional style."

Grace said she hoped Sweet Pea liked apple juice. Before she had to explain herself, blue and red flashing lights came on behind them.

Mac pulled into the parking lot of a small church, and the Mallard Bay patrol car followed them. Seconds later, Tremaine Harper appeared at his window.

"Chief! I mean, Mac. Glad I found you!"

Grace and Mac exchanged glances. The young officer was clearly shaken.

"Chief Grassley and Detective Marbury sent me to find you." Tremaine emphasized the MSP officer's name, leaving no doubt who'd really given the order. "I went to your place, Grace, but Niki said you were at the furniture mart. When I got there, the manager said he saw you heading toward town."

"What's happened?" Mac asked.

"Can you follow me over to Americus Street? There's been a death."

"I'll drop Grace off—"

"No, sir!" Tremaine looked over his shoulder as if checking for witnesses. "Chief won't like me telling you, but Grace should come, too. I think Ellender York needs her."

CHAPTER TWENTY-FIVE

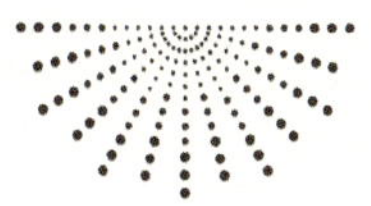

Tremaine would only say that Ellender wasn't the victim, which left Grace and Mac to wonder who was.

"I can take you home first," Mac offered as Tremaine trotted back to his patrol car. "Five minutes won't make any difference now. I'll call Cyrus for Ellender, if she needs him."

"I'm fine, and if you take me home, I'll only worry. If she doesn't want me, I'll call Cyrus, but I want to make sure she's okay."

He didn't argue with her, but wore the air of a man who'd known the response when he made the suggestion.

When they turned the corner onto Americus Street, there were enough spotlights and headlights from emergency vehicles to read a newspaper.

"Good thing Halloween isn't until tomorrow and most people are out at the fireworks at the VFW tonight," Mac said. "Awful lot of personnel for a natural death."

Grace had been thinking the same thing. "How do we work this?" she asked.

"I'm winging it, too. This is my first crime scene as a civilian."

They parked behind the cruiser, then followed Tremaine to Natalie Wilkens's front door. Two sheriff's deputies acknowledged him, and greeted Mac with a nod and polite "Evening, Major". The younger officer made a comical face and glanced at the house as he used Mac's former Maryland State Police title. His meaning was clear enough. Tate Grassley was the chief of police in Mallard Bay and as such, was in charge.

Grace didn't even rate a smile. The senior deputy said, "Sorry, ma'am. I can only let the Major go in."

A voice inside the house rose in anger. Grassley was dressing someone down. Immediately, both deputies straightened their shoulders.

"No problem," Grace said and turned toward the York house.

"You'll need to leave the area, ma'am. I'm sorry, chief's orders." This time, Grace got an apologetic nod.

"I understand you have instructions," she said. "But I'm Ms. York's attorney." She left the men without waiting for permission and crossed the yard. No one stopped her and the bluff worked again with the deputy stationed at the York house.

She found Ellender and Tyler in the den with an MSP detective sergeant who was not pleased to be interrupted.

"How did you get in here?" Desiree Marbury demanded.

Grace kept a poker face while trying to work out why a senior detective was grilling the couple. "Good evening to you, too, Desi," she started, then backtracked when the detective's frown deepened. "Detective Marbury," she corrected, then added to Ellender and Tyler, "we know each other."

"Which doesn't answer my question, does it?" Marbury snapped. "Why are you here?"

Grace said she was Ellender's attorney and hoped the pale young woman wouldn't contradict her and demand to see Mosley. But, far from complaining that the wrong lawyer had shown up, Ellender jumped to her feet and rushed to Grace, who glanced at Marbury as she accepted her client's bear hug.

The detective was now embarrassed, as well as angry. The last time a client of Grace's made a move like that, it had ended badly. Perhaps that was why Marbury didn't tell Grace to leave. Or maybe, Grace thought, she didn't want to have to peel Ellender off her pregnant attorney.

Whichever, the detective gestured to the chair she'd been sitting in and said, "Be my guest," to Grace. She left after giving them all a warning to stay put until she returned.

Marbury had barely cleared the doorway when Tyler said, "Thanks for getting the cops off our backs, but we don't need you. I can take care of everything."

Grace didn't respond to him, but shut the door before taking the seat Marbury had occupied. "Tell me what happened," she said to Ellender.

She was rewarded with a grateful smile from Ellender and a scowl from Tyler. Then they both started talking, the story spilling out so fast, Grace wished she had a recorder going.

"I've been trying to avoid her, Natalie, I mean," Ellender said. "But yesterday I answered the phone when she called. She demanded I pay her lawyer's bill for talking with you. Do you think it looks bad? That she and I argued so much and had lawyers?"

"Probably," Grace said, "or they wouldn't be questioning you. What happened next door?"

Tyler jumped in. "Natalie's dead," he said. "I came right over when I heard the call for an ambulance come over my emergency scanner. It was a huge relief when I saw which house they went to, but now we have a new problem. The old bitch is dead and the police think Ellender killed her."

THE POLICE DID, INDEED, HAVE QUESTIONS ABOUT Natalie Wilkens's death, and before Grace could get more information, Marbury returned with the senior deputy Grace had encountered earlier. In short order, Ellender and Tyler were separated and taken in for questioning. Grace made it clear she was there as Ellender's attorney, only, and was told she could follow them to the State Police Barracks in Easton.

If Tyler objected to her abandonment, he didn't show it. "Don't worry, little sister," he called over his shoulder to Ellender as he was led away. "I'll do whatever it takes to make sure nothing happens to you."

The officers exchanged glances, and Grace wanted to slap the officious little twit for the message he'd sent. *I don't need an attorney because I didn't do anything.* You, *on the other hand . . .*

Ellender looked horrified.

Grace was sure she saw a fleeting look of satisfaction slide across Tyler's face.

LEAVING MAC TO GET A RIDE, SHE FOLLOWED THE State Patrol cars out of Mallard Bay, but soon lost them as they raced away from her on Route 50. While she drove, she ran through everything she knew about Ellender, her family, Tyler Forester, and the Wilkenses. She also called Mac to tell him where she'd be and was grateful that she didn't get an earful about running around late at night in her condition. She rubbed the spot on her side that had been kicked relentlessly until a few days ago. Now her ribs got the most attention, but they were harder to massage with a seatbelt on. Her adrenaline rush was making the baby extra active.

"Go to sleep," she whispered, imagining the tiny foot beneath her hand. A series of short, gentle spasms started near her belly button. Sweet Pea had hiccups. "Well, since you're awake, send me some bright ideas, okay? Mama needs to be on her A game."

She refocused on the job that lay before her, glad that she'd had a late afternoon nap. She needed to get Ellender released and some place safe. Preferably without the obnoxious Tyler. Something more than an irritating personality was off about him, and it was time to find out what it was.

Having been on both sides of the process in the recent past, Grace was familiar with the routine the State Police followed with persons of interest and arrestees. The latter group faced more invasive procedures, but just being questioned was unnerving. After a brief wait while her credentials were checked, she was taken to a small interview room where a furious Ellender sat alone and unrestrained.

"Are you aware they're searching my house?" Ellender demanded when they were alone.

Grace nodded.

"If they find anything, that awful Chief Grassley planted it during the search. He treated us like we were killers. You have to do something! They won't let me see Tyler and he isn't well. He needs his medicine." Ellender sounded panicked.

"What's wrong with him?"

"It's all from the accident. He's on a painkiller and it makes him unsteady and, frankly, he gets too emotional and says things he doesn't mean."

"Things like what?" Grace asked, although she could guess.

"Like how nasty Natalie is and how much trouble she's caused me. I was so scared when the police showed up, especially when Tyler started running off at the mouth, telling them that anything Natalie had said about me was a lie and that he'd warned her to leave me alone. He didn't even shut up when they told us she was dead. Everything he said made them suspicious. But he didn't do it, Grace!"

"Listen to me," Grace said. "You don't know what he did when you weren't with him. If you want to help him and keep yourself out of trouble, be quiet unless I tell you to talk."

Ellender did as she was told. By the time Desiree Marbury joined them, Grace thought they had a fighting chance.

"My client will answer questions, but then I want her released," she told Marbury.

To her surprise, after a half hour of interrogation, the detective agreed. Two hours later, Grace was driving back to Mallard Bay with Ellender sitting beside her, talking on the phone to Tyler's frantic mother. Nervous, nonstop Tyler had taken a swing at the deputy who was questioning him and had been arrested for assault. Grace doubted that would be the only charge he'd face.

NATALIE WILKENS HAD BEEN A SMALL WOMAN IN life. Sprawled across her kitchen floor, she seemed larger, which was the opposite of how Mac usually saw dead bodies. He'd been at far worse scenes than this one, but it was clear unnatural death had occurred here. The large dent in Natalie's head made that obvious.

This wasn't his investigation. He shouldn't be on the scene, but he couldn't refuse Desiree Marbury's request for help. She was butting heads with Grassley, and the next most experienced officers were her own staff. Grassley wanted them all gone so he could "wrap things up and file murder charges." McNamara wondered if the man had forgotten everything he'd ever learned about police work, or if he thought Marbury had.

"All we *know* from her injury and the blood splatter is that she hit her head on the corner of the kitchen island," Marbury said to Grassley, enunciating each of her words slowly and carefully.

"What we don't know, yet, is if she was attacked, had a medical emergency, or fell accidentally."

Grassley started to argue, but stopped when Tremaine Harper said, "Chief?"

Reflexively, McNamara turned from his inspection of the pantry and caught Grassley's gaze before they both looked at Harper. The young PFC had been looking at Mac when he spoke and had to endure his boss's sharp rebuke.

"Sorry, sir," Harper said in a tired voice. "I wasn't addressing either of you. I just recognized what this is." He was on one knee, flashlight shining under an oak hutch.

Marbury reached Harper first and looked at the shiny gold star he'd found. They all saw Grassley's hand fly to the collar of his uniform shirt.

"Lose something?" Marbury asked.

It got ugly after that.

CHAPTER TWENTY-SIX

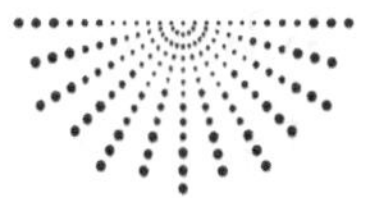

For the first time anyone could remember, the town council's meeting room had been commandeered by the Police Department.

"He knows the MSP are in charge, doesn't he?" Mac asked Mayor Ruby Blanchard.

They watched from the hall as Grassley untangled cords for two printers and a large computer monitor on the long mahogany table used by the council. Tremaine Harper was unpacking the bags from his latest run to Staples in Easton, while listening to his boss rattle off items they still needed.

"Are you happy being retired?" the Mayor asked, a hopeful note in her voice. "I mean, really happy? Because there's a little village that needs you. Great place, you'll like it. Sleepy in the winter, fun in the summer, and you already know all the residents."

"You gave him a contract, Ruby."

"I remember. And I remember you told us not to."

Mac had another thought. "Does he understand all this will have to come out of his budget?" By his estimation, Tate had already spent several thousand dollars in office supplies, and then there was the overtime for Tremaine, who looked like he'd been up all night.

When Ruby didn't answer, he said, "You gave him a blank check, didn't you?"

"He wasn't supposed to spend this much. He said he had to have at least a basic setup if he was going to solve the murder."

"Natalie Wilkens's death hasn't been declared a murder, yet. That's the whole point of turning it over to the MSP. This is what they do, especially for small jurisdictions. They are the experts, Ruby, and besides, there are additional complications. Tate should be completely hands off."

"He says it'll look bad if we pass our responsibility off to the state."

Grassley caught sight of them and waved them into the room, saying, "Mayor, thanks for coming. This little meeting won't take long. You're both busy people and I'm up to my badge in alligators, as you can see."

He cleared two chairs, then perched on the edge of the table, looming over them when they took their seats. "This is a terrible situation, but PFC Harper and I are on it. I'm making progress, but I'm going to need some extra bodies in here while I run the investigation. Of course, there's no budget for it, so you'll need to find the money, Ruby."

Even for Tate this was brash, but Ruby took over.

"While I'm glad you're bringing Mac in," she said, "as I told you last night, I think this is a job for the State Police."

Grassley leaned forward and gave her a thin smile. "I took an oath, Ms. Blanchard, and I intend to live up to every aspect of it. That means up-holding the laws of this town, the state, and the Constitution of the United States of America. I will not shirk my responsibilities."

Mac wondered if patriotic music was cued up.

"I understand," Ruby started, but Grassley rolled over her.

"I have not asked *Mr.* McNamara for help, and I have no intention of doing so. I wanted him here to tell him that in your presence." They turned to the subject of their argument.

Mac said, "You asked me to come to the Wilkens home, and you asked me here this morning."

"Last night, Detective Sergeant Marbury insisted on having your opinions," Grassley countered. "Perhaps she can find something else for you to do since you're such good friends." A leer accompanied his last words.

Mac let the insinuation go, but it opened the uncomfortable conversation they needed to have. "I'm not working the investigation, Tate. Detective Marbury needed an extra pair of hands at the scene, as you well know. Or maybe you don't since you seem to be confused as to the protocol in an unattended death. The medical examiner hasn't declared it to be murder, yet, has he?"

The Mayor looked from one man to the other in confusion. "What's going on here?" she demanded.

When Grassley didn't respond, Mac said, "The cause of Mrs. Wilkens's death hasn't been officially determined."

"Is that what your friends up in Baltimore tell you?" Grassley snapped.

Mac shook his head. "Mrs. Wilkens has been dead less than twenty-four hours."

"I know exactly how long she's been gone." Grassley's words had a dangerous edge.

"Then you also know it's too soon for the autopsy results to come in."

"Wait a minute," Ruby broke in. "Tate, you told me she was murdered."

"You weren't the only one he told," Mac said. "Half the town is buzzing with his descriptions of the scene at the Wilkens house."

"Not again!" The mayor slapped her hands on the table and stood up. "Tate, you said you were an experienced investigator. That's the only reason I agreed to let you set up this room. You blew your annual budget buying all of this stuff, and now I'm hearing you might not have any use for it?"

Grassley ignored her and turned to face Mac. "Nat was murdered. Anybody looking at her could see that, and I'm going to find out who did it." To Ruby, he added, "He's just trying to malign me, and distract you. A star from a chief's uniform was found in Natalie's kitchen."

"You'll find my hardware sealed in a frame in my den," Mac said. "The State Police determined last night that the star was yours. If you hadn't admitted being in that kitchen earlier in the day, you wouldn't be walking free right now. You and Mrs. Wilkens were in an intimate relationship. Until the circumstances around her death have been resolved, I'm recommending Mayor Blanchard place you on administrative leave."

Grassley was on his feet, hands clenched. "Take your recommendation and get out."

"I'm sorry for your loss," Mac said in a calmer tone. "But you can't be involved in the investigation."

"Well, I've heard the rumors. Is this true, Tate?" Ruby's tone said any answer other than 'yes' would be suspect.

Again, Grassley ignored her. "It's my job, my town. I'm in charge. Now, get out."

But Ruby Blanchard had other ideas. At her request, Mac stood to one side while she put Grassley on leave and took his badge and gun. He did not go quietly.

The mayor wasted no time rounding up the other council members. They contacted the MSP and the sheriff's office for duty coverage, but it was another hour before Mac could leave. He had just reached his truck when his phone rang. He didn't recognize the number beyond identifying the Annapolis area code, but he took the call anyway, welcoming the break in his bleak thoughts.

"Major McNamara? My name is Zara Wingate. I'm Tyler Forester's attorney, and I'm hoping you can help me."

The woman had his former MSP title, which meant she'd read up on him. Mac didn't know how he could help the man who might be the main suspect if Natalie Wilkens had been murdered, but he also didn't want to brood about Grassley. He said, "What do you need?"

THEY SAT IN A BACK BOOTH OF THE EASTON Diner, coffee cups in hand and slabs of apple pie sitting between them. Mac liked the forthright attorney immediately. Wingate, a small woman with a neat, graying cap of curls and a genuine smile, thanked him profusely for meeting with her.

"How can I help?" he asked.

"I understand you were first on the scene of the wreck that killed Hank and Verity York?"

He sat back in surprise. Maybe she wasn't as upfront as he'd thought. "I assumed you were representing Forester on his current charges."

"I am. Or I'm trying to. This is an unusual

situation for me. I am a criminal defense attorney, have been for twenty-five years. Cases like Tyler's are difficult in the best of circumstances, and his is further complicated by our relationship. His mother, Betsy, and I have been best friends since our freshman year of college. I'm Tyler's godmother." She gave him a rueful smile and shook her head. "Put that look away, Major. The boy can't stand me, and frankly, it's mutual."

"Call me Mac," he said. "The major retired years ago."

"Well, Mac, the truth is I can't get out of this, much as I want to. Betsy is a devoted mother—too devoted, in my opinion. She's had a hard life and I won't abandon her, so Tyler's stuck with me as long as she is paying the bill, which Tyler thinks is enormous."

"But which is actually on the house?" he guessed.

"Imagine how thrilled my partners are. I'm not only away on a pro bono case, it's one I'm not likely to win because my client won't talk to me. But, that's my problem, not yours. You're wondering if I'm fishing around looking for an opportunity to prove Tyler was permanently damaged in that accident. Possibly to such an extent he could lash out at a police officer, or even commit a murder."

Mac was back to his first assessment: forthright and scary smart. "Am I right in what I'm wondering?" he asked.

"It's not the plan as I sit here, but I have to look at everything that might impact the charges against him. He's a difficult personality at the best of times and jail is bringing out his worst traits. He's already been in one fistfight and he's not been there a full day, yet."

"Personality traits. Doesn't sound like his poor choices result from an injury."

"When I talked with Tyler and Betsy this morning, they repeatedly brought the wreck into the conversation. It was the only thing he'd talk about, even though he was sitting in jail for assaulting a state trooper. If you can just describe what happened the night of the wreck, it would be helpful. Tyler's made some claims, and I'd rather hear your version before I share them."

He sipped his coffee as he ran dates through his mind. Tyler still had time to sue Ellender York for damages before the statute of limitations ran out. Or Betsy Forester could file a civil suit for her own emotional distress. Zara Wingate probably had good reasons for her questions, but he wasn't sure they were the ones she'd given him. He stuck to recounting the basics she would find in any newspaper's back issues.

"It was raining when I arrived at the accident. Ellender had been driving her father's car, a Cadillac equipped with an emergency notification system. I was responding to the alert forwarded to 911. I assessed the scene, called for backup and medical personnel, and took care of Ellender while we waited for help. She was in shock and her arm was injured. Hank and Verity York were dead." He stopped. For weeks after the accident, he'd seen Verity every night in his dreams. "Tyler was in the backseat, unconscious. He was breathing on his own, so I didn't touch him. The big buck Ellender hit was off the road."

He asked a passing server for a fresh cup of coffee and waited for Zara to ask the question that would tell him what she was really after.

When they both had been served, she said, "Did Ellender say anything to you that night?"

"Such as?"

"Did she say who was driving the car when it crashed?"

He studied the attorney's impassive face and rearranged the theory that had been growing as they'd talked. She'd surprised him again. "You'll have to explain that one," he finally said.

"Against my advice,"—a pointed look underscored her uncomfortable position—"Mrs. Forester has instructed me to find out if Tyler was driving when the York car hit the deer. He says he has recently had a 'reawakening.' His word, not mine. It's in his best interest if I can determine if there's any truth to his sudden recollections."

The lawsuit scenario rose to first place. He decided to stay with the details Wingate already had. "I'd be surprised if Tyler remembers anything."

"That's it?"

"What does he say happened?"

Wingate frowned. "He has vivid memories of the wreck and the death of Verity York. He claims she died in his arms. Nothing we were told at the time or have learned since substantiate such a scenario."

He considered this. "Are you concerned Tyler isn't competent to assist in his own defense?"

"I'm concerned about everything, Mac."

He left the diner and went home to go through his old notebooks. Tyler was lying, and he needed to prove it. He also needed to know why. He was going to revisit the nightmares.

CHAPTER TWENTY-SEVEN

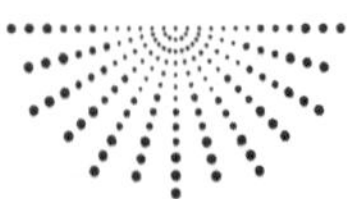

Grace spent most of Saturday morning with Ellender and Mosley fielding questions from the State Police. Ellender's explanation of Tyler's promise to protect her seemed to establish his motive for Detective Marbury, but Grace kept that observation to herself. The focus of the inquiry was clearly on Tyler.

"He's always looking out for me," Ellender said. "I keep telling him he doesn't have to. I can take care of myself. But since my sister and father died, he feels responsible for me. All he meant was that he would keep me safe. It didn't have any deeper meaning. He says it all the time."

When Marbury asked the nature of their relationship, Ellender hesitated before responding,

"Good friends." Grace was sure her client was lying, but she didn't know in which direction. Ellender and Tyler could be lovers, or she might not be his friend at all.

The search of Ellender's house had resulted in all the opened food in her kitchen pantry being collected by the MSP, along with the lawn and garden products in her garage. It wasn't hard to conclude that the police suspected Natalie Wilkens had been poisoned.

Despite Ellender's pleas, neither Mosley nor Grace would agree to act as Tyler's attorney. Mosley pointed out that Tyler had representation and Ellender still needed them. Then he warned her to stay away from Tyler, his mother, and lawyer.

She flatly refused. "I was serious about cutting my ties with him, and I will when this is over. But I won't leave him while he's in trouble. He didn't leave me when he had every reason to, and I won't do it to him."

When their client, looking equal parts defiant and guilty, had gone, Mosley said to Grace, "You're off this case, m'dear."

She struggled to contain her irritation. "We've discussed this. Ellender came in as my client and I want to keep her. If the situation gets to be more than I can handle, or runs into my maternity leave, I'll turn her over to you."

"I'm sorry," he said, "My decision is final." The smile he gave her as he left the office was dismissive, and he was gone before she could react, which was probably for the best.

Furious and worried about her blood pressure, she made herself sit down and think through the past few weeks with Mosley. What was he up to? She decided it didn't matter. She wasn't playing this game anymore. When it suited him, Mosley referred to her as his partner. When it didn't, he called her what she was, an employee. She hadn't forgotten Mac's warning about Grassley, but she wouldn't allow Mosley to treat her as if she were twelve.

This was another decision she'd put off for too long. She'd refused to commit to Mosley's firm, preferring instead to work as he needed her, which, until she got pregnant, had been nearly full time. Eventually, she would need permanent employment, but her instincts had been right—it couldn't be here with Mosley. She wasn't content to guide rich clients through estate planning and property acquisitions, and he fought her on any changes to his practice. She knew she wouldn't be happy working for anyone else, either.

The cantankerous old lawyer had just given her the shove she needed. She'd help him until he and Jake were on their feet and she had childcare set up for the baby. Then she'd open her own firm. She'd decide the details later. It felt right. Wherever her practice took root, she'd be her own boss and win or lose by her own decisions.

She would win, she told Sweet Pea. She was sure of it.

HALLOWEEN ROLLED ON DESPITE NATALIE WILKENS' death, or, depending on where you heard the gossip, her murder. Having been removed from anything to do with either scenario, Grace found herself at odds with no work and Mac preoccupied with some kind of project. He was vague, and she didn't push him. Wasn't this the whole point of not living together? They each had plenty of space.

Niki provided a distraction by giving her a job she didn't want, mainly since it involved wearing a white rabbit costume the size of a bedspread. The guests at the first large party at the Inn at Delaney House would be in costumes for the Halloween theme, and Niki wanted eyes out front to make sure everything came off smoothly. Grace agreed to help, partly so she could safeguard her house, but mostly because Niki promised it was the last event until spring. Except, of course, for Bridezilla's Thanksgiving wedding.

"Stay put, Sweet Pea," Grace said, glaring at Niki and rubbing the new sore spot under her ribs. "Auntie has every day booked until Christmas and she needs your cooperation."

She expected Niki to laugh, or at least protest that nothing was booked after Thanksgiving, but Niki held out the invoice for the party. Under a bold red PAID stamp was an amount that would cover Delaney Inns' expenses for the next two months.

"What's the profit margin?" Grace asked and braced herself for a sob story.

Her cousin's response was to hand over a check that brought them even through the end of the year. "All for you, this time," Niki said. "The profit on Bridezilla is when I turn the bend on the business."

Grace blinked away a rush of tears and hugged Niki. "Congratulations," she whispered. "But I'm still not wearing the rabbit suit."

"You'll be darling in it." Niki produced another piece of paper, this one a list of party details.

"All you have to do tonight is walk around and check these areas. Leah Smith is the host. Keep her in view, in case she needs anything when I'm in the kitchen. She's happy so far, but the guests are her husband's clients and she's nervous."

"I can do that in my own clothes," Grace protested.

"You'll stand out and be a buzzkill."

"Only for the doctors in the room. No costume and no more arguing."

She cut notches in the waistband of her largest black maternity slacks and squeezed into a black silk tunic. The look worked, she decided. She would go as a rotund maître d'.

Chores occupied the afternoon, and as the party got underway, she had to admit that after years of searching for her professional niche, Niki may have found it with her new business. Her waitstaff was well coordinated, the food delicious, and the drinks free flowing. Delaney House had been built for entertaining and hummed with the party's energy. Grace smiled, watching her cousin in action. Gone were the days when the big, empty rooms echoed any movement. Reservations were coming in daily, and her investment in what had been a crumbling pile of bricks was beginning to pay off.

Relieved as she was with the successful party, she was ready to call it a night by eight.

"You can't quit now," Niki said when she found Grace loading a plate in the kitchen.

"Sorry, kiddo. Here's a lesson: don't hire your rapidly aging, overly pregnant cousin to work big parties. I'm going upstairs."

"But, you can't!"

"I'll use the back staircase," she said, knowing that wasn't what Niki meant.

"The music will keep you from sleeping. Grab a snack and then give me a hand with the dessert trays, please? One more hour and I'll carry you upstairs, myself."

Grace considered it. The baby had been quiet all evening. Maybe she could manage a little longer. But her back was hurting and now that she was standing still, climbing the three flights of stairs was out of the question.

"You don't want me out there barefoot and these shoes have to come off. I'll go over to Avril's and spend the night." Ignoring Niki's protests, she added a handful of cookies to her dinner plate for Avril, and two of Leo's favorite biscuits for the dogs, then covered it all with a tea towel and left out the kitchen door. The cool night air felt wonderful as she walked from her yard into the woods. There was a faint scent of wood smoke from a nearby house, and Grace hoped it was Avril's. She could sit by the fire before trying out the nursery suite.

Something moved in the shadows off to her right.

"Who's there?" She stopped, listening over the sound of her thumping heart. She was on a well-worn path, halfway through the narrow strand of woods, but nothing felt familiar in the dark.

Something snapped right behind her. She dropped the plate and ran.

A tree root came out of nowhere, and a second later, she was sprawled on the ground. She screamed and tried to move, but the pain in her back was too much. The last time she'd fallen in these woods, she'd landed in a grave. Tonight, she had more to worry about. The baby wasn't due for five weeks.

She heard her name being called, and yelled, "Something's out here!" A light appeared from the direction of Avril's backyard.

"*Gracie!*" From the opposite direction, Niki's voice joined Avril's as both women reached her in a chorus of yelling and conflicting directions. She tried to sit up, then just as quickly sank down again, startling both of her saviors into silence.

"Back," she said through clinched teeth.

Niki leaned away, but Avril said, "I'm not leaving her. Call 911."

"No, no," Grace gasped. "It's my back, not the baby."

"You're out traipsing around in the dark. What the hell do you know about anything?" Avril snapped. "And *you*," she said, rounding on Niki, "call 911, now!"

Bedlam resumed and continued until Grace was being lifted onto a stretcher. No one saw anything suspicious in the woods, but Niki said she'd get Avril home safely, which started an argument about which of them, exactly, needed looking after.

Grace didn't tell the paramedics she wasn't in labor. She wanted them to take her some place quiet.

CHAPTER TWENTY-EIGHT

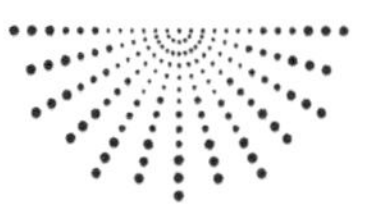

The ER doctor agreed with Grace that all seemed well with the baby, but in light of the severity of her back pain, kept her overnight before releasing her on Sunday morning to Niki, Mac, and Avril. Avril won custody with the argument that she would be on hand if Grace needed anything, while Niki had reservations and Mac would have to take leave from work. Grace was happy with any solution that didn't require her to recuperate in Meri McNamara's house or climb three flights of stairs.

Mac spent the rest of the morning combing the woods where Grace had fallen, but found nothing out of the ordinary. After that, Grace quit insisting she'd heard someone or something. She knew what she knew, but Mac was worried enough for both of them.

Sweet Pea's room at Avril's turned out to be as comfortable as it looked. The landlord, however, made Grace reconsider the emotional price of her refuge. Two nights in the nursery suite got her up on her feet. She returned to work on Tuesday and shamelessly wrung every bit of sympathy from her coworkers. Even Marjorie was subdued and brought her decaffeinated coffee without being asked.

Work proved to be a sufficient distraction from her aches. With only minor arm-twisting, Mosley shared news he'd gotten from Ellender, who'd been briefed by Betsy Forester, who quoted Tyler's attorney. If the information train was correct, preliminary reports on Natalie Wilkens showed she had fallen during a seizure and died after striking her head on a table corner. The cause of the seizure was the ingestion of a pesticide.

The reports bolstered the case against Tyler. The arguments he'd been so proud of having with Ellender's tormenter and the details he'd freely shared of his last visit to the Wilkens house were now evidence against him. With this development, Grassley was reinstated as chief after three days of leave, but was under orders to not interfere with the State Police investigation of Natalie's death. The Mallard Bay Police Department was not a happy place.

Mosley told Grace to forget about the investigation and Ellender, and work on a zoning issue that had been sitting on a back burner. Once again, he shut her protests down with a finality that offered no compromise.

The morning passed uneventfully, and although she chafed under Mosley's patriarchal attitude, she was grateful for the respite. Her back was tender, but nearly healed, and she'd almost decided she could get used to calm and boring when the buzzer on her desk phone burst to life. Marjorie's special long ring signaled an emergency in the outer office.

The emergency's name was David.

"I don't understand why everyone connected to you is so rude," he said, glaring over his shoulder at Marjorie as she stomped out of Grace's office, shutting the door with more force than necessary.

Grace thought this was amusing until he turned his attention to her.

"I came as soon as I heard you were injured."

She couldn't tell if he was disappointed that

she was up and moving, or surprised. "Who told you that? I'm fine, as you can see."

"You fell. In the woods. In the middle of the night. That was incredibly irresponsible." He looked as if it took all his self-control not to explode. "If you don't care about your own well-being, consider our child's."

He wasn't saying anything she hadn't been torturing herself with, and she told him so.

"Well, then," he said, startled for a moment. Then he reached for her, pulling her into a gentle hug. "You're really okay?"

"Yes. We're fine as we can be." She pushed him away, hoping a smile and a few platitudes would send him on his way.

He shot down that hope with his next words. "Since I'm here, I want to talk about the schedule."

"Yours or mine?"

"Be serious, Grace."

He was still standing, something she couldn't do for long stretches. She waved him toward the conference table and eased herself into a chair. "Let's have it."

"I want you to have the baby at Holy Cross Hospital."

"In Silver Spring? That's seventy miles away!

You want me to drive over the bridge when I'm in labor?"

"Of course not. Come home with me today and stay until the baby is born. We can discuss what happens after that, later. I even have a room for him. Look."

She waited as David thumbed through screens on his phone and produced a video of a circus-themed nursery.

"Do you think he'll like it?" David asked, surprising her with his anxious tone. "I know I bought too much, but once I got started, it was hard to stop."

She stared at the crib, dresser, rocker, and a showroom full of toys and accessories. "It's a beautiful nursery, David. And when we visit, the baby will love it."

Visit lay between them, a chasm that seemed impossible to bridge.

He closed the picture. "Any chance I can talk you into a few days of pampering in DC? If you won't stay with me, I'll get you a suite at the Willard. You'd enjoy that, wouldn't you?"

To her surprise, he only nodded when she declined. Which meant she was off-balance when he moved in for the kill.

"I love you, Grace. I think I've made that

clear, so remember it in the weeks to come. I'm not giving up or backing off. We are a family. This child belongs to me. I can't make you love me, but he is mine and always will be. Do you understand?"

She remembered this expression and tone. Her mouth went dry as he talked, and Sweet Pea squirmed. "You're threatening me!" She hated that her voice shook.

"Did that sound like a threat? My apologies. I wouldn't want any eavesdropping secretaries to misunderstand me." He stood, straightened his already perfect shirt cuffs, then in one quick move, bent down and kissed her, hard. "I'll do whatever I have to keep my kid," he whispered in her ear. "Don't make me prove it."

He left her then, but his touch and scent lingered on her skin until she ran to the bathroom to wash her face.

"Is he going to be popping in like that often?"

Grace was startled to find Marjorie waiting for her when she returned to the office. Her face was still damp, but The Bat didn't ask what she'd been up to.

"Unless you want to catch a baby on your lunch hour, stop surprising me," she said. But in an odd way, she felt better. She knew where she stood in this situation.

"That child is staying put for a little while, anyway," Marjorie said as she settled her bony backside on the edge of a chair.

"And you know that, how?"

"Raised on a farm."

Grace didn't ask any more questions. She knew the answers were unlikely to be flattering. "Okay, then. Back to David. I'm sorry if he upset you, but yes, he's likely to be here from time to time. Handle him however you want, but I appreciated the heads-up."

Marjorie frowned. "You mean the long ring on the intercom? That key gets stuck sometimes."

"Okay." Grace shrugged and kept her smile to herself.

"Are you moving in with Lee?"

How did she do it? It was as if Grace's internal debate had set off an alarm on The Bat's radar. "Why do you ask?" It was weak and whiney, but she really wanted to know.

Marjorie looked upset. "He gave me some

things of Meri's. Claimed he was rearranging furniture."

"I'm not moving in," Grace said, relieved that she could be truthful with Mac's sister-in-law.

"He put their wedding pictures away. He's moving on." Marjorie stood. "But I wish it wasn't with you. I wanted someone more like Meri for him, but I won't cause trouble. I just want you to understand that however you and Lee end up, I'm his family and that won't change. "

Her speech echoed David's threat, but Grace didn't think she'd eavesdropped on them. There was no fight in Marjorie, just a sadness that tugged at Grace's conscience. She and Marjorie were in complete agreement. Mac did deserve better than a woman who was constantly in crisis, which is how she would always be if she couldn't settle the problem of David.

CHAPTER TWENTY-NINE

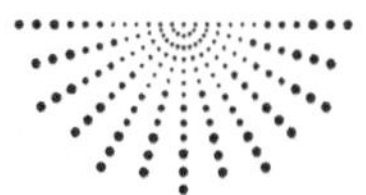

The morning moved along like a bad movie. Once one painful scene ended, another began. The next surprise was the arrival of the Maryland State Police.

Mosley asked Marjorie to show the two officers to the conference room and to put Ellender in his office when she arrived. When they were alone, he turned his attention to Grace. "I suppose you're going to demand to know what's happening?"

She gave him a pass for stress. "I'm not making demands. I'm worried, Cyrus. I want to be included in the meeting."

He frowned. "And as I've told you, I, alone,

am representing Miss York. End of discussion. You have other work to do."

This was not the Mosley she knew. He left, and she heard male voices in the hallway. When his office door shut, she swallowed her pride and joined a flustered Marjorie in the reception room. "What—"

"I don't know," Marjorie burst out. "He won't tell me anything. We could ask Jake, but he's at a school conference. Oldest kid, I think."

That Jake could be in Mosley's orbit while Marjorie and she were excluded would have been unthinkable a month ago. Grace said she was going to pack up and work at home for the rest of the day, but instead of stopping in her office, she slipped into the file room.

Searching the computer files would leave a footprint, but Grace thought the information she wanted would predate electronic storage. She found nothing in the first three drawers she checked. She'd thought there would be a file on at least one of Ellender's parents. A history with the York family could account for Cyrus's secretive behavior, but nothing turned up under their names.

On a whim, she checked for Owen and Natalie Wilkens, then groaned and straightened her aching back. Files on the couple filled the entire bottom drawer of the archived records. It would take hours to go through them, and when Cyrus found out what she'd done—and he would—he'd explode.

So, he'd had been the Wilkenses's attorney, and now he had taken Ellender as a client. So what? He must think that representing Ellender didn't present a conflict, but then why hadn't he mentioned the situation to Grace? The answer to that was easy: he wasn't talking with Grace about anything these days.

What had driven such a wedge between the Wilkenses and the Yorks? And why didn't Cyrus want her anywhere near Ellender? She wasn't his kind of client, and this wasn't his kind of case. So why did he want her?

All the reasons Grace had for leaving his practice rushed back, fueled by the daily irritation of Jake sitting in Lily's seat and Marjorie's blatant insults. She was an experienced attorney with an impressive resume. Why was she putting up with this insanity? Without bothering to close the over-stuffed cabinet drawer, she left the file room, grabbed her tote and jacket, and left without a word.

She would give Cyrus notice tomorrow, finish up the projects on her desk, and leave. He'd made it abundantly clear Jake could step into her job, so her departure should make everyone happy.

She felt a thrill of excitement. The timing couldn't be worse, but she would be free.

SHE POINTED THE BMW OUT OF MALLARD BAY and tried to keep a light foot on the gas pedal. The perfect next scene for this horror show of a day would be for Grassley to pull her over for speeding. She had no destination in mind, just a need to move while she sorted her thoughts. Her options had narrowed in the last few hours, but her vision had cleared. It wasn't a sudden reaction to the morning's events, but a recognition of the lessons she had learned while she'd been busy fighting for a life she realized she no longer wanted.

The long months of pregnancy had given her more than a new person to love. Her perspective was different. Some of it was Mac. Their romance was a boost to her ego, but loving and being happy with a good man changed everything. Whether she and Mac stayed together, and what such a union might look like, was still hazy, but it was possible. And that was more than she'd had six months ago.

Somehow, she would handle David, and her child would have a happy home.

She loved and was loved. She was strong. She was smart.

She would think of something.

THE RESOLVE GRACE FOUND ON HER DRIVE lasted long enough to get her home. She was in the downstairs kitchen at Delaney House, eating pretzels and doodling on a to-do list, when she heard Niki talking in the hallway. Seconds later, her cousin burst into the room, chattering at top volume to someone in an area with worse cell service than the Eastern Shore.

"Let me check . . . Did you say *four*?" When she caught sight of Grace sitting at the table, Niki froze while the shrill voice at the other end of the phone chattered on.

Grace rolled her eyes.

"Well, at the last minute like this, I don't know if I can manage it," Niki said. "And if I can, there would be a premium. We're closed for the season, as I said. Double? Let me put you on hold just a sec." Without giving Grace a chance to say no, she begged for mercy. "*Please*, Gracie! It's only tonight. They want four rooms. At double rates. That's . . ."

Grace watched her try to add the numbers in her head.

"A lot of money," Niki finally said. "And you won't even know they're here. I promise. Maybe you could go to Avril's?" They both knew if Grace hadn't heard the call, Niki would have rented the rooms without hesitation.

"I'm not going anywhere tonight, so don't you dare rent my apartment."

Niki blew her a kiss and returned to her call.

Grace smiled and cleared away the remains of her snack. She had taken action on one of her decisions, and it felt good.

"Can you stay a few minutes and give me a hand?" Niki said as Grace slipped her notes into her tote and picked up her keys. "The rooms are clean. I just need to do a little spiffing up."

Grace shook her head. "Sorry. You only get the house, not a maid." She left Niki scrambling to order food while simultaneously running a dust mop down the wide side hallway.

Once upstairs, she tried to continue planning the upcoming changes in her life, but the sounds from the floors below were distracting. She was too antsy to nap. There was so much to do, even choosing which step to take first was daunting. She ended up doing nothing at all until one decision was made for her.

The extended family who occupied the second floor of Delaney House that night wasn't loud, but noise still drifted up to Grace's apartment. The increase of plumbing sounds and footsteps on the stairs reinforced her concern that this was not the right place to live with a baby. What would an infant's cries do to the guests' experience in the authentic three-hundred-year-old inn they'd paid to enjoy?

She had five months left before the Inn at Delaney House reopened in the spring. Five months to give birth, adjust to motherhood, and to move. There. Another decision made—she would find a new home. There really was no other choice. She and Mac had agreed not to live together, and Avril's suite was not a long-term solution.

None of this kept her awake. She knew she was on the right path and she slept well. Which was good, because the next day her personal problems were once again swept aside as the outside world rolled over her. Changes that had been bubbling away under the surface of daily life exploded in Mallard Bay on Wednesday morning.

∾

THE DAY STARTED WELL ENOUGH. SHE STOPPED BY the bakery and bought a dozen of Jeannie Harper's special macadamia cookies. At the office, she cheerily offered them first to Marjorie, who wanted to know who'd made them before taking one, and then to Jake, who looked confused but happily scarfed down three. She was pleased to see that Cyrus was in his office. She wasn't in the mood to be nice to him. With cookies for fortification, she plowed through every open account in her office, littering the paper files with sticky notes and the electronic ones with memos regarding the work to be done. She was so engrossed she missed seeing Tate Grassley arrive and stride, unannounced, into Mosley's office. However, the yelling that started minutes later got her attention.

Grace and Marjorie met up outside Mosley's closed door.

"Don't you have a microphone planted in there? I can barely hear them," Grace whispered as The Bat made swatting motions in her direction.

"You loathsome jackass!"

They had no trouble hearing the rest as

Mosley ripped into Grassley, but unfortunately, nothing he said explained the conflict. Jake joined them, and then they all had to scramble out of the way as Grassley flung the door open and barreled down the hall.

"What in the world!" Marjorie cried, then jumped back another few feet as Mosley came out of his office. His bright red face said his blood pressure was at an unhealthy level.

"Keep that reprobate out of here!" He pointed a shaking finger at Marjorie. "If he returns, call the police. The *real* police. Call, call . . ." he stood clenching and unclenching his hands as the women exchanged worried looks.

"I'll call Mac," Grace offered. "He'll know what to do."

"I *know* what to do," Mosley sputtered. "But it's illegal, and Mac would do it, so don't call him." He rubbed his bald head, massaging the area that had once been covered by a pompadour. "Jake," he barked, making them all jump. "My office."

Grace and Marjorie were left behind, angry and mystified. Whatever was going on didn't include them.

CHAPTER THIRTY

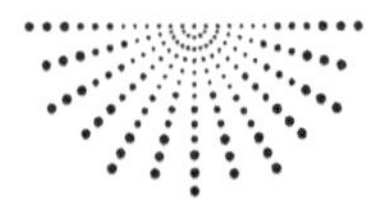

Mac called as she was leaving for work the next morning. "Marjorie told me what happened yesterday. You okay?"

She realized how much she'd missed him. "I'm going into the office for a little while. I've got to plan how to handle the next few weeks."

He saw right through her. "Tell me."

And that was all it took. She put the keys and her tote down, settled in the old rocking chair and told him everything.

Marjorie had given him the sordid details of the Grassley blow up, so Grace explained how Cyrus had been behaving, and the decision she'd made to leave her job immediately. "Except now, I can't leave him," she said. "He's up to something involving the State Police and Ellender and he only has Jake for backup."

"How do you propose to protect him?" Mac asked. "He won't cooperate and stand behind you."

"You don't understand how upset he is," Grace insisted.

"I do understand. I understand because both you and Marjorie have told me and I respect your instincts. And, I've had several conversations with Cy. He's not being dismissive of you, Grace. Paternal, yes. Dismissive, no. You really can't help him, but you could make things worse. Do you want to take that risk?"

"You're not telling me to drop it because I'm pregnant, are you?"

"Of course not."

She smiled. Not because of his answer, but because she believed him.

When she arrived at work, she was calmer and ready to blast through the small projects she hadn't turned over to Jake. With a bit of luck, she would walk out tomorrow afternoon with a clear conscience. She'd offer to coach Jake by phone, or he could come to her. However they worked it out, she'd be out of Cyrus's firm.

She'd barely settled in at her desk when the noise started. At first, she tried to ignore it, telling herself whatever was going on across the hall didn't concern her. If her help was needed, The Bat wouldn't be shy about demanding her presence. She heard the scrape of furniture, and arguing from Marjorie and Cyrus, with an occasional placating word from Jake. By the time things were quiet again, her attention was on the office calendar.

She'd finished reviewing a will Jake had drafted and was trying to get into the main calendar app. Her password had been kicked out three times. Her own calendar opened without a problem, but she saw nothing had been scheduled after her maternity leave. That didn't make sense. No one but Grace, and now Mac, knew she wasn't coming back in April. She reached for the intercom button, then hesitated. She'd enjoyed a relatively peaceful morning, and even an innocent mistake with the calendar would lead to an argument with Marjorie. It could wait.

By noon, satisfied she'd made enough progress to stop for lunch, she was punching in the numbers for the deli when Cyrus knocked on her door.

"A moment of your time?" he asked.

"Just about to order lunch. Want something?"

"No, thank you. I'd like to have a word, please."

"Sure." She studied him, but he had that implacable, closed expression he assumed when working on something unpleasant. "Everything okay?"

He gave her a curt nod and said, "Everything will be fine."

His unusually bad behavior of late, the noise of furniture being shuffled around, and her suddenly empty calendar all kicked in. "I want to talk to you, too. If I might go first?"

"I'd prefer to take care of my business and then if you have questions, I'll try to answer them."

He clasped his hands behind his back and remained standing as he talked. At first, he praised her work, but his expression said nothing good would follow the compliments. He moved on to upcoming plans for the firm, telling her Jake was on track to graduate from law school and take the bar. Mosley proclaimed him qualified to work as a junior associate with oversight.

When he paused for breath, she jumped in. "I'm so glad to hear this, because I need to leave the practice, Cy. I'm sorry for the short notice, but it doesn't look like you need me."

He held up a leathery hand that had been quelling younger attorneys for years. "We are more alike than you think, Grace. You are very astute."

He'd been about to fire her. The lump in her throat threatened to choke her. Then she noticed a thick envelope in his hand. After a second, he slipped it into his jacket pocket and said, "You're one of the best attorneys I've ever worked with. It has been an honor to have you here, but you deserve better than an aging practice in a small town. You're sliding toward the seamier side of our profession because there isn't enough work for two heavy hitters in this office. Take this time off with the baby to think about what you'll do later. I'll help you however I can."

Not even his exaggeration of his golf course practice made her smile. He not only wanted her gone, he didn't want her to come back. She barely managed a croaky "Thank you."

"Well! We're in accord. Good. I believe you're due two months of vacation and holidays and I'll add another six months of pay for family leave."

The urge to cry vanished more quickly than it had appeared, and she found her voice. "You can't even pretend to consider my resignation? You already had my severance package worked out! Do you have a check ready in that envelope?"

Mosley looked shocked. He went to his go-to courtroom move of tugging at his belt and rocking back on his heels—which meant he was serious and not going to be shifted. "Grace, I'm proud of you, and I admire your work. I will always be here for you, but we aren't partner material right now. This isn't a good place for you to be."

She agreed, and it was over. A few minutes later, she was driving home, free and shaken to the core. Had Jake and Marjorie known what their boss was planning to do? The only words she'd exchanged with Jake this morning were critical of a letter he'd drafted for her the day before. She'd gone overboard on the corrections, and knew it, but he had taken the criticism without comment. Probably because he knew that he'd soon be able to write however he liked, while she would be unemployed. And now that she thought about it, Marjorie had been subdued, too, bringing her mail as soon as it arrived, and shutting the door behind her as she left Grace's office. Both of them had been out to lunch when she left.

What was really humiliating was the relief she saw on Cyrus's face when she was leaving. Not anger or resignation, but relief. What had caused that?

The fight with Tate Grassley was the only thing that made sense. She thought of Mac saying she could make things worse for Cy. She turned the situation over again and again in her mind, but none of her thoughts brought any relief. For once, she was going to have to let go and trust someone else to solve the problem.

When she broke the news to Mac over dinner, she knew she was right. "How long have you known?" she asked.

"Cy called me this afternoon after he talked to you," he said. "That's why I've been trying to reach you. It didn't seem like something to discuss in voice mail messages."

Grace thought of the three calls she'd missed. Missed because she'd refused them. She'd wanted to be alone in her apartment, where she could think. When she finally called Mac late in the afternoon, she'd tried to back out of their plans for dinner, but had compromised on carryout Chinese.

So far, she'd picked at her Hunan shrimp and mashed the rice on her plate into a paste. "Did he tell you why he wanted me to leave?"

"He said you worked too hard and you wouldn't slow down any other way."

"And?"

"And he's tried to talk to you about it, but you won't listen."

"That's ridiculous. I know there's more. I was only working half days, for heaven's sake. This is the result of Tate blasting into the office yesterday. Cy was furious and he wouldn't talk to Marjorie or me. Only Jake. If you know what's happening, you have to tell me." She stopped and concentrated on not crying.

Mac sighed and reached for her.

"I can't," she whispered, folding her arms across her chest. "I don't want to dissolve into a hysterical pregnant mess."

"Too late," he teased in a gentle tone and pulled her to him, anyway. "Cy has loved you all your life. You know that."

It made her feel worse to think Cyrus loved her, but didn't trust her with the truth. "Why did he tell Jake, but not me? Don't make me slap the Boy Wonder around, because I will."

"Let it go, Grace. Tate's digging his own grave

as fast as he can, so let him finish the job. It doesn't concern you anymore."

"It does if their fight is why Cy wanted to fire me."

"Now who's being ridiculous? He didn't fire you. He wants to keep you safe." His smile disappeared. "Cy has been slaying dragons for more years than either of us has been alive. He's got a problem that he's handling by himself, and I won't break his confidence. You should know him well enough to trust him to do what's right."

He left after dinner, trying and failing to get her to go with him. As a compromise, she promised to set the alarms when he left and thought he looked almost as relieved to escape as Cyrus had been when she left the office.

She climbed the staircase to her apartment, which would soon be a bridal suite. Everything was evolving, and one way or another, she'd caused most of the changes.

"Time to get a plan, girl," she told herself, and picked up her pace.

CHAPTER THIRTY-ONE

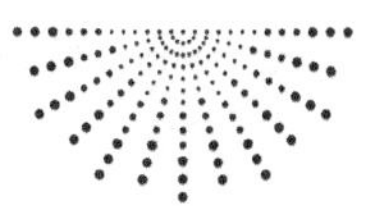

Mac wished he could get his house key away from his sister-in-law without a fight. Moving in the middle of the night might work, but then again, this was Marjorie, so probably not.

"You're not dressed." Her mouth was turned down so far, the edges nearly reached her chin.

"I'm not?" He checked his pajamas. "I have on pants. That's good enough for six thirty in the morning in my own house."

"Catch the front door, will you?" She sailed past him and into his kitchen, her arms full of still-warm muffins, half a cake, and a casserole. "What kind of job do you have again? I guess you set your own hours."

He considered leaving but there was the pajama problem.

From the kitchen, Marjorie yelled, "You don't have coffee made? I'll do up a pot."

She was staying. He braced himself for A Problem and went to take over the coffee chores. Marjorie made battery acid caffeine, and he already had heartburn.

When he had their cups ready, he interrupted the list she was making of chores that needed doing around his well-tended house. "I'm not awake enough for small talk, Margie," he said. "So let me have it. What's bothering you, and it better not be about Grace."

He rarely used that tone with her.

"I'm not standing in your way anymore," she finally said. "I told Grace awhile ago."

"I appreciate that." He didn't add that Marjorie's disapproval had never slowed him down in his pursuit of Grace. He was fairly sure his determination had been obvious to everyone.

"Yes, well," she said dramatically. "What's the point? And as for her child—"

"Marge."

"I only mean you'll be a good influence on the poor little thing. Lord knows—"

"Mar-jor-ie."

"It's Cyrus."

It could be a trick to pull him into office gossip, but that wouldn't rate an early morning visit. "Is he sick, again?"

"No, but something's wrong. Lee, I'm not sure how much Grace told you, but Cy fired her. Well, she quit, but only because he was going to fire her." When this got no response, she added. "It wasn't right, and I told him so."

"What did he say?"

"The usual. Told me to mind my own business."

"Which stopped you in your tracks, I'm sure. *Is* it any of your business?"

"Everything to do with Cy and the firm is my business. My life. You know that."

He didn't argue with her.

"Whatever's wrong has to do with Tate Grassley," she continued. "I believe the argument they had a couple of days ago was why Cy wanted Grace to leave. He's protecting her."

Hoping to buy some time to think, he said, "From what?" then drained his cup and got up for a refill. He should have been prepared for this. Damn Cy, anyway.

"She won't be able to find a job before the baby comes, and setting up her own firm will take time. I think Cy suspected she'd try to keep her hand in his practice while she was on maternity leave, so he made sure she couldn't. And if she isn't working, she'll be out of Tate's way." Marjorie stopped for a breath and to judge his reaction before adding, "Grace was snooping in the archived files."

"Did Cy catch her?"

Marjorie grabbed a paper towel and polished the spotless stovetop.

Mac saw the evasion for what it was. "Did you catch her and tell Cy?"

"Who knew he'd react that way? And I only told him because I was worried, too. Tate hates Grace, and she was in the Wilkens files. I was afraid she was getting close."

"Close to what?"

"Whatever you and Cy have been trying to keep from us. Something that would be in the old Wilkens file."

This was just great. Now he was going to be blamed when Grace found out what her ex-boss had done. He wanted to call Cyrus and tell him to come get his troublesome secretary, but then he'd have to deal with their argument, too. He went to offense instead. "Why do you say Tate hates her?" Marjorie blushed and he knew whatever was making her uncomfortable ought to be good.

"I dropped into the station week before last to take him some of my muffins. Sort of a late welcome gift to smooth over the rough time Cyrus and Grace had given him. I thought Tate was a nice guy, even if he had insulted Grace, which I now agree was wrong. Very wrong, okay?"

He managed not to laugh, and Marjorie rushed on, misinterpreting his expression as irritation.

"Anyway, I was intending to invite him to dinner, but when I walked in, he was yelling at Tremaine Harper. Tremaine! That young man's never done anything in his life to deserve that kind of treatment. I was shocked at that, but then Tate turned on me and said if Grace thought she could buy him off by sending me over with muffins, she was wrong. Then he said if I knew what was good for me, I'd get out. You better believe I got out of there fast."

"You tell Cy?"

She nodded. "That's when I was sure something was up. Ordinarily, he'd just tell me not to flirt on the firm's time, then help me figure out what was going on. But he yelled at me—really yelled, not like our usual back and forth—and told me to stay away from the station and to watch my speeding. He said he didn't want to have to get me out of jail for doing thirty in a twenty-five zone. It was like watching the old Cy twenty years ago. Then he made Grace leave, and she hadn't done anything to warrant that. I mean nothing beyond the usual, which is plenty, but still. Yesterday, I heard him on the phone and he said, 'She doesn't work here anymore, so leave her out of this.' I'm sure it was Tate he was talking to."

"You don't know that," Mac said, but it was a force of habit to contradict her gossiping.

"Who else would it be?" she snapped. "It's not like he has shouting matches with anyone else. Cy's protecting Grace. He loves that girl like a daughter. He's been irritable lately, but get rid of her? If anyone could make him do that, I'd have pulled it off ages ago." She grinned at the glare Mac gave her. "Just checking to see if you're taking this all in."

"I've heard every word," he assured her.

"There's more. He's gone at it with Grassley several times, including warning him off Ellender York. I, uh, overheard that, too."

"I'll talk to him, Margie."

She recognized the dodge for what it was. "But you won't be in a hurry, because you know what's going on, right? You and Cy are infuriating."

He laughed and squeezed her hand. "You give as good as you get. And speaking of problems at work, aren't you going to be late?"

After she left, Mac finished the coffee, dressed, and called Cyrus.

Things were getting out of hand.

CHAPTER THIRTY-TWO

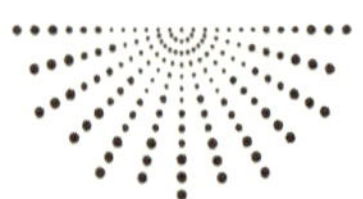

As Grace predicted, the news of her departure from Mosley's office traveled quickly, if incorrectly. According to Niki, the story buzzing through the pre-town meeting gossipfest was that Grace had tired of working and wanted to be a stay at home mom—in Paris.

"You're gonna have to spiff up your wardrobe, girl," Niki said as they ate breakfast. "You can't go to Paris in the clothes you wear around here."

"If it's good enough for shopping at Three Pigs and Baldy's Market, it's good enough for Paris. Besides, Provence is where I'm supposed to be right now."

Had the year turned out according to plan, she would have been in Paris next month, just about the time Sweet Pea was due. "I can't remember when anything went as I planned it."

"Don't sweat this, Gracie." Niki reached out and took her hand. "Whatever dumb thing Cy is going through is his problem. And this break will be good for you. When you're ready, you can open your own firm and I'll help with the baby and so will Mac and Avril. We're all family. Better than, actually."

Tears sprang to Grace's eyes. Before she could stop herself, she told Niki about David's last visit. "He said we are a family and the baby is his. He said he'd do whatever he had to in order to keep it."

"He threatened you?"

Hearing the words from Niki made Grace feel worse. She nodded and wiped her face.

Niki's response was immediate. "I'll bet you didn't tell Mac, did you? Call him now."

"No!" Grace stopped and took a deep breath. "I shouldn't have told you. It wasn't that bad, I'm just emotional. He was mad because I wouldn't give in and have the baby at Holy Cross. I can handle David."

Niki's mouth fell open. "Oh, my God. It's like a bad soap opera. Do you realize those are exactly the words my mother uses? 'I can handle your father. No one knows him the way I do. I'll be fine.' Did David hit you, Grace? You know that's what Dad . . ." she stopped. After two years and several almost breakthroughs, she'd finally exposed her family's biggest secret.

"Oh, honey." Grace reached to hug her.

Niki's blond curls fell across her face and she pushed them back angrily. "Mom says that, too. 'Oh, I fell, honey. I'm so clumsy.' How many times can the woman fall down three steps to the patio?"

"Listen to me," Grace said. "David has never touched me in anger. If he had, I'd have left, and had him arrested, and he knew it. He had nothing I wanted except his love, so that's what he used against me."

"But, don't you see? It's still abuse, even if he didn't touch you!"

"All right! I was abused. I was belittled and demeaned and ignored. I put up with raging tantrums and took care of him and sacrificed my happiness. He and I are very skilled at hurting each other." Grace sat back, spent.

Niki absorbed this, then said, "How much? Can you hurt him, I mean? If he tries to take the baby, can you hurt him enough to stop him?"

"Don't make it worse than it is," Grace said.

Sweet Pea stretched, flexing those busy little feet, and she thought about Niki's question. "I can handle David," she said. There was no bravado in her words, only determination.

The cousins looked at each other, each making decisions. "I'll help you," Niki finally said, reaching across to take Grace's hand. "Whatever you and the baby need, I'm here. Understand? What*ever* you need."

The doorbell rang, but Niki didn't let go until Grace nodded.

~

NIKI AND ELLENDER KNEW EACH OTHER, something that Grace hadn't realized until they greeted each other at the front door. Niki's cool tone when she excused herself said there would be a story later.

"I guess I knew she was related to you," Ellender said once Niki had returned to the kitchen. "She was in school with Cherish and my sister, Verity."

Grace ignored the comment and suggested they talk in the front parlor. It was close by, and she hoped Ellender wouldn't be staying long. She was Mosley's client, and the last thing

Grace wanted was a turf war with her former boss.

When they were seated across from each other on the love seats that flanked the fireplace, Ellender said, "I understand you don't work with Mr. Mosley anymore."

"It was always a temporary arrangement," Grace said. She'd decided that was enough of the truth to be a good answer.

Ellender nodded as if this pleased her. "I want to hire you, and before you say no, please hear me out."

"There's no point. You're Cyrus's client and I can't represent you."

"I'm not asking you to. I want to hire you for Tyler. He's been charged with premeditated murder. Natalie had a seizure and fell, but because the seizure was caused by the pesticide in the flour Tyler took her, they're saying he's responsible. Even the attorney his mother hired wants him to plead guilty to involuntary manslaughter. He won't do it and everything's a mess. He keeps getting into fights and he's got injuries."

"Who's the attorney?"

Ellender looked impatient. "Does it matter? Tyler's innocent, and he won't plead guilty." She dug through her purse and produced a business card.

"Zara Wingate." Grace tapped the name into the search bar of her phone and read the first response that popped up. "She's well qualified. Experienced, and she specializes in criminal law. This is the type of attorney he needs, but if he won't use her, he should get someone with similar qualifications."

"He hates her and won't deal with her. He's agreed to hire you on my recommendation."

"I'm sorry." Grace stood, grateful for the sturdy arm of the love seat and making a note not to sit on its soft cushions again until after the baby came. "I'm not taking on any clients or doing any work for the next six months. Tyler needs a good criminal attorney, not a friend."

Ellender smiled, and said, "Oh, he doesn't like you."

Despite her irritation, Grace laughed. What was it about this girl?

Ellender was still sitting, head tilted up to meet Grace's gaze. "That sounds awful, but I'm being honest with you. He needs an attorney, and he'll accept you because I trust you. Also, he was impressed by the way you handled that detective on the night that Natalie died. And he thinks you'll stand up to his mother. This Wingate woman is a friend of his mother's."

"Is that a real goal for him? He's in jail charged with murder and his concern is defying his mom?"

"No. Not exactly. She smothers him and always has. Her solution to everything is to get him into therapy, preferably, inpatient. That way he's confined somewhere, and she doesn't have to worry about him. He, *we*, believe she wants him to take a plea deal so he'll be off her hands."

"He must cause her a lot of trouble. Does she think he's guilty?"

Ellender's shoulders slumped. "I'm afraid so. There's no doubt he hit the officer, and Betsy thinks he killed Natalie, too. He causes everyone trouble, as you've noticed. I'm sure his mother is worn out, but she wouldn't be if she'd leave him alone, instead of trying to fix him."

"Do you think he's guilty?"

"Of killing Natalie? No." Ellender's answer was unequivocal. "Tyler has problems. You already know that. He says he'll get time served for the assault, and the longer he stays in jail on the murder charge, the better chance he has of coming out with a successful lawsuit. It's a thing with him. He looks for grounds for lawsuits the way other people look for jobs." She stopped, embarrassed, then added, "We argue about that a lot. I keep telling him he can't sue when he's the one starting the fights, but he doesn't listen. He says he has a plan."

"Any idea what it is?" Grace asked.

"It changes a lot. Anyway, he said he'll represent himself if I can't talk you into taking him on."

Grace tried to be kind as she again refused. "Ellender, I appreciate your confidence in me more than you realize, but I'm having a baby soon. I can't help him."

"But he's innocent. Of murder, anyway."

Grace kneaded the tense muscles in her lower back as she considered this. Even though she didn't want Ellender to stay, she sat down again, this time in a straight-back armchair. "I can't do it. I'm sorry. But tell me why you believe he didn't kill Mrs. Wilkens."

"Tyler isn't good at expressing his feelings, or at getting what he wants without offending people. I'm sure he didn't kill Natalie, because he can't lie. He will say things that aren't correct, but only when he believes they're true. He can't deliberately lie."

Grace shook her head. "Why not? Anyone can lie. Everyone *does* lie, in one way or another."

"Not Tyler. Not deliberately, anyway." Ellender was emphatic. "He is so full of emotion, all the time, if he feels something, he says it. He also always has to be right, as you may have noticed. He couldn't maintain a lie past the first telling, so he doesn't bother. Believe me, he isn't truthful because of his scruples."

"Do you think he's capable of killing someone?"

"Yes." Ellender looked unhappy. "I believe he could. But he didn't kill Natalie. He was so proud of their argument and how she'd capitulated to him, he was planning to confront her again."

Grace waited to see if there'd be more of an explanation. When there wasn't, she said, "The best thing you can do for him is to tell this Zara Wingate what you've told me."

"Please." Ellender reached out to Grace, then just as quickly pulled her hand back. "I'm really asking for myself as well as Tyler. Until he's taken care of, I can't leave him. And I have to cut my ties to him."

"I'm sorry. I can't say I like Tyler, but I admire your loyalty. If I could help him, I'd do it for you. Ask Ms. Wingate to recommend another lawyer, it's her field and she'll know the best person for the job."

Ellender didn't argue further, but followed Grace into the entry hall. She turned at the door, looked around and up at the domed ceiling. "This is a beautiful place. Which one of you owns it?"

"What?" Grace asked, surprised. "This is my house."

Ellender shook her head. "It's not your home, though, is it?"

CHAPTER THIRTY-THREE

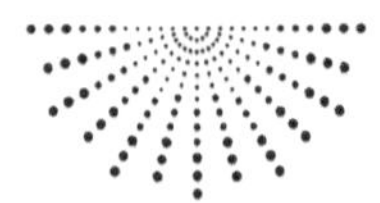

Niki pounced on Grace as soon as the front door closed behind Ellender. "She's delusional. You know that, right?"

"Is that your professional opinion?" Grace asked. She headed for the kitchen without waiting for an answer. She knew Niki was on her heels.

The kitchen turned out to be a mistake, because once inside, Grace couldn't pretend she hadn't seen the disaster. Niki had been busy during the time Grace had spent with Ellender. Graham cracker crumbs and powdered sugar covered most surfaces, and a strong scent of alcohol filled the room.

"Rum balls," Niki said, brightly. "For Bridezilla's reception."

"Looks like you're planning on an army of rum fans," Grace said, wondering how her cousin had managed to get crumbs on the edges of the glass-front cabinets.

"Just twenty dozen. Half vanilla, half chocolate."

"Twenty *dozen*?"

"Well, you need something to keep you busy, so grab an apron and let's get to it. I can fill you in about the York sisters while we work."

Because she'd waited until the last minute to prepare them, Niki had been worried the rum balls wouldn't have enough time to age properly, and she'd increased the amount of Bacardi in the recipe. "The flavor won't be as smooth," she said as she pinched off a bit of the dough and popped it in her mouth. When her eyes stopped watering and she could talk again, she added, "But no one will care when they can get a buzz from candy."

Grace put on a face mask so she wouldn't smell fumes. She knew if she wanted information on the Yorks, she'd have to work for it. Niki kept her end of the bargain, jumping right into her story as soon as they had the rum ball operation underway.

"Verity was a few years behind me in school, but she was really pretty and smart and one of those rare girls almost everyone likes. She was on the homecoming court with me as a freshman the year I was queen, and we had some other activities together. She always seemed older than she was. Dated older guys, too."

"Like Tyler?" Grace asked as she dusted a pastry mat with powdered sugar.

"Well, no. Believe it or not, he's only two years older than Verity. Or was."

Grace did the math. She knew Ellender was twenty-four, which meant Tyler was thirty-one. He looked at least five years older.

Niki said, "I didn't know him well. He was really cute, though, and they looked great together. That's how I remember it, anyway."

Grace shook her head, thinking of the thin, nervous, and obsessive man who drove everyone around Ellender crazy.

"I ran into him in town a couple of weeks ago," Niki went on. "I hadn't seen him in ages. I recognized him, but he's aged so much."

"So how did he end up with Ellender?" Grace asked. "Didn't she have a boyfriend in the picture when Verity died?"

"Not that I know of, but I didn't keep up with her. Back in school, she was like the flip side of Verity. It must have been hard for her, to have an older sister who looked so different. Verity was tall and slim, with long, straight, dark hair. Ellender's auburn hair may be straight, but that's the only thing those two had in common. Ellender pretended to be a mind reader, but I think she was just lonely. The other kids made fun of her, Ellender I mean, but not in front of Verity."

"Ellender was ostracized for pretending to read minds? I guess I can understand that with high school kids."

"According to Verity, the other kids stayed away from Ellender because she really *did* read their minds. Freaky stuff. The story that got the most attention was when she told a teacher to be sure and check her tires before she left school."

Grace rolled her eyes and said, "Let me guess —she had a flat?"

"A blowout, doing sixty. Nearly died in the wreck and lots of people had heard what Ellender said. Right after that she told a kid who was teasing her to go home and ask his mother who Bill was and why he came by on Wednesdays. After that, the Yorks decided on homeschooling for Ellender."

"You don't buy that, do you? I mean that she could read minds or see the future. Whatever." Grace scooped up a teaspoon full of the sticky dough, rolled it into a ball, and then dropped it into a mound of powdered sugar.

On the other side of the old farm table, Niki repeated the process with sweetened cocoa powder. "I hadn't thought about Ellender in years. But I remember this one time when she freaked me out. She and Verity were waiting for their dad to pick them up after school and I was waiting on Aidan to get out of football practice." At the mention of her former boyfriend, Niki's features softened. "He was walking across the parking lot toward us and Ellender turned to me and said, 'You can't love him.' She didn't say it like 'You can't be serious about a goofball like him.' She said it like she was sad, because there was something wrong with me. I just wrote her off as a brat, but Verity poked her and told her to stop it. They got into an argument and I left them to it. But I didn't forget what she said, and the awful thing is, she was right. I've never been in love."

This was a common theme of their girls' night conversations. Grace didn't feel compelled to repeat her "Give It Time" speech, and before she could respond, Niki turned the conversation back to David.

"Why don't you ask Ellender what to do about the big jerk? If you don't want to get all personal with her, just ask if he's going to be a good father."

"We already know the answer to that," Grace said. "She has enough problems without me adding to them. Besides, I think Ellender's just observant. Once rumors start about someone being psychic, it's easy to twist any kind of coincidence into a vision."

"Maybe," Niki said, and dropped a handful of rum balls into a jar. "Unless the rumors and visions are true, then it's just weird."

It was hard to argue that point, and Grace didn't try.

DRAINED BY THE MORNING'S EMOTIONAL EVENTS, she wanted nothing more than a nap, but knew if she closed her eyes, her mind would go back to the first conversation she'd had with Niki. She could worry, or she could do something about David. She fired up her laptop and went to work. Two hours later, she had a plan. When she finally lay down, she immediately fell asleep.

Zara Wingate woke her a little after three. Tyler Forester's attorney sounded short tempered when she asked for a meeting. Grace, who was having a hard time covering her yawns, saw no point and said so.

"I won't take long, Ms. Reagan," Wingate insisted. "Please."

The small woman Grace found on her front porch a few minutes later didn't look like trouble. At five-foot nothing, with short graying hair and brown eyes magnified by wire-rim glasses, she seemed efficient, calm, and determined. It was the determination that set off Grace's internal alarms.

She led the way to the front parlor, offering the lawyer the same seat Ellender had occupied earlier. Unlike most people who bill by the hour, Wingate was quick to the point. She'd come on the same errand as Ellender.

Grace returned the favor. "My baby is due in a few weeks. I'm not working."

Wingate said, "I've talked to Ellender York, and I understood that was your initial answer, but I have a proposal for you. I want to hire you to be the go-between for Tyler and me. I'll remain counsel of record, but you'll join me as an associate."

"I thought he wanted to fire you."

"That's true, but his mother doesn't, and right now, he's letting her make the call."

Grace didn't want to go over the same ground Ellender had covered. "Is he under guardianship?"

"No. And I can't go into more detail unless we have confidentiality."

"Is he a danger to Ellender?"

Zara shook her head. "Not in my opinion. He's gone to great lengths to protect her."

"Which doesn't answer my question."

"No, it doesn't. The truth is, while I don't think he's a danger to anyone but himself, I can't state that for a fact."

Grace thought about all the information that sentence conveyed. "Ellender said he's been charged with premeditated murder. What's your position for defense?"

"Obviously, if I can prove it was totally accidental on Tyler's end, and someone else put the poison in the flour, we'll go with that. If I can't make it work, I'll go with manslaughter, without premeditation or intent to commit murder."

"And if neither works?"

"If he's found guilty of the current charges, we appeal. However, with Tyler's personality, I wouldn't give odds on him making it to the first round."

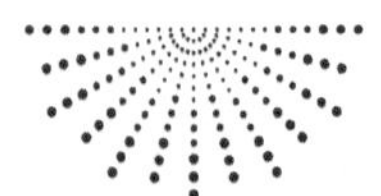

CHAPTER THIRTY-FOUR

"But you think he did it?" Grace asked. She wouldn't help Tyler get away with murder.

Zara looked surprised. "I thought you'd handled criminal cases. I don't decide what the truth will be. I decide what's best for my client and proceed accordingly. Which is why I will try to get a diminished capacity ruling. It will make the rest of the defense easier."

Grace refused to be embarrassed. She hadn't asked for the work and felt no need to assume a professional detachment. "You're asking me for help. I'm not working now, and every aspect of this situation is important if I'm going to change my plans." She watched the attorney consider her response.

"I just need you to help me for the next two weeks," Zara said. "As a liaison, hell, as translator, if you want to look at it that way. Tyler sees me and he shuts down. I need you to communicate with him for me."

"Why two weeks?"

"If he'll agree to manslaughter for delivering the poison to the victim, and I can show diminished capacity to the court's satisfaction, then I should be able to work out a minimum sentence in a facility with treatment programs."

"So, you do think he's guilty. Will he agree to that?" Grace couldn't imagine the self-aggrandizing Tyler allowing Zara to say he was anything less than perfect–and a victim.

Zara smiled. "We'll see. But people do many things you wouldn't expect when they're facing a prison sentence."

Grace's mind raced, piecing bits of information together in this new light. There were still huge holes in Tyler's story and in Ellender's. "I won't do it without knowing everything. Also, I'll have to have Ellender's permission, since I was her attorney at the time of the murder, and your client made some potentially damaging statements against her."

Zara nodded. "She doesn't think Tyler should

plead. She wants you to take his defense because I think pleading to manslaughter is the best way for him to come out of this with something left of his life. She may not agree to you helping me convince him of that."

Grace said, "If she doesn't, it's a nonstarter, and even if she does, I won't do anything against her interests."

"I'll take what I can get."

"Is there a chance he's innocent?"

"There's always a chance." Zara's expression softened. "That's why I do this job. If any evidence, no matter how small, points to Tyler being innocent, I'll fight for exoneration. You have my word."

"Then hire me for an hour and convince me that he should plead to manslaughter."

"And you'll reconsider?"

"I'm not promising anything."

After a moment, Zara set her phone to record, identified herself and Grace, and noted the conversation was to prepare for the representation of Tyler Forester. As she continued to talk about her client, most of Grace's questions were answered.

He was an only child of a woman whom Zara described as over-protective. The combination of a narcissistic personality and lack of discipline had, in Zara's opinion, created a young man who was controlling and manipulative.

"His injuries from the accident that killed Verity York and her father threw him into an emotional chaos," she said with a sigh. "Tyler fills his life with drama. Verity was good at keeping him steady. He obsessed over her, but somehow she handled it. Betsy believed Tyler had grown up."

"When did she realize she was wrong?" Grace asked.

"She and I have been friends for more than thirty years. She's not great at hiding her emotions, and I know she thought he had changed. When Ellender called with the news Tyler had been arrested, it was a shock. Betsy turned to me, and I couldn't say no, but Tyler and I aren't a good fit." She gave Grace a rueful smile. "Plenty of people don't like me, including some of my clients, but that rarely plays into whether I can get them out of trouble. Tyler barely speaks to me. He hasn't fired me, yet, but he will. He's agreed to hire you, and we don't have time to audition attorneys to see who else he might accept. Will you help me try to save him from life in prison?"

Later, when she was alone, Grace knew she'd made a mistake. Despite her best intentions and her instincts, she had joined Zara Wingate's team.

~

ELLENDER'S RELIEF AT HEARING GRACE WOULD help Zara faded when the attorney refused to discuss Tyler or his defense.

"You were happy to talk to me when you needed my help," Ellender said when she finally tracked Zara down after several unreturned calls. "Why won't you tell me what's happening next? When will he get out?"

Zara didn't budge. "I'm sorry, I can't discuss Tyler with you, because you don't have any standing in the case. And please don't bother Betsy. I've advised her not to talk to you or anyone else. I'm sorry to be so harsh, but the defense is always at a disadvantage, and confidentiality is paramount."

Ellender knew what this meant. "You're going ahead with the guilty plea, aren't you?" she demanded. "Tyler doesn't want that! He didn't kill Natalie, and you and Betsy can't make him say he did."

Zara made some soothing noises and was off the phone before Ellender could say anything else.

She was knee deep in packing boxes and wrapping paper, with a china closet that was only half emptied. She didn't want to keep the delicate rose-patterned bone china. Verity would have gotten all the frilly stuff, but now everything was Ellender's. Everything, including Tyler.

"What a mess," she said, not referring to the piles of packing material around her.

When her cell rang, she answered it without checking the unfamiliar number, remembering immediately why that was a bad idea.

"Thanks for the help, Baby," Tyler said, sounding much too cheerful for a man in jail.

She gritted her teeth against his use of her father's nickname. Ever since the day he'd frightened her, he seemed to use it at every opportunity.

When she didn't respond, his tone changed. "Have you talked to my lawyer?"

"Zara or Grace?" she asked, swallowing her useless anger.

His one-word description left no doubt he meant Zara Wingate.

"She says she can't discuss your case with me. And she's told your mom not to talk to me, either." Which, now that she thought about it, wasn't all bad. She couldn't strategize with Tyler if she didn't know anything.

"Better make her tell you what's happening. I need to know and she'll never tell me the truth." His mood was like a light switch flipping on and off. "Eventually, they're going to figure out I didn't do it, and then guess who they'll be coming for?"

It wasn't the first time he'd suggested she could be charged with Natalie's death. Like a dog with a bone, he kept circling and returning to the same point: Ellender was the real object of Natalie's hate and had suffered years of abuse by her neighbor. Who had more motive than she did? There would be no getting him off the topic, but she tried, anyway. Since her conversation with Grace, she'd reconsidered the possibility of Tyler's guilt. What if he had killed Natalie, but had blocked it? Tyler could only tell the truth as he understood it, after all.

"Is Zara still talking to you about pleading guilty to involuntary manslaughter?"

"Why would I do that, Baby?" He sounded genuinely curious. "*I* didn't kill anyone."

She almost hung up, but at the last second, she said, "You took her the flour with the pesticide in it, Tyler. You admitted it to the police."

"No, no," he said. "You don't want to tell it that way. How was I to know you kept pesticide in your baking supplies? I suggest we stick together or we both could be in big trouble. But just out of curiosity, why did you put poison in the flour?"

She wanted to throw up. Was this why Zara wouldn't talk to her? Was this going to be Tyler's defense?

"El? Listen, Baby, that's not why I called. I'm sorry, I don't have much more time. Are you still there?" It was the old Tyler who was begging.

Her hand shook as she punched the speaker icon and set the phone on the table next to her. "I'm listening."

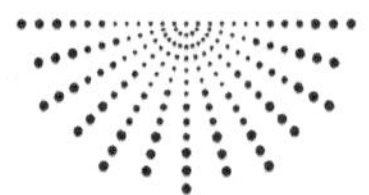

The fire in the den of Mac's cottage was overkill on an evening in the high fifties, and Grace tried not to sweat enough for him to notice. He was drinking Scotch, and she was envious. Her decaf coffee was a poor substitute and no help at all in the argument they were having.

It had been her turn to cook, but she was still avoiding Meri's kitchen. Barbecued ribs from Three Pigs, along with potato salad, and a pint of Cherry Garcia for dessert had solved the problem. The food was the only bright spot of the evening. Mac was quiet, and she didn't want to add her problems to whatever was bothering him. Keeping the conversation light during their meal was difficult. When he asked if she'd heard from any of her clients, she broke the news about her temporary status as Tyler's attorney. They'd been arguing ever since.

She suggested drinks and the fire to change the subject, but he wasn't ready to let it go. He also wasn't accepting her explanation for agreeing to assist Zara Wingate.

"You'd already said no. Why didn't you leave it at that?"

"Tyler's getting hurt in jail, Mac. It's totally his own fault, from the accounts I've heard, but what does that tell you about his mental state? He can't be around other detainees and he can't stand to be alone. He can't afford bail, and Zara is worried he'll get himself killed before the trial. He won't listen to her, and won't agree to a deal for involuntary manslaughter. If she can't change his mind, the state will go ahead with premeditated murder."

Mac's frown didn't lift. "Why is that your problem?"

She wanted to shout "Because he isn't guilty!" But if she did, then she'd have to say that her only proof was her belief in Ellender's argument that Tyler couldn't lie. Better not to bring that up, since it sounded ridiculous. So, instead, she said, "He's a difficult person, but Ellender and Zara think he'll talk to me. It's a good fee, and Zara only needs me for two weeks. After that, whatever happens, I'm done."

"But you're defending an unstable man against a murder charge. And have you forgotten what I said about Grassley?"

"No, but Zara says if Tyler pleads to unknowingly poisoning Natalie, she can work a deal with the prosecutor. Grassley should have some satisfaction from that."

"Great. Then Tyler gets out and you're connected to a guy with a bad temper who's already killed once and a cop with a bad temper who blames you."

Grace looked at him in surprise. Unlike most police officers she knew, he'd never complained about the justice system within her hearing. But then, he wasn't a complainer, period. She'd never considered how he might feel about the violent aspects of his career.

"Just for once," he continued, "couldn't you let trouble go by without grabbing it with both hands? You should figure out where you'll live, have the baby, and get your feet under you before you take on a psychopath."

This was the downside to letting him into her heart. It would be much easier to yell at him if she didn't love him. The heat had become unbearable. "I need some air," she said abruptly, and tried not to run as she left the stuffy room.

He caught up to her on the patio. "You've got to stop doing that."

"Sorry," she gasped between deep breaths of the cool night air. "I'm hot. Sometimes I'm simply overcome when I'm near you."

"Is that so?" He pulled her into his arms, then just as quickly released her. "You're burning up. Are you sick?"

"Only a faulty thermostat. Another bonus of motherhood."

As usual, he read between the lines. "You're not comfortable here, are you?"

"I'm just hot, Mac. It happens. I'll be fine in a minute."

"You aren't comfortable in my house." This time it wasn't a question.

How could she have thought he wouldn't understand?

They sat on the glider, holding hands. After a while, he said, "I love you, Grace, and I don't want to change you. I wish you could believe that. I'm not looking for Meri. I know exactly where she is. You and I are here, alone. There's no one else. Not Meri, not David, just us. And when

David is present and there are reminders of Meri, it's still just us. Just you and me, as long as you love me."

"I'm not hot anymore." She scooted closer, pulling his arm around her, and snuggling into his neck before whispering, "Everything's changing. I'm scared I won't be able to handle what's coming."

"You can do anything," he said, and kissed the top of her head. "I can prove it. Which one of us is about to give birth?"

"Let's see . . . me?"

"That's good. It'd be hard to hire someone to do that at this late date. What else are you going to do?"

"Too much, I'm afraid." She had a long list.

"Do you know why I gave up my job as chief?"

She tried to read his expression in the dark. "Because I keep embarrassing you?"

He laughed. "Tempting to allow you to think that, but no. I resigned because I knew I could do that job. Most days, I could handle it in my sleep. I wanted to try something I wasn't sure I could do."

"Teach?"

"It's harder than it looks, sweetheart. But actually, I was referring to having a normal life with you. I realize *normal* isn't exactly flattering, and God knows it isn't a word I've ever applied to you before. But, when I'm with you, I feel whole and happy. Even when you make me crazy, I'm happy."

"Does your happiness require me to live here?" For a moment, she thought she'd ruined the gift he'd just offered her.

He turned to face her. "No. I only need you to do one thing." He lifted her hand to his chest. "Live with me here."

With a grateful sigh she said, "I can do that."

BREAKFAST WAS A HAPPIER MEAL THAN DINNER the evening before. Their lighthearted banter took a serious turn over the last of the pastries, but this time there was no arguing.

"We need to talk about Tate and Ellender," Mac said. "If you're determined to get involved with Tyler, I want a half hour with no interruptions. Your full attention."

"Like you haven't had it until now?"

"I don't want you yelling because I didn't tell you sooner. Let me get through the whole story. I just put it all together yesterday, after I talked with Marjorie and Cyrus."

"I don't yell," she said primly, and waited until he stopped laughing. "You met with Cy and The Bat and there's a 'whole story'? Are you sure you aren't still a cop?"

"Some days it feels like it."

She waited while he mashed muffin crumbs with the back of his fork, scraped them off, and repeated the process. Sweet Pea stretched, and Grace said he had about five minutes before she needed a break.

"Tate threatened you and Ellender."

She stopped fidgeting. "With what?"

"He was more crude than specific. He and Cyrus got into it—that was the confrontation you and Marjorie heard. Tate says Natalie told you Ellender was threatening her. He also said Ellender knew Tyler was violent and that he intimidated Natalie."

Grace stared at him. "Natalie told me that Ellen hurt her. I told you about talking to her at Three Pigs. Is that why Cy wanted me out of the firm? Because of negative gossip from Natalie?"

"Remember the part about no interruptions? Cy wanted you out because Tate is going after anyone who helps Ellender or Tyler. He scared Cy pretty badly, and getting you out of the office was the quickest way to make sure you would be safe. You're Cy's priority. You and Ellender."

"Then why isn't he telling me?"

Mac looked uncomfortable, but he said, "Cy won't change his mind. He's convinced Tate's dangerous and I agree with him. Tate hinted he was in the woods watching Delaney House the night you fell. Cy's been in contact with the State Police and I'm talking with Ellender today to talk to her about leaving town for a while. I'd like for you to stay here, at least until this business with Tate is settled."

"You two are overreacting." The response was automatic, but she was remembering the dark woods and the sensation of someone moving up behind her. Tate. She shuddered.

Mac said, "It's not an overreaction, but Tate can deny it all and we don't have any proof. The night I went to his house, I saw a man capable of carrying his threats out. I'm not willing to risk finding out I'm right. Please consider staying here."

"I'm going home this morning," she said. "But I'll think about it."

"You're going to represent Tyler, anyway, aren't you?"

"Mac, It's a couple of visits to jail and ferrying some papers back and forth for his signature. I'll be careful."

"It'll be the first time," he grumbled. But he didn't try to stop her.

CHAPTER THIRTY-SIX

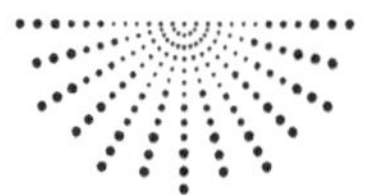

Ellender agreed to meet Mac without asking why he wanted to see her. That in itself told him a lot.

He'd have preferred a meeting location closer to Mallard Bay, but he'd asked her to choose a place where they could talk privately. She named a waterfront park in Stevensville and sent him directions. He arrived early, looked around, and walked down to a narrow beach without seeing anyone. Not too surprising on a blustery November morning. He only took a second to admire the view of the Bay Bridge before returning to the truck and turning the heater on high.

Ellender arrived and asked him to drive

around, directing him to a rear exit at the opposite end of the lot. He did as instructed, saying nothing as they wound through an adjacent office park and exited out onto Route 8, headed toward Romancoke.

She broke the silence by asking why he'd asked to meet with her.

"I'm worried about you." It was true. It also wasn't the only reason he'd wanted to talk with her.

"You're a nice man. You were good to me after the wreck. I wish we'd kept in touch."

He nodded. "You seemed to be doing well, though, until this rough patch."

"Is that what you call it?" Her laugh was short and harsh. "Are you looking for evidence against Tyler?"

"I'm not a police officer anymore, Ellender."

"Then why did you call me?"

"Cyrus Mosley says you don't want him to represent you any longer, and he's worried about you." He waited, hoping Cy had read the situation correctly.

"Isn't that illegal or something? I mean, for him to talk about me like that?"

"Our conversation was about Tyler Forester.

We're both acquainted with him, which is why we're concerned."

"You believe he's guilty."

"Cyrus thinks Tyler hurts you."

They drove past tract housing and mansions and fields and shopping centers. Once Ellender started talking, he wondered if he'd have to cruise around all of Kent Island. She had a lot to say. When she was finished, there was only silence until he pulled into the parking lot of a large farm stand. He backed the truck around until they faced the road and then killed the engine.

"Do you dream much about the night of the accident?" he asked her.

She blinked, but answered without hesitation. "In batches. I'll relive it every night for a few weeks, and then nothing for a long stretch."

"Where are you in that cycle?"

"Dreaming." She closed her eyes. "It's awful."

"What was happening in your life the last time you weren't dreaming?"

She thought for a moment, then looked surprised. "I was looking at apartments in Annapolis. It was fun, planning such a big change. Is that it? That I don't dream when I'm happy?"

He thought this poor girl hadn't known real happiness in a long time. Instead of answering the question, he said, "Was Tyler with you when you went house hunting?"

"No." She looked out the window. "Will the dreams stop if I get away from him?"

It was an interesting choice of words. He thought Cyrus might be right about the abuse. "I'm a cop. Was a cop, but once is always in that business. I have my own dreams from time to time. Everyone does. If you can accept the truth about what happened, I don't think you'll have them as often. But, every time you doubt yourself, you'll be back on the side of that road, in the dark, on the worst night of your life. It's what we humans do. When in doubt, or scared, we want to repeat a pattern. Until you create a new pattern, a healthy way of handling your guilt, you'll dream."

"Is this where you tell me it was an accident?"

"Are you going to tell me you aren't guilty?"

She shook her head.

"Then if I say you weren't at fault, you won't believe me. If you feel guilty, make it work for you. Let it drive you to put good out into the world." The words were hard—or trite. It would all depend on how she heard them.

Her eye roll said "trite." "You sound like Cherish. Why can't either of you understand that no matter what I do to help Tyler, I'll still owe him."

"You've just spent an hour telling me how he's changed in the last two years, and why you know he didn't kill Natalie, and why you're afraid of him but have to help him, anyway. Did you leave anything out?"

It surprised him when she said she had.

"He wants me to prove he's innocent. If I don't, I'll be arrested, too, because I'm the next logical person for the police to suspect. He might even implicate me."

"Are you guilty?"

"No." This time, she managed a sad smile. "And no, I didn't help him do it, either."

"Then be smart about this. Can you go somewhere out of town to stay for a week or two? Making yourself available for him to threaten isn't helpful."

"I'm moving in two weeks. I have to pack and empty the house so I can list it for sale."

He thought of options. There was a more imminent danger than Tyler's big mouth, and no way to keep her safe if she stayed in Mallard Bay. "Did you know that Natalie and Tate Grassley were lovers?"

"Uh, *no*."

As he expected, her expression registered somewhere between shock and "yuck."

"Grassley thinks he knows who killed her. He believes it's you, or you and Tyler, so he'll probably have you under surveillance, even though he's not part of the investigation into her death. You need to leave town before he comes up with some trumped up reason to harass or arrest you."

"But I can't move into the apartment until . . ."

"Go stay with friends or rent a hotel room somewhere and don't tell anyone but Cyrus Mosley where you are." He handed her an envelope. "There's a debit card in here with enough on it to cover all the expenses. Fly, but don't drive your car to the airport. Call an Uber and fly wherever you're going, but don't tell anyone. If you need more money, call Cyrus. That's how serious this is."

He watched her weigh his suggestion and discard his offer, all without saying a word. She wasn't ready. He tried one more time. "Tyler isn't doing well in jail. He's an angry man accused of a terrible crime, and he's digging himself in deeper. You can't help him, Ellender, and if you don't stay away from Grassley, things will get worse for you."

"Worse than what? Worse than the nightmares?"

"Yes."

Instead of making her see reason, his answer seemed to make her angrier.

"Worse than knowing I'm responsible for Tyler's limp and the pain he's in?" she demanded. "Than knowing it's my fault when he cries and talks about holding Verity's broken body as she died? She was in a ditch! My sister died in a filthy ditch with her neck twisted and..." she couldn't take in enough air to finish.

Mac said, "Put your head down and breathe slowly." He pushed gently on her shoulder until she complied. When he could hear her breathing ease, he said, "Now listen to me. That's not what happened. Not even close." He let his words sink in.

"But he told me," she argued, gasping for each word. "You weren't there until later!" Her head came up. "He, he had to hold her while she died. All the blood everywhere—"

"No." Mac let the single word lie between them.

"I saw them!"

"No." It was gentle, kind. Unmovable. "Remember the dreams. They can't hurt you if you look at them closely. You're here with me, and you are safe. What do you see?"

Tears ran down her face, and her voice jerked. "Her neck is twisted and her eyes . . . Dad's are open, too." She watched the busy road in front of them, but he knew what she was seeing had happened two years ago.

"Who's there?"

"She's dead, but she's still looking at me."

"Where is Tyler?"

After a time, she whispered, "I don't know."

He said, "I do," and waited for her to ask.

"I . . . he had to be there."

"Tell me what you know. How does it start?"

She winced. "Dad's dead. I'm with him for a long time, trying to brush all the glass off him, until I'm bleeding, too. Then I see Verity. I try to get out to her and I fall a lot. She's so cold."

When he thought she was finished, he asked again, "Where is Tyler?"

She shook her head and came back to him. "I block a lot of the details."

"No, Ellender. You don't. Not in the dreams, anyway. Tyler was unconscious. Unconscious and strapped in the back seat. He didn't wake until his ambulance reached the hospital. I can get the records if you want proof. He didn't see Verity at the accident scene."

"You're wrong," she cried. "He described everything to me."

"Before or after you told him about the dreams?" He watched her as she considered the question and saw doubt in her eyes. "I was the first one to arrive, and I called it in. There are recordings you can listen to. I found you holding Verity. You, not Tyler. She was dead, but you kept talking to her. You were the only person in the car who didn't lose consciousness."

"I don't remember that."

"I think you do. I think you remember every time you dream. You're in the car. No one answers your calls, and you get out to find Verity."

"There was so much blood," Ellender whispered.

"Most of it was from the deer." He risked touching her shoulder, but she flinched and he pulled back. "It was quick for Verity, I promise." He reached for a box of tissues in the back seat.

"Tell me the rest," she said.

"You fought with the paramedics who tried to help you. You didn't want to leave her. They had to sedate you to keep you from making your own injuries worse. You were holding her up out of the ditch water, even though you had a broken wrist—you had to be in agony, but you didn't let go of her."

He let her cry until she wound down. He still had to make her understand about Tyler and Grassley, but first, she had to grieve.

CHAPTER THIRTY-SEVEN

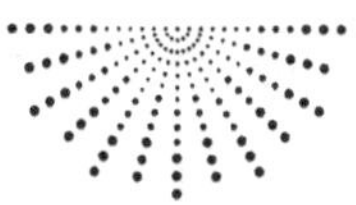

Zara called with the news that Tyler had been in yet another fight, but Grace wasn't prepared for what she saw when he was escorted into the visiting room at the County Detention Center.

"What happened?" she asked, not waiting for an answer before asking if he'd received medical attention.

The correctional officer escorting Tyler said, "He's been to the ER."

"Sergeant Bauman," Grace said, reading the nameplate on the officer's uniform. "Mr. Forester clearly needs help." She stepped toward Tyler to examine his face, but stopped when Bauman raised her hand.

"His other lawyer's already been informed.

The hospital released him. He's being housed in our intake section, so he's not within sight of the inmates he riled up. If you could advise him to keep his mouth shut, we'd all thank you. He seems intent on making the worst of things. Real good at it, too."

"I want to see the hospital discharge papers and any instructions for aftercare," Grace said. "Those wounds on his face are dry and cracking. They need medication."

"I'll check with medical. Ask for me when you're ready to leave. More medicine won't help, though. He keeps washing it off."

Grace thanked her and waited until they were alone before questioning Tyler.

"Dudes thought they were something," he mumbled. At least that's what Grace guessed he'd said. The words had to make their way between split lips.

"Looks like they *were* something," Grace said. "What caused the fight?"

"Hurts to talk. Told El. Get from her. When can you file the suit?"

Grace ignored the question and pulled out Zara's notes. "Let's work on the charges against you, first. That's why I'm here. I've agreed to assist—"

Tyler shook his head. The movement looked painful. "You. My attorney."

She wouldn't misrepresent the truth, even if only by omission. "I'm one of your attorneys, for now. Ms. Wingate is the trial counsel, Tyler. And it's not something that arguing with me will change. But I'll help you any way I can."

"Don't need it."

"Yes, you do."

He dropped his head and refused to meet her gaze. She thought he said, "Be fine."

"No, you won't, not unless we handle everything right." When he didn't respond, she added, "You have to watch yourself in here. That means staying quiet. Can you do it?"

The battered face came up to glare at her.

"We have a lot to go over. You've admitted to taking the poison to Natalie . . ."

He kicked the table with such force that Grace jumped.

The door immediately opened, and an officer twice Tyler's size barked, "Do it again, and you're back in the cell."

Grace was glad that her client's damaged mouth distorted his reply. The officer withdrew, but stayed on the other side of the door, and didn't take his eyes off them.

"Are you capable of controlling your behavior?" Grace asked. "Because if you aren't, you won't get out of here."

His blackened eyes flared. "Not guilty."

"Then why does your mother believe you are?"

It was a risk, one that she and Zara had argued about. Grace had promised not to use it unless she couldn't get him to talk any other way. "She's your mom, Tyler, and she believes you killed Natalie. Why is that?"

"El knows I didn't," he said, cracking open a cut at the corner of his mouth.

She tried from every angle she could think of, but his response remained the same.

THE DISCHARGE FORM AND THE ER DOCTOR'S instructions showed Tyler's injuries weren't serious, despite the gruesome pretreatment photographs. Assuming he let his wounds heal and quit picking fights, most of the damage would heal before he made it to court. She scanned the report and sent it to Zara, but didn't answer her responding call. There was only one thing she could tell the attorney that might help Tyler.

El knows I didn't. Her former client had released her, but just as Grace had feared, representing Tyler could hurt Ellender. She hadn't expected the complication to arise this fast, but here it was.

She was halfway out the front door of the Detention Center lobby when she heard her name called and turned around to find Jake hurrying to catch up with her.

"Glad I caught you," he said. She got the low-beam Jake Special, but it quickly dissolved under her withering look.

"What are you doing here?" she snapped.

"Believe it or not, a client." He nodded at the reception area behind them. "I'm delivering some papers for Mr. Mosley. But I'd like to talk, if you can spare a minute."

"Here?" She didn't want to talk with him. If she did, she might ask him how he was enjoying her office.

"The lobby's empty. I would appreciate it."

"Jail is an odd place to apologize," she said when they were seated. "Would you have bothered if you hadn't seen me?"

"I have nothing to apologize for." No smile this time.

"Then what do you want?"

"To get straight with you on several things. I haven't been open about Lily, or why I accepted Mr. Mosley's offer, but I thought you knew all about both situations."

"You were wrong."

He nodded. "Yes, I was. I'm sorry you're not at the office anymore, but that's not an apology because I had nothing to do with the circumstances. I've learned a lot from you, and I'm grateful for that. I can't say I'll miss you, though."

"Wow. When you drop the smile, you really get serious, don't you?" She had to admit she'd channeled a lot of undeserved frustration to him.

He wasn't finished. "Being around you these past few months has been hard. Lily and I talked last night for the first time in a while, and she agreed we should be honest with you. I would have called you today, anyway."

"Don't stress yourself. I'll talk to Lily. I've got to be somewhere." She started to rise, but Jake reached out and tapped her arm.

"Please. I need to explain—"

"You did what you needed to do. Let's just leave it at that."

"No."

She'd never seen him angry before. It stopped her protest and piqued her interest. This wasn't the too-happy guy who drove her crazy with questions and a perpetually sunny attitude. She waited while he studied his feet, presumably finding the words he wanted.

"I only found out last night that Lily didn't tell you she left me for someone else."

She wasn't sure she'd heard him correctly until he straightened up and looked her in the eye.

"An attorney in her new firm. She's still struggling with everything, and I'm sure she'd explain it in different terms, but that's what happened." He flushed, his neck turning scarlet. "Just when I thought things would work out for the kids and me, we're going through another breakup. Lily asked me to keep the details quiet, but I assumed you knew and that was why you didn't like me."

She was stunned and struggled to make sense of what he said. "But you told me—"

"That we weren't together anymore, but we were still friends. 'Friends' is a stretch, I'll admit. Also, I didn't take a job that should have gone to her. Mr. Mosley thought Lily would get a better start at a larger firm. He knew she had an excellent offer, but that she'd stay if he asked her to."

"Does she know that?"

"She does now. She's furious that he made the decision for her."

"I feel her pain," Grace muttered. "I wish she'd told me."

"She was already in Annapolis and falling in love by the time she figured it all out." The scowl that clouded his face aged him. "And as for her not telling you, well, she said you hadn't exactly been close recently."

It was true. She and Lily had parted with hurt feelings, both too stubborn to do anything about the rift. It had been easier for Grace to blame Jake. "I'm sorry," she said. "No excuses. I'll call Lily, too."

"That's up to you. But while we're at it, I don't have your job, either. Mr. Mosley's made that perfectly clear. He's been generous with me, but he won't turn your clients over any time soon. I hope you didn't quit because you thought he would. It's true that I'm in your office now, but only because he wants a bigger conference room. A construction crew is coming tomorrow to take out a wall and expand it into my old space."

Her second apology was just as embarrassing as the first. They spent a few minutes touching base on the open cases she'd left, and he promised to call when he needed help.

"Good thing you ran into me," Grace said as he walked her out to her car. "You might've exploded trying to hold all of that in for much longer." It was a lame joke, but the best she could do at the moment.

"I told you because you were judging me without all the facts. Now if you still don't like me, so be it. I can deal."

"Jake, I—"

"No, drop it. Really. There's something else I want to tell you while you're uncomfortable and think you owe me."

"What?" She did a double take, and this time got his real smile, dimples and all.

He checked the surrounding area before continuing, smile gone and worry lines showing again. "I'm hoping you'll listen to me, because it's been hard to decide what to do."

"You mean there's more?"

He nodded. "Mr. Mosley doesn't want you and Marjorie to worry, but you two need to know that Tate Grassley is angry with all of us. Especially you. He's telling everyone that you're helping Ellender and Tyler get away with the murder of Natalie Wilkens. He may be right about Tyler being the killer, but he's not acting rationally. Certainly not professionally, and I'm worried about his lack of self-control. You should stay away from him. Just my opinion, of course."

She looked at him for a long moment, then said, "Thanks."

"I hope one day we can start over."

It would take awhile to consider all the things she disliked about Jake without her misconceptions coloring her opinions. She put her hand out. "Good luck, and don't forget the floor fan trick. I have a feeling you're going to need it."

She watched him walk away and wondered what else she had been wrong about.

CHAPTER THIRTY-EIGHT

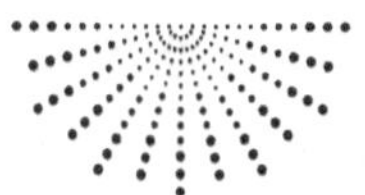

Mac answered her call on the first ring. "You okay?"

She didn't like the concerned note in his voice. "Fine," she said slowly. "I'm sitting in my car at the Detention Center parking lot. Are you okay?"

"Are you coming home? To my house, I mean."

Now he was worrying her. "I was going to make a stop and see Ellender. I have a couple of questions after talking to Tyler."

"We'd better talk first." He described his meeting with Ellender.

Grace thought about Tyler's manipulative personality, but it was still hard to believe what he'd done. "He lied to her about holding Verity when she died? Are you sure?"

"It was all there in my notes. Reading what I wrote when it was all fresh brought small details back. Like the cuts on Ellender's palms. When she told me she dreamed about brushing glass off her father's body, I knew she was remembering what really happened.Tyler was unconscious after the wreck, and strapped in the car. His leg was mangled, he couldn't have moved if he had been awake."

"She must be so upset. Why would he lie to her? That's disgusting!"

"Disgusting, but lucrative. Look at all the money Ellender's given him. Guilt was a sure-fire way to keep it flowing. If she sticks with him after this, it's her choice, but right now he isn't a threat. My concern is Grassley. She's agreed to go to visit friends in North Carolina, but she wouldn't leave until tonight. Maybe you can feel her out and make sure she's going?"

"Will do."

"But Grace—"

"I'll be careful. I'll call you if anything looks wrong and I'll check in when I leave her."

～

The York house looked smaller to Grace, and she wondered if the old white clapboards felt the last member of the family preparing to leave. She believed buildings took their character from the individuals who inhabited them. Delaney House had taught her that as she restored it and uncovered her family—people she'd never known, but without whom, she wouldn't exist. She'd returned the historic mansion to its original glory, and she hoped someone would do the same for this house once Ellender made her escape.

Two suitcases sat just inside the front door. Grace hoped they signaled Mac had been successful in persuading Ellender to leave town. She resolved not to stay any longer than it took to ask her question, but Ellender insisted they sit on the patio.

"For years I haven't been comfortable in my yard or anywhere that Natalie could see me," she said. "I'm moving in two weeks, so I come out here every chance I get. This used to be a fun place." A wistful smile lit her face and, just as quickly, disappeared. "What's happening with Tyler?"

Grace described his injuries, stressing that they would heal. She repeated Sergeant Bauman's statements that he'd started the fight and was washing off the medicine.

Ellender said she wasn't surprised. "He can be self-destructive, especially if it gets him what he wants."

"And what is that?" Grace asked.

"Sympathy from me and evidence for his lawsuit against everyone involved in his arrest. I've tried to talk him out of it, but he wouldn't listen."

"You *knew* he was deliberately provoking fights?" Grace asked, surprised.

"He called me Friday night, and we had an argument. He wanted me to help him get out of prison. I told him I couldn't put up bail, I don't have it. We argued some more, and he said he had no choice but to make sure he had plenty of proof that he'd been hurt while he was being held. He also wants to stay in a hospital until he's released, so don't be surprised if he does it again. He doesn't have money, his mother can't raise enough without putting up her house as collateral, and I'm tapped out."

"That's unbelievable!" Grace said.

"Not really. I've given him a lot of money since the wreck. What's left is tied up until my birthday in February. That's why I'm renting an apartment instead of buying. He knows all of this, but is insisting I sell something to get bail. I don't own anything worth the amount he needs and I can't mortgage this house, because I won't own it until February. If I could, he'd insist I do it."

Grace thought if Mosley heard this, his head would explode. "I'm not questioning why you aren't giving him money for bail. I don't think you should give him anything. But why didn't you tell us what he was doing?"

"Oh. He talks to his mom every day. I thought he'd tell her and she would call Zara. Neither one of them likes me and Betsy would use it as an opportunity to ask for money, too."

Ellender had changed. Her frantic need to protect Tyler was gone, and Grace knew Mac would be glad to hear it. She said, "Well, he's isolated now, so he should be safe."

"Isolation is the worst thing they can do to him," Ellender said. "He needs to be the center of attention and he'll keep pushing boundaries until he is. Zara is recommending he plead guilty to manslaughter. She says he'll get a lighter sentence. Betsy thinks he might even get mandatory mental health treatment instead of prison. Is that possible?"

Grace thought Tyler's mother was nearly as delusional as he was. "The last time we talked about this, you insisted there was no way he was guilty, because he can't lie."

Ellender gave her a level look. "You've talked with Chief McNamara." It was a statement.

"Yes. He's worried about you."

"He's asked me to call him Mac, but I've always called him Chief. Hard habit to break. He's a wonderful person. And you're wrong. He told you what I said because he's worried about you. He doesn't think it's safe for either of us to be involved with Tyler or Chief Grassley and he's right."

Grace didn't deny it. It was unsettling, though, to receive two warnings in as many hours.

"It's okay," Ellender said. "I told Mac he could talk with you and Mr. Mosley. He can tell anyone he wants. The more people who know, the safer I am, don't you think? I can use all the help I can get." She picked a spent bloom from a straggly geranium, releasing its pungent scent. "Tyler told me Chief Grassley came to interrogate him in jail Friday morning. Grassley said he could prove Tyler killed Natalie, and he'd see him in hell for it. Tyler's frantic. He doesn't know what Grassley has."

"That's what he said? Not that there couldn't be any proof, just that he didn't know what it was?" Zara wouldn't be happy with that, Grace thought. She could charge Grassley with intimidation, but what if his claim was true? It would make his obsession with Tyler and Ellender, and apparently Grace, understandable.

"Yep. That's the first thing I thought, too, but I didn't say that to Tyler." Ellender rose and said, "I have water or coffee to offer you. I'm going to have a Bloody Mary. I usually drink alone, but I'm not picky about it." She looked at her watch. "Hey! I waited until two o'clock."

Grace held up her hands. "I'm not judging you."

"Sure you are." Ellender smiled with her words. When she returned with her glass of water and a tall, pale pink drink, she said, "You can lose the anxious look. I'd never drink and drive, not with my record. I have an Uber coming at five o'clock. You can tell Mac I'm taking his advice. He'll understand."

"So, you are leaving," Grace said. "He'll be relieved. I am, too."

"Yes. I'll nap on the ride to the airport. No more alcohol until I'm in my hotel in Raleigh. Tomorrow night I'll be in Myrtle Beach. Don't tell Mac, but there's no college roommate. It's a solo vacation. Woo-hoo. Anyway, I have stuff to do, and you said you had a question. Let me guess." She paused dramatically, drained half the glass, then said, "You want to know why a psychic like me wasn't able to see Tyler for what he is?"

"Nope. But you're not a psychic, are you? And even if you were, emotions can blind us."

Ellender smiled, and another inch of the drink disappeared. She set the glass down and said, "Let's get this over with. Ask your question, then I'm off to the beach."

"Notes or tape?" Grace took out her phone.

"I'm only telling it once."

"This morning, Tyler said you knew he was innocent. What did he mean?"

When Grace hit Record, Ellender talked.

CHAPTER THIRTY-NINE

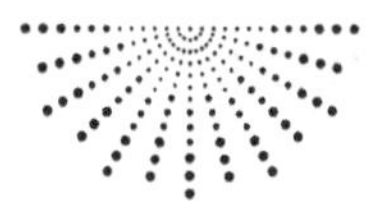

"He thinks I'll lie for him. Tyler still calls me his little sister when he wants to remind me of the connection we have. I felt like his sister when I was ten. I thought he was great back then. I didn't have friends in school, so my family . . ." She rotated the now empty glass, making wet circles on the worn maple table top. "They were all I had when I was a kid. My family, Tyler and Cherish. Now my family's gone, and even the Tyler I knew has disappeared. All gone except Cherish, and I feel like a burden to her."

This was becoming a therapy session. "Do you want to stop?" Grace asked.

"No." Ellender leaned over to speak directly into the iPhone. "Dad and Verity died and Tyler's more screwed up than he was before the wreck, and I'm to blame for most of it. Period." She tapped the screen to stop recording.

"That's it?" Grace asked.

"There's more, but you and Zara will probably wish you hadn't asked." Ellender tapped the phone, gave her name again, and delivered the rest of her statement, speaking with clinical detail and no embellishments, just a chronological recounting of the day Natalie died. The day she'd come home to a ringing phone and Tyler hiding in the shadows of the hallway. After a break for a fresh drink, she moved on to kill Tyler's chance of escaping a murder charge.

"Friday, when he called me from jail and I told him I couldn't pay his bail, he said I had to tell the police that he was with me all afternoon the day Natalie died. He said if I told them we both took the flour to her, and that we saw her later and she was fine, we would be each other's alibi."

Grace reached out to stop the recording, but hesitated. If she let Ellender talk and her statement further incriminated Tyler, she'd have sabotaged her current client. But what Tyler had asked of Ellender didn't add up.

Ellender said, "Leave it running. You wanted this, remember? Tyler asked me to say that he'd stayed with me until six, and that I watched him walk away from my house through the backyard and down the alley until he was out of sight."

Grace frowned. "But it would have been dark at six."

"Yeah." Ellender gave a thumbs-up. "Not so good at the little details, is he? I couldn't have seen him go very far in the dark alley, and both of us taking the flour to Natalie wouldn't prove anything. This kind of thing is why I thought he couldn't lie. He's too scattered to plan beyond his next meal, never mind remember the details of something that didn't happen."

"So, when did he leave you?"

"I threw him out around three thirty and, believe me, I didn't care where he went as long as it was away from me. I got my house key back from him and double-locked the door after he left."

"But when I got here later that evening, he was with you."

"He showed up just as I realized something bad was going on at Natalie's. Yesterday, Mac said that we repeat patterns when we're scared. Whatever. I let Tyler in and let him stay."

"So, what do you think happened to Natalie?"

"I don't know, okay?" Ellender's eyes filled. "Tyler told me he went to her house because she'd called here and asked to borrow flour, so he took her a bag from my cabinet. The idea of Natalie asking me for anything, then allowing Tyler to deliver it, is ridiculous. She complained about him constantly."

"But the flour in your pantry contained the same pesticide as the flour on her counter."

"It has to be Chief Grassley who planted it. Tyler is all impulse. Thinking about poisoning someone, deciding what to use, how to do it—that takes planning and secrecy. Tyler has no filters or self-control. He'll say and do anything on the spur of the moment, but plan and keep a secret? No. Plus, if he'd killed her, he'd have asked me to cover for him as soon as he did it, not a week later."

Grace looked at the remains of Ellender's drink and wondered how long the girl would be willing to talk. "If he lied to you for two years about being with your sister when she died, he's capable of keeping a pretty big secret, isn't he?"

Ellender shook her head. "It might not be a lie in his mind. He was badly injured in the wreck, after all. I mean, I blocked the whole thing, myself. Even now, I'm not sure what's a memory and what's a part of the nightmares I have. If Mac hadn't been there, I'd still believe everything

Tyler told me." She stopped the recording and left the room, returning with her own phone. "I've sent you a text with some photos. I may have to give them to the police because I'm telling the truth when I testify. I don't think he killed Natalie, but he wasn't with me before one thirty, or between three thirty and seven on the day she died."

Later, when Grace was home and studying the pictures, she was amazed Ellender hadn't broken with Tyler earlier. The three photos showed bruises on Ellender's torso and legs. All the shots were attached to one caption: *Tyler. I'm really not clumsy at all.*

Grace squeezed her eyes shut as she remembered Niki's tearful recounting of her mother's injuries. *How many times can one woman fall down three steps to the patio?*

Was this why she was pulled toward Ellender? And why, when the chips were down, she always came to her aunt's defense? The three of them had been victims, and they were all dealing with the fallout from their bad choices.

She punched Zara Wingate's number into the phone. Tyler Forester had the right to a good legal defense, but he wouldn't get it from her.

CHAPTER FORTY

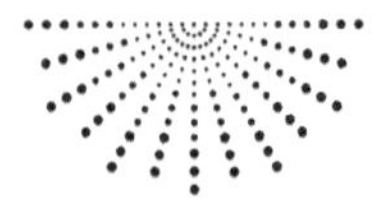

With Ellender out of town, Grace enjoyed a pleasant Sunday with Mac. Grassley, Tyler, and David were never far from her mind, but she tried hard to enjoy what would be one of the last days they'd have alone. They had a leisurely brunch, a walk on the beach, and a late afternoon nap in front of the fire. The magical day was over too soon, and Monday returned her to real life with a traffic-clogged drive to Annapolis.

"This is exactly the sort of stunt I was afraid Tyler would pull," she said to Zara Wingate as they walked along the harbor front. It was a warm day, but the breeze off the water held the bite of cold weather to come. She buttoned her sweater up to her neck, knowing it was only a matter of time before she overheated and it came off again. Zara's office was only a few blocks up Fleet Street, but she'd agreed to walk with Grace, who was having leg cramps after the drive from Mallard Bay. Zara had also offered to buy lunch, but Grace wanted to get back across the Bay Bridge before traffic reached its afternoon peak. Her work for Tyler Forester would be finished once she'd made her report, and she'd felt compelled to give it in person.

"I thought he was odd from the first time we met," she continued, talking down to the gray curls on Zara's bowed head. "Now I know he's abused Ellender, and he's attempting to blackmail her."

The shorter woman walked quickly, her hands clasped behind her back and eyes on the sidewalk, with occasional glances at the water as she listened to Grace explain why she was backing out of their agreement.

"First, he demanded Ellender bail him out, but she didn't have the money to do it. Now he wants her to lie and give him an alibi for the afternoon of the murder."

Zara was quick to correct her. "I think the state's moving too fast. I don't consider the evidence to be conclusive for homicide, and so far, the chief of police has just been a lot of noise. He gives me a new avenue for appeal every time he opens his mouth. If it is foul play, the chief is the first place I'm looking. I assume you've heard the rumors about him. The affair with the victim, and his intimidation tactics?"

"Lots of rumors. I can help you with that if it comes to it, but I have more to tell you." Grace pointed to a nearby bench. When they were seated, she pulled up the photographs Ellender had given her.

Zara studied them from different angles, then returned the phone. "Have you handled many domestic abuse cases?" she asked.

Grace held her temper. "Why is that relevant? Those bruises don't look life threatening, but Tyler scared her enough to photograph them for evidence."

"And you're sure that's Ellender in the photos? Her face isn't visible."

Grace scrolled through the photographs and showed Zara the shots she had taken when she and Cyrus met with Ellender after her arrest. "These are the bruises I saw, and she told me there were others."

"How'd she explain the bruises you saw?" Zara asked.

Grace watched the wake line from a water taxi and forced herself to consider Zara's point. If the pictures were used in court, she'd have to answer the question. She relayed Ellender's original explanation of a fall during a boating outing.

Zara nodded. "In one of our few conversations, Tyler said if Ellender should turn against him, the bruises weren't what they looked like. I tried to talk to her about it and got the same story you did."

"Did you believe her?"

"Not my job," Zara said. "Right now, Tyler's charged with assaulting a state trooper and murder, not abusing his girlfriend. Let's not do the prosecution's work for them."

Grace dropped it. She would be off the case as soon as she left Annapolis.

"So," Zara continued. "There are a variety of potential motives that the state's attorney can throw at us. We know Natalie was poisoned by handling and breathing a toxic chemical that was in the flour she was baking with. Flour identical to the kind our client admits he delivered to her from Ellender York's pantry. He also says he argued with the deceased frequently, including when he delivered the flour. The same chemical compounds found in the flour in the Wilkens kitchen were in the bag in the York pantry and in an open box of weed killer in the York garage. And the weed killer is one of the products Mrs. Wilkens claimed made her sick when Ellender used it last summer. Tyler could easily have known about it."

"Lots of holes in that narrative."

"Yes," Zara agreed. "And, I've got the argument that Grassley killed his lover, but that'll be a stretch if she was poisoned by something found in the neighbor's house. Try this theory on. Tyler's covering for Ellender because he knows she did it. It would explain a lot. And, trying to get himself hurt in jail so he can sue could just be a bonus. Save Ellender and make money doing it."

Grace had known they'd get here sooner or later. She said, "You'd have to get the jury to believe that someone who graduated with top honors and is in a master's program at UMD would poison her neighbor and keep the tainted flour on display. That's more Tyler's speed." She described how he had lied about Verity's death. "Ellender could easily counter that he tried to frame her for the murder he committed."

Zara shrugged. "I didn't say it was my best argument, just an option. He's broken, Grace. His childhood, his parents, whatever. Time doesn't heal all wounds. Sometimes they fester."

"He's dangerous! I won't help him because of what he's done to Ellender and I believe it's possible he committed murder."

Zara stood and stretched, then gave Grace a sad smile. "Decisions like that are a luxury I don't have, unfortunately. But I understand. You're finished."

As they resumed their walk, Zara changed the subject. "I'm dealing with Detective Marbury since the MSP took over the investigation. She seems efficient."

"Very," Grace agreed. "By the book all the way."

"I met the former chief of police the day after the murder. McNamara seems like a good guy, too."

Grace smiled. "Very."

"I'm not surprised to hear you say that." Zara laughed at Grace's expression. "He is a popular guy in law enforcement circles. Gossip travels, even across water. In this case, I'd say it was good news. Congratulations."

Grace didn't ask if she was talking about the baby or Mac, but returned to the topic of Tyler, asking if Zara thought he was guilty.

"Immaterial. His fingerprints are in her house, including the kitchen where she was found, and he confessed to some pretty incriminating acts. But, in our last conference, when I explained the manslaughter plea, he went ballistic. Said he'd kill himself before he pleaded guilty."

"What happens next?"

"I get to make him change his mind and either plead, or start cooperating in his defense. And I don't have long to do it."

"I'm sorry. I feel bad about abandoning you, but I think he could be guilty." She patted her abdomen. "This baby is the most important thing to me, and I'm not tainting her start in life with a murder trial. I hope you understand."

"Three times over," Zara said with a smile. "My youngest is the same age as Tyler. They grew up together, and I knew the little boy that Tyler was. It's a heartbreaker, Grace, if I let myself think about it. So, I concentrate on what I can do right now. Logically, I see the prosecution's case as potentially winnable. I also see a possibility of getting Tyler some much needed help, even if he's convicted."

"What does he have? Is there a diagnosis?"

"Probably would be if Betsy had ever followed through with a treatment plan. I used to believe he was just spoiled rotten. But with the added information you got from Ellender about his behavior, well, I'm not sure how it all adds up in medical terms. My grandmother would have said 'mean as a snake,' but I'll have to do better than that for court."

They reached the lot where Grace had left her car, and she found herself suddenly reluctant to part ways. She wanted to tell Zara to be careful, but felt silly. Instead, she said, "Neither Tyler nor Ellender know that I'm resigning from his defense. How do you want to handle it?"

"I'd like to leave you on for the record, if you'd let me. It's good to have someone who knows all the players to bounce things off. No more actual work except to listen to me now and then. You can bill that against the balance of the retainer for your time, and I'll pay by the hour if I run through it."

Grace agreed. Sitting on the sidelines felt safe enough.

The drive over the bridge was bumper to bumper, but her heart was lighter as she left murder and the responsibility for Tyler Forester's fate behind her.

CHAPTER FORTY-ONE

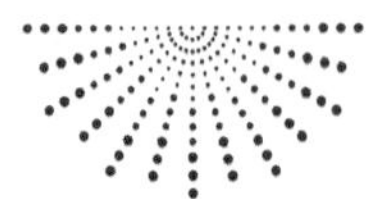

Once over the bridge, Grace gave into temptation and stopped to shop at the outlets. The BMW's backseat and trunk were full and her bank account much lighter as she drove the last fifteen miles to Mallard Bay. A warm bath and early bedtime were her immediate plans. After two nights at Mac's, she was ready to go home, despite his protests.

"Who'd be crazy enough to take Niki and me on?" she'd argued. "Not to mention my state-of-the-art, hear-it-in-Delaware alarm system?"

He eventually dropped the argument, but he wasn't happy. And when she had to park down the block because she couldn't find a spot closer to her own home, she regretted her decision. She didn't remember Niki talking about any event scheduled for tonight, and their shared calendar app was empty. Still, a dozen extra cars and enough wattage to blow their utility budget said something was happening. Light poured from every window of Delaney House.

When she walked into the front hall, a woman she didn't know met her with a cheerful "Hi! Come on in. The bar's set up right through those double doors, and the owner's around somewhere giving a tour. You can probably catch up with her on the second floor."

Grace thanked her politely and went to find her cousin.

"You weren't supposed to be here," Niki said for the third time as she brought a tray of leftover appetizers into the kitchen. The last guest had departed ten minutes earlier, and Grace was filling a dinner plate from the picked-over silver platters. At the moment, her mouth was full of crème brûlée, so Niki had to worry a bit longer. "I'm sure I told you weeks ago that tonight was the open house for the Chamber of Commerce. You said you'd stay with Mac."

Grace polished off the brûlée and picked up a Smithfield ham biscuit. "You claim I don't listen to you, but this one's not my fault." With her free hand, she held up her phone calendar, which was empty for Wednesday. "You told me the open house would be the week that Mac's off work. That's when we're planning to go to Cape May."

"Right! And you said—"

"That he's off next week."

"Are you sure?" Niki asked, defeat in her voice. "Okay, I'm sorry. I got it wrong. I'll do better." All the glitter and excitement that had been in her face earlier faded as she turned to scrape and stack dirty plates.

Grace decided the time wouldn't get any better than this. "You're doing fine, Nik. I'm moving out."

"No, no." Niki whirled around, tears in her eyes. "I want you and the baby here."

"You're doing a great job," Grace insisted, and felt ashamed when she saw the surprise on Niki's face. "You'll do even better without me hanging around your neck. Go ahead. Open the Inn at Delaney House for good. Book away to your heart's content. I'm going to look at some rentals tomorrow, but I'd like to stay here until the baby comes.

I can move into Avril's new guest wing if I don't have a place by then."

Niki gave her a "Who are you?" look. "You sound as if you mean it. You don't have to do it, but don't say you are and then change your mind." She flushed, but didn't take her words back. "I love you, Gracie. And I know what this place means to you. You shouldn't be making big decisions right now."

"I knew this could happen when we agreed to set up Delaney Inns. It's not that I can't live here. I don't want to live here once it goes commercial. I feel a responsibility for the house, but it's a building and I'm just a caretaker, the latest Delaney to dust it off and patch it up. None of us have really owned it, have we?" It was the way she'd always felt about the house and she wondered why she'd been avoiding the subject.

"I think the house has owned some of us," Niki said. She poured a glass of wine and sank into the rocking chair by the kitchen staircase. "I used to play for hours on these steps. I pretended it was a Barbie apartment building."

Grace had more recent adult memories of the staircase, but made herself pay attention to her cousin.

"I've always loved this place, but never as

much as when I saw you peeling away the years of Gran's neglect. The parlors and dining room are glorious and the entry hall! I wish you'd been here earlier tonight to hear the compliments. I gave you all the credit, just so you know."

Grace smiled. She'd heard Niki's version of the renovation work, and it always made her tired. "You didn't tell them I did the plumbing and wiring, too, did you? You know that makes people nervous."

Niki laughed. "The truth makes a better story. I told them how much you paid to have that work done."

"And now they think I'm insane."

"No, ma'am. They ran out of here to tell everyone where their next party will be. I actually had to turn down two bookings tonight. One woman was so upset she couldn't have Thanksgiving next year, she booked for New Year's Eve. Almost all the holidays have something penciled in for twelve months out. We'll see how many hold up when I ask for deposits, but tonight, I couldn't be happier. Except for the part about you leaving."

"Delaney House is going to be a tremendous success," Grace said. "All the more reason for me to move out for now. I'm not saying I'll never live here again, but I don't see it happening anytime soon. I've been stubborn and unwilling to face certain facts where this baby is concerned, but it's getting real, fast."

Niki looked skeptical.

Grace laughed at her expression. "Seriously. If you can manage not to rent out my bed until I move, go ahead and change the website. Fill the place up."

"Book Christmas parties?" Niki asked warily.

"And New Year's Eve parties, and Valentine Day soirees, and every holiday in between. But until I've moved my stuff out of the apartment, don't rent the third floor. Deal?"

"Don't toy with me." Her cousin's voice was husky.

"It's your inn, kid. Knock yourself out." Grace maintained her smile until she shut her apartment door behind her. It was done. Delaney House was Niki's.

TIME PASSED IN A BLUR. GRACE MOVED FROM ONE task to the next without letting herself think about what she'd done, or what she was about to do. By Wednesday afternoon, she'd seen five rentals, approved Niki's changes to the website, packed half her apartment, and was sitting on the edge of the exam table in the obstetrician's office.

"A week. Maybe a few days more, but I doubt it. You're very close." Dr. Allyson smiled at her. "Come on now, don't look so shocked. You had to know this kid would show up one of these days."

"But you said December second! She can't be this early!"

"Baby's a good weight and your blood pressure is on the high side, so I'm fine with a couple of weeks early. You should be, too."

"But what if her lungs aren't developed enough?"

"They should be fine, but if needed, we'll administer oxygen."

"But I'm supposed to go through a nesting period first, right? I'm packing to move!"

"I'm going to let you in on a secret." Dr. Allyson winked at her nurse, and in unison they said, "Baby doesn't care!"

Grace listened to the instructions for rest and gentle exercise, but her mind was on house hunting. Suddenly, all the faults she'd found with the places she'd toured seemed trivial. After a quick weighing of the pros and cons, she contacted the real estate agent and rented a small brick house near the harbor with a pretty backyard and a six-month lease. It had little in the way of character, but it was clean and available the first of January. Best of all, it was in town and close to Avril, and there was a fenced yard for visits from the dogs. The short-term lease was renewable at her option, and would give her some breathing room.

Mac took all the news in stride, and offered to come home from Sykesville when she told him the baby would be early. With a bravado she didn't feel, she insisted he stick to his class schedule for the week. All the changes would eventually crash in on her, and she didn't want him to be around for the panic attack she was trying very hard not to have.

Avril made no pretense of being calm. She yelped with excitement, then told Grace to take deep breaths and not upset Sweet Pea until she could finish their rooms. She hung up while Grace was telling her not to go to any trouble.

She decided that telling David could wait. Once he knew she would deliver early, he would hover and make her crazy. She didn't want to think about how he'd take the news of her living with Avril while she waited for the rental house. She was exhausted, not from all she'd done, but in anticipation of what was to come. A week. She could be a mother in a week.

The doorbell was a welcome distraction, but it meant she had to get up from the too-soft love seat in the parlor. Chastising herself for sitting there again, she finally got to the front door to find a cheerful FedEx driver who needed her signature for a thick manilla envelope. "Farquar, Mitchum, and Stoltzfus, P.A., Attorneys at Law" filled the upper left corner. David.

"What now?" she asked herself as she ripped the envelope open and pulled out a sheaf of papers. The document on top was a resume with a brief note in David's distinctive scrawl.

She will arrive in two weeks, unless you need her sooner. I'll cover all costs. D.

He'd hired a nanny, and not just any nanny, either. The resume described a registered nurse/midwife who also had a master's degree in early childhood development. Her last charge had just graduated to a Swiss boarding school. Grace knew there would be an ugly scene when he learned she wouldn't have room for a nanny in her two-bedroom cottage, and Sweet Pea would be in daycare.

There was another piece of paper in the envelope, an Affidavit of Parentage. Grace's name and

David's were filled in the appropriate boxes, and a red arrow-shaped sticker pointed to the space next to "Signature of Mother." When she read the note clipped to the back of the form, the sadness she felt was the only thing that surprised her.

Complete this at the hospital after the birth. I'll be there to pick you up and handle everything else. D.

She hadn't had a paternity test performed, because there hadn't been a reason to. Since they weren't married, the Affidavit of Parentage would legally establish his responsibility for the child. It would also give him standing to seek custody if he could find grounds. He wasn't trusting her to name him on the birth certificate.

Sometimes she forgot how well he knew her.

CHAPTER FORTY-TWO

The four days Ellender spent at the beach gave her perspective, and with it came a plan to free herself from Tyler.

Myrtle Beach was warm, the hotel was lovely, and her phone was shut off. She fired it up on Wednesday afternoon to find a series of increasingly frantic messages from Tyler, capped off by one from his mother. In less than an hour, she had checked out and was on her way to the airport, arriving home a little after nine. Tyler's mother was at her door soon after that, unannounced and in tears that became hysteria as soon as Ellender let her in.

"He's fired Zara and insists on representing himself. He says you agree with him and you're helping him. How could you do that?" Betsy said, sobbing.

Unable to calm the woman or get rid of her, Ellender led her into the kitchen and poured two glasses of merlot.

"I don't drink." Betsy pushed the glass away.

"No problem." Ellender picked up the rejected glass and downed the wine, enjoying the scandalized look on Betsy's face. She hoped the woman would take the hint and talk faster, or better yet, leave.

Neither happened. Instead, Betsy said, "Well, I guess you're under a lot of stress."

Ellender groaned, then said, "Not going to lie to you. I like wine, and I like vodka. I'm drinking more these days, thanks to your son, but Tyler or no Tyler, I drink."

"It's all right." Betsy wiped her eyes and sank onto a barstool. "We'll get you help with that down the road."

"Now, listen—"

"About Tyler." Betsy cut her off. "He says you'll pay his bail. Is that true?"

"No. I don't have the money to do that."

"That's okay. It's probably best if he stays where he is, and you handle everything, anyway. He says you know who really killed that woman and you'll be able to prove it, soon. You'll still need to get him some medical help, though."

Ellender's alcohol infused bravado faded. She'd never thought of her own mother and Tyler's in the same light, but tonight she saw something familiar in Betsy's pain. Ellen York spent the last months of her life teaching her daughters everything they'd need to know in the years after she was gone. If the girls changed the conversation to a less depressing topic, Ellen would look as distressed as Betsy did now. Both mothers wanted to change their children's futures, and neither accepted the inevitable failure of their plans.

"There's nothing I can do to help him," Ellender said, lying about the plans she had.

"You owe him!" Betsy lost the resemblance to Ellen York. Eyes narrowed to slits, she made the threat Ellender had been expecting. "And you owe me. You're not even close to paying us off."

She stood firm, saying she had made her last payment to the Foresters. Twenty minutes and many tears later, Betsy was gone and Ellender was an emotional wreck. She told herself that she needed to forget about Betsy and get ready to execute her plan. Crying and drinking wasn't a good way to start her life of crime.

~

THE NEXT MORNING ARRIVED MUCH TOO SOON. IT took ages to get everything ready and rehearse her act. The first bit of good luck was that her white, six-year-old Ford Focus was innocuous enough to blend in with the other vehicles parked near Tate Grassley's house. That was a relief because she was pretty sure she would suck at surveillance, and wouldn't be any better at breaking and entering. In the early bright sunshine, her plan felt stupid, but if it worked, all her problems might be over.

Grassley's front door opened, and she snapped out of her reverie, first sitting upright, then just as quickly scooting down behind the steering wheel. That was one fear realized. She really did suck at surveillance. By the time she'd inched her way up and could see what was happening, he'd driven off in a big black SUV. She spent another twenty minutes gathering enough courage to leave the safety of her car.

She was a fan of Sue Grafton's alphabet mysteries and had tried to think like Kinsey Millhone in preparing for her first crime. She wore tan slacks and a white polo, and stuffed her red hair under a navy ball cap. A clipboard and pen rounded out her ensemble. She wore a bored expression as she strode up to Grassley's porch and rang the bell. If she was wrong about him being gone, her only plan was to run.

Seconds ticked by and she breathed easier. Ostentatiously, she looked at her watch, checked her phone, and rang again. After more foot-tapping, she pretended to make a call and strolled around the house, looking up at the roof and gutters. She talked into the inactive phone about shingle shedding and dry rot and other contractor lingo she invented as she walked along.

The shades were down on the front windows, but when she reached the backyard, things got easier. High fencing meant the neighbors would have to be on the roofs of their single-story ranchers to see her, but she hurried, anyway. She didn't want to be caught breaking into the chief of police's house.

~

"You did *what?*" Cherish forgot about talking Ellender out of having another Bloody Mary.

They were sitting in the same spot where Betsy Forester had met her match the night before.

The York kitchen with its eighties decor and half packed boxes was becoming Operation Central of Ellender's new criminal enterprise. Cherish wasn't absorbing the latest turn of events very well.

"It's possible Tyler is innocent," Ellender repeated. "If he is, Tate Grassley has to be the killer, so I broke into his house to find evidence."

Cherish stared at her. "I can't believe you!"

"This is the last time I'm helping Tyler, I promise, but I have to do it. I have to give him a chance to prove he didn't kill Natalie."

Cherish found her voice. "Don't give me that 'He can't lie' crap. He's been lying to you about how Verity died."

"Not how she died, Cher, just about what he and I did after the wreck. And he's lying again now, telling his mother that he was driving that night so that she won't sue me. Look, I know he's seriously messed up, but if only half the gossip in town is right, the only other person who had a motive to poison Natalie is Tate."

"*Chief* Grassley."

"None other. And if I can prove he did it, Tyler only has the assault charge to deal with and will eventually get out of jail."

"So, you broke into Grassley's house."

"I did."

"And you're telling me because, why?"

"I need help." Ellender hoped if she kept the conversation simple, she'd sound like she knew what she was doing. She also hoped a workable plan would occur to one of them.

"No." Cherish shook her head. "Help is me giving you advice to dump Tyler and move to Annapolis. Help is you giving me a hand with the chickens and explaining the life lessons you claim are in my cards. Help does not mean going to jail because your best friend has lost her mind."

Ellender reached for Cherish's hands and held them, knowing there would be no shock or fizzle, only steady — if sometimes ditzy — warmth. "If it goes wrong for me, I want you to know you've been right all along about him. I couldn't see it because I owed him, and I always will. He had a chance with Verity. He could have changed. She said he was changing. I took that away from him when I killed her."

"You didn't kill her! You know it upsets me when you say that."

"But I did. I didn't mean to. I loved them both so much. And if Verity were alive today, Tyler might be the brother-in-law I didn't like, but who made my sister happy. Or maybe they would be divorced, but he would have had his chance with her. I'm finished after this, Cherish. I swear. If he's innocent, I'll clear him. If he isn't, then he pays for what he did. I can live with myself either way."

Cherish wasn't happy, but she stopped arguing and said, "Tell me no one saw you and you didn't leave any evidence behind."

"I wore gloves, but I had to break a windowpane to get in."

"Then he knows someone got in." Cherish moaned.

"Yes, but not who did it." Ellender tried to sound more confident than she felt. "If he knew, I'd be arrested by now."

"The day's not over. Did you find anything?"

"Yes." She took a file from a box on the table and handed it to Cherish. "This was in his desk."

"Oh, sweetie." Cherish paled as she looked through the contents. "How did he get these?"

"Took them from Natalie's house, I guess. Those photographs go back to when Mom was alive, but most of them are of me. I almost missed the file. I was looking for weed killer, but there was nothing. Then, as I was leaving, I saw the desk and had to look. It was in the first drawer I opened."

"But why would Natalie have these, and why would she give them to him?"

"I don't think she did," Ellender said, suddenly furious and not a little drunk. "I think he took it out of her house when he killed her!"

A tap on the kitchen window startled them, and Cherish unloaded a string of curses as Tyler came in through the unlocked door.

The next second, he was between them and hugging Ellender. "You can leave, Cher," he said over his shoulder. "I'm back and I'll look after our girl."

His mother had come up with the money for Tyler's bail. He wouldn't say who'd given it to her. All Ellender knew was that she was stuck. She could order him out, but he'd never leave her alone. At least if he was here, she could watch him.

"We have work to do," she told Cherish with a pleading look Tyler didn't see. He was so excited, the silent communication between the women went over his head. Cherish didn't stop objecting until Ellender handed her Tate Grassley's file. "I know how important this is to you, but I can't work on it now. So just put it away and as soon as I can, I'll see if Grace will help you as a favor to me."

Cherish looked confused, but took the file, shoving it into her purse just as Tyler reached for it. "Do you mind?" she snapped. "I'm having family problems."

Tyler said he wasn't surprised and slammed the kitchen door behind her.

"Let's eat," Ellender said, trying to distract him. Food was a safe bet. He was always hungry. "Tell me what's been happening."

She baked a frozen pizza while he talked non-stop, apparently happy to describe each minute he'd been away from her. She used the time to plan her next steps.

It took two hours, an entire pizza, and three beers for Tyler to slow down. While he rambled, she consumed a pot of coffee, hoping to flush as much of the vodka as she could from her system. When she thought they were as ready as they would ever be, she told him she knew he'd lied about Verity's death. Later, when she remembered the scene, she wondered what had kept her talking when every nerve ending in her body was telling her to shut up and run.

When it was much too late for her to take her

own advice, he said, "Little sister, let's go for a ride."

He took the car keys from the hook by the door and smiled when she refused to go with him. He lifted the hem of his shirt to show the pistol tucked into his waistband, and the argument was over.

"You drive," he said. "We're going to the scene of the crime. I'm gonna show you exactly how you killed them, and then I'm gonna tell you what's next for us."

CHAPTER FORTY-THREE

"Why are you doing this?" Ellender asked. It was the first thing she'd said since they'd gotten in the car. Tyler was unusually quiet, but he drummed an erratic beat on his left knee while his shaking right hand held the gun on her.

"Because it's time," he finally said, looking around as they drove through Mallard Bay.

No one took notice of them.

Ellender looked for any opportunity to draw attention and was rewarded with a red light. She inched her finger to the window control. One scream—

"I'll shoot the first person who looks at us."

The light changed. She picked up speed and in

seconds, they were out of town. She was on her own.

"That's better." He lowered his shaking hand to his lap, but kept the gun pointed toward her. "You haven't been listening to me, El. You listen to everyone else, and tell them what they want to hear, but my words mean nothing to you. I've been telling you what has to happen and now I'm going to show you. Today you're going to understand."

Ellender tried to concentrate, but she was too angry. Too scared. The man next to her wasn't Tyler. That boy had been slipping away for years, and he was right—she hadn't been listening to him. Now, here they were, about to face a truth she wouldn't be able to block out.

She didn't need directions to the clearing in the woods where her father and sister had died. She came occasionally, usually when the cycle of bad dreams started. Begging for forgiveness in the place where she'd killed them never made the nightmares go away, but it gave her a little more strength in the daylight hours.

"Stop here," he said. "We'll walk the rest of the way. I want a dramatic entrance."

His chuckle reinforced the only distinct feeling she could get from the myriad of emotions around him. Tyler was enjoying himself. She slowed the car, then eased it off the shoulder, taking care not to let the wheels dip into the muddy roadside drainage ditch.

"Try again, Baby. I'm not getting my feet wet and you're not running off while I climb over the gearshift."

She found a wider spot farther on. There was no getting away now, so she concentrated as hard as she could and tried to stay calm.

"Pick up the pace." He ground the gun into her back. "I've got a spot picked out where we can sit and look at our tree while I explain a few things. You killed my girl here, Baby, and you still owe me."

He described her debt and how it would be paid. Neither of them saw the car that stopped a hundred yards behind them, or the man who got out of it.

AVRIL PROVED TO BE AN ENTHUSIASTIC PLANNER, rapidly organizing most of the details for Grace's move into the new nursery. They made a morning of shopping in Easton for the last of the baby necessities, hitting store after store until Grace called for a break. After a leisurely lunch at Banning's Tavern, she was ready for a nap.

Avril had other plans. After stopping at the post office, Easton Hardware, and several other stores for errands, Grace announced they were going home. "You took so long in Lowe's, I need to eat again," she complained. She reminded Avril that the wood floors in the dining room and twin parlors of Delaney House were being polished. "Do you have anything to eat at your place, or should we stop for carryout?"

Avril's response was to look at her watch for the third time in ten minutes.

The lightbulb finally clicked on. Grace sighed and said, "Is it possible to develop dementia while you're pregnant? I can't believe I didn't see this. What time is my shower?"

"Don't be ridiculous." Avril's answer was a second too slow. "You said no fuss, and no shower."

"Okay, but when are you supposed to have me at the party?"

"Soon. You'd better step on it and practice acting surprised."

Grace tried to look pleased, but she wished she hadn't insisted on driving. They were in Avril's ancient Mercury Marquis and, despite its wide, comfortable seats, she couldn't find a position that would ease her aching back.

"I know a shortcut," Avril was saying. "Take a left at the light at the airport and turn right at the dead end."

~

TATE GRASSLEY WAS SWEATING AND LOOKED ILL, but neither of his prisoners challenged him after he fired a bullet into the ground at Tyler's feet.

In the silence that followed the echo, he said, "Ellender York, I'm arresting you for breaking and entering and theft. And, as for you, punk, I'm arresting you because I can. If you keep quiet, I may change my mind when we get to the department."

He tossed two zip-tie restraints at Tyler. "Hands together in front of you!" he barked at Ellender. When Tyler had her wrists secured, she clumsily did his.

She meekly followed instructions as they walked to the Explorer. Tyler had a jerky limp and muttered to himself. Once they were on the road, Grassley regretted putting him in the front seat, but he couldn't leave him behind, handcuffed. It would raise too many questions. He had to get them to Mallard Bay and get Ellender's arrest on the record. It was the only thing that mattered. He had promised Natalie everyone would know she'd been right about the Yorks.

He hadn't gotten up any speed at all when he realized his fingers were going numb and he couldn't feel his feet. The Explorer slowed and jerked to the left.

"Hey, man, watch it!"

Neither Tyler's warning or Ellender's scream penetrated the fog that took Grassley's vision. The last thing he saw was the yellow center line as they crossed it.

~

"WE'RE LOST," GRACE SAID, INTERRUPTING Avril's monologue on the importance of bright colors in a baby's room.

"The next turn off is in a quarter mile," Avril said, irritably. "Just past that bend. Are you okay?"

"The doctor said a week, or more, so stop asking me. I'm uncomfortable, and a little queasy, too, nothing unusual. I may not stay long at the shower. Do you think Niki will mind?"

"If Niki is giving you a shower that I know

nothing about, then yes, we'll all mind if you bug out. Pull yourself together."

Grace never got to answer. They rounded the curve and ahead of them, an SUV sat half-on and half-off the asphalt, its nose buried in a ditch. The big Mercury screeched to a stop mere inches from a collision.

For a moment, neither of them said anything. Then Avril pointed to the mud-streaked Mallard Bay Police Department emblem on the driver's-side door. They stared at the white Ford Explorer that had once been Mac's department vehicle. Grace pulled off the road, and they scrambled out.

The Explorer looked empty at first, then Grace found a handcuffed woman unconscious on the rear seat. A mass of auburn hair covered her face.

"Ellender?" She was reaching to check for a pulse when Avril shouted. A dozen feet away, another body was in the ditch.

"It's Tate," Avril yelled over her shoulder. "I think he's been shot. See if there's a first aid kit in the car!"

The Explorer was well stocked. Grace found the kit, delivered it to Avril, and hurried back to set a string of warning flares before the bend in the road. That done, she returned to the Explorer and awkwardly leaned inside to pick up Ellender's hand. Finding a weak but steady pulse, she pulled her phone out of her pocket, then froze when a quiet voice behind her said, "Put it down." Something hard and cold hit her arm. "Put it down and turn around." The words were barely above a whisper.

She dropped the phone and turned. The pistol clasped in Tyler's hands looked huge. A quick glance told her Avril hadn't seen them and wouldn't as long as she stayed focused on Grassley.

"I need a ride," Tyler said. "A ride, and some help with that." He nodded in Avril's direction. "You two will come with me and in a couple of miles, I'll let you out. You won't have any problems getting someone to stop for you, not in your condition."

She quickly agreed, but said, "Just take me and leave Avril here."

"No. You'll be more cooperative if she's along. Now, grab Ellender and get her into your car."

Grace turned to do as he said, then stopped. "I think I'm in labor." She wished to God she was lying, but the backache that had been growing was now spreading to the front.

"Okay," Tyler said. "How about this? Anyone who stays here, dies."

She reached for Ellender. A sharp pain raced across her abdomen and she backed out of the car, losing her lunch and splattering Tyler, who yelped and jumped backward. Grace grabbed for the gun and held on with a strength fueled by the onset of another pain. Not even the gun's firing weakened her grip. It took several gasping breaths for her to realize she was on the ground, on top of Tyler, and he wasn't moving. The next thing that registered was Avril saying, "Give me the gun, Gracie. I think you killed him. Good girl!"

Suddenly, it didn't matter what else was happening; Grace curled up, all of her focus on her body.

Which is why she didn't notice the still very much alive Tyler make the foolish decision to get up, only to be tripped by Avril and forced to crawl at gunpoint to the trunk of the Mercury.

After a time, the yelling stopped. Then strong hands grasped her, and she heard Avril's voice. *Stand up, Gracie. Another step. You can do it. Two more. You're okay. An ambulance is coming.*

She made it to the Mercury's back seat, but before she could assess her situation, the car began to rock. Avril left her to pound on the rear quarter panel. "Move again, you sadistic moron," she yelled, "and I'll shoot you through this trunk. I've got five more bullets."

After that, the only sounds were Avril's low murmuring and Grace's panting.

When state troopers and paramedics arrived, they found three women in varying degrees of distress, an unconscious chief of police in a ditch, and a mangled bad guy locked in the trunk of an old land yacht. They also found a newborn baby screaming its displeasure.

Sweet Pea had arrived, and her lungs worked just fine.

CHAPTER FORTY-FOUR

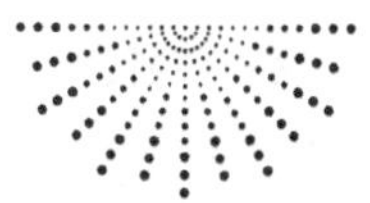

Mac studied the video frame by frame, then at normal speed so he could listen to a pale but smiling Grace talk about her daughter. He tried to make out the details she described in the red-faced, squinty-eyed infant, but quickly decided it was best to accept her assessment and hope her view was better than his.

The video and FaceTime calls were all he'd see of mother and daughter until they were released from the hospital. Policy was immediate family visitors only, and one person at a time. The police presence outside Tyler's room on the floor above the maternity ward meant there would be strict adherence to the rule. Niki managed an in-person visit, but Avril's claim of midwife status hadn't gotten her past security. David was in Bermuda, scrambling for a flight back to the states. Small blessings, Mac thought. Grace's delivery had been traumatic enough without an apoplectic new father to deal with.

He clicked the phone off and changed his jeans and sweatshirt for nicer jeans and a flannel button-down shirt. He had an appointment with Ruby Blanchard, and he wasn't doing anything to make the mayor think he was ready to go back to work. Mac was determined that he wouldn't step into the chief's job, even temporarily. Tremaine Harper had two experienced sheriff's deputies helping him and the sheriff herself monitoring all of them. They would be fine until a new chief was hired.

RUBY WAS IN THE COUNCIL'S MEETING ROOM, DEEP in conversation with MSP Detective Sergeant Desiree Marbury. They demanded baby details before moving on to the topic of their meeting. He felt awkward discussing Grace's child, and changed the subject as quickly as he could, asking Marbury for an update on yesterday's events.

"There are still some missing pieces, issues in

the timeline, mainly. A few things don't add up," Marbury said. "Chief Grassley didn't regain consciousness until late last night. The account he gave differs from Tyler Forester's, but is closer to Ellender York's. He said he saw Ms. York's car abandoned on the side of Holloway Road, in a heavily wooded area about a mile from Route 50. He recognized the car as hers because she was parked near his house shortly before it was vandalized."

"He's saying Ellender broke into his house? That seems unlikely," Ruby said.

"He claims to have video from a home security camera," Marbury said. "Anyway, Grassley stopped. When he got out, he heard voices up ahead, but didn't have a clear view. When he followed the noise, he saw York and Forester arguing. He arrested York and had words with Forester, who tried to intervene. He put them both in the patrol car, intending to bring them here. At some point, Grassley lost consciousness and caused the car to wreck. When he woke, Forester was out of the car and had a gun. Grassley pulled his own weapon and Forester shot him."

Mac frowned. "Can't picture the little guy in a shootout with Tate, but a gun is an equalizer, I suppose."

Marbury shrugged and gave them the high-lights of Ellender's statement, which stunned Ruby and made Mac furious.

"We were supposed to be notified if he was released. What happened?" he demanded.

"I'm afraid I wasn't specific enough about which department was to get the call, and by default it went to Mallard Bay," Marbury said with a sigh. "Grassley kept the information to himself and tracked Tyler down. He found him at Ellender's and followed them."

"Has Forester said why he forced her to go out to the accident scene?" Mac asked.

"He talks nonstop, but doesn't make a lot of sense. Says he and Ellender are getting married and she can't testify against him."

"He's not the brightest bulb, is he?" Mac shook his head.

Marbury flipped through her notes. "Ellender backs up most of what he says about the encounter with Grassley, who she describes as sweating and clumsy. She also said Forester threatened to kill her if she tried to leave him. She didn't see Grassley get shot because she was knocked out when the car wrecked."

Ruby said, "Wait until you hear the stories coming in, now that people know Tate's out of commission. He's had several erratic episodes lately."

"Why didn't Ellender tell Grassley that Tyler was armed?" Mac stopped, too angry to go on. Tyler could have shot Grace and the baby as well.

Marbury said, "She was more afraid of Tyler than Grassley. She said he wouldn't have hesitated to kill both of them."

"How'd she know that?" Ruby asked.

"She knows him pretty well," Mac said. "Hard to believe Tate missed the gun."

"Not when you consider the shape he was in," Marbury said. "Ma'am," she turned to Ruby Blanchard. "Do you have next-of-kin information for the chief?"

"I thought you might need it," Ruby said. She slid a piece of paper across the table. "I shouldn't be surprised that Natalie is listed as his emergency contact, but none of this seems real. Can I do anything for him?"

Marbury added the paper to her folder, then said, "I'll contact our personnel division and his former department in Pennsylvania. They might be able to find some family. If anyone contacts you regarding him, please let me know."

"It's not only the gunshot that's the problem, is it?" Ruby asked. "He hasn't looked well, lately."

"He's a very sick man," Marbury said, then stood and thanked Ruby. "Major, could you walk me out to my car?"

Mac followed her in silence until they reached the parking lot.

"We don't have much time, sir," Marbury said. "Grassley is dying, and he knows it. The doctors say there's a widespread cancer, and the gunshot just finished the job. He's stopped talking to us, and I'm convinced he knows how Natalie Wilkens died."

"He won't talk to me," Mac said.

"I know," she said. "I've got a plan, but I need help."

"Name it."

And just like that, he was back to work.

CHAPTER FORTY-FIVE

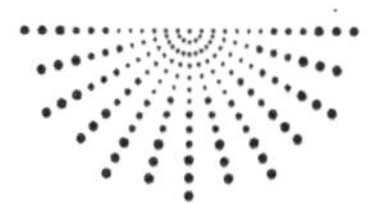

"Five minutes. If she's asleep, don't wake her up, she's had a rough time."

Ellender nodded. She was in no position to make bargains; the detective sergeant was being kind. From the way the woman kept glancing over her shoulder, Ellender guessed they weren't supposed to be on the maternity ward. She slipped into Grace's room before she lost her nerve, but stood back from the bed. It hurt to see the bossy, fast-talking woman who had saved her life lying motionless.

"It's okay," Grace said. "I'm awake. Just can't lift my head right now."

Ellender had promised herself she wouldn't cry in front of Grace, and it was a minute before she could speak. "I came to thank you," she finally managed and moved to the chair next to the bed. "I'm not sure what's going to happen to me, but I wanted to see you before I left the hospital. I listened to you and I tried to do what I thought was right. And I'll keep trying. I'm so sorry you and your baby—"

"Shhh. No. We're fine."

"Please let me say it," Ellender begged. "Dad and Verity can't hear me apologize. Let me tell you." She closed her eyes, and it all came out, soft words pouring from her broken heart.

When she fell quiet, Grace reached out and took her hand. "Look at me, Ellender. It's over. You can keep looking for ways to atone and make yourself miserable, or you can live a life that's worthy of them."

Ellender shook her head. "I don't think I can."

"You're already doing it. You give pretty good advice yourself." Grace wiggled her hand.

Ellender looked up in surprise. "No shocks?"

"Nope. Now tell me how I am. What do you see?"

"Pink." She laughed. "It'll take some explaining, but pink is good." A light tap on the door ended the visit, but she had what she'd come for.

~

TATE GRASSLEY LOOKED UNCOMFORTABLE, AND Ellender didn't think it was because of the tubes and wires connecting him to the machines around his hospital bed.

She stood close enough to encourage conversation, but far enough away to prevent him from touching her. Not that he was in any shape to try. Looking at him made her skin crawl, and the memory of his hands on her nearly broke her resolve.

Be worthy of them.

She didn't want to be here, but there was no choice. She'd known that when Mr. Mosley said the State Police wanted her cooperation to find Natalie's killer. That had been a week ago, and they thought she'd be trapping Tyler. She knew better and was happy to prove it, but Mr. Mosley had refused. Today, when the MSP asked again, she didn't have a choice. She watched the machines monitoring the man who had terrorized her. Despite everything, she felt sorry for him.

"You got something to say?"

He was awake.

She forced the words out. "I heard you asked to see me."

He made a sound that might have been a laugh. "I don't remember. Damned docs shoot stuff into me, but it isn't helping."

Ellender's unease increased. *Keep him talking.* The small recorder she wore was an uncomfortable reminder of the agreement she'd made.

"I'm sorry," she blurted out. "For what Tyler did, shooting you, I mean."

A bit of Grassley's cockiness surfaced. "Winged me, is all. Cheap shot."

Detective Marbury had told her Grassley understood his condition. He coughed, and she instinctively backed up, even though she couldn't catch what he had.

"You're a thief," he said. "Water."

She hesitated. Then, not wanting him to ring for the nurse, she picked up his cup and straw and stepped closer to hold it for him.

After a sip, he lay back on the pillows and studied her. "Breaking into my house was stupid. It's still a crime, even if what you took is worthless. Got you on tape. Security camera." Another cough shook him, and he groaned. "You'll go to jail. Everyone will know Nat was right."

Sweat beaded up on his face. She made herself follow her instructions. Looking into his jaundiced eyes, she said, "You could have arrested me at my house."

His response was another bitter smile, then he was coughing again. When he stopped this time, he took shallow breaths. He was dying, and Ellender knew she'd dream about this, but it would be much worse if she left. He had the answers, both Marbury's and hers. She skipped to the most important questions.

"Why did you follow us out of town?"

"Watched the punk manhandle you out of the house. You were happy enough when I showed up."

What she'd been was relieved when Tyler slipped the gun under his shirt. He said if she spoke, Grassley was dead, and she believed him. He'd already explained how he would kill her if he didn't get Verity's half of the inheritance. He was going to prison, and today, in the daylight, she was okay with that.

No one had a gun on her now, but she still had a microphone in her bra. Detective Marbury's threat of arrest on theft charges was persuasive, too.

"Why were you watching my house?" she asked. It wasn't one of the questions on the detective's list, but Ellender wanted to know.

He didn't hesitate. "Why'd you steal that file from my desk?"

"You had pictures of Mom and me! Did you take them from Natalie's house because they proved she'd been spying on us? Or did she give them to you?"

Ellender had to wait while Grassley's laugh turned into coughs. When he got his breath, he said, "I did a lot for her. And for you. Saved you twice."

She looked into those awful yellow eyes. He was fading. She spoke quickly and tried to sound respectful. "Chief Grassley, please help me. I didn't kill Natalie, and I don't believe Tyler did, either. If you killed her, tell me. It can't hurt you, now."

He didn't try laughing again, but eventually said, "*Me* kill *her*? That's rich."

She wasn't sure she'd heard him correctly and leaned closer. The little microphone poked her like the tip of a knife. "Please," she begged. If Grassley wouldn't give her the truth, she at least had to satisfy the police that she'd done all she could.

He smiled. "Loved her."

"You must have loved her a lot. I know it hurts and I'm sorry for your pain."

He closed his eyes, and she thought she'd lost her chance. She forced herself to reach out and touch his hand. He was still there, so she pulled up a chair and waited.

When he woke the next time, he looked different. "You won't like it."

She knew it was the truth. Suddenly, she wanted him to die now, and take all his hate with him. It took everything she had to say, "Tell me."

Smiling, he said, "She hated you because you had the bad luck to look like your father."

At first, she didn't understand. "But I don't look—"

"You wired?" he wheezed.

Despite Detective Marbury's instructions, she nodded.

"Good." He gestured for her to move closer, then said, "All of us hurt her. Your mother got away, but Nat made sure Owen paid. I paid, too, and never saw it coming. But she shoulda been more careful. Hard to enjoy your revenge if you're dead."

No, no, no . . . Ellender turned away, but he grabbed her arm.

"She hated you most of all. Every day you were there, reminding her of what Owen had done. I tried to get you away from her by arresting you. I thought it would make her happy and keep her from killing you. But she said I just slowed her down. See? I saved you twice." His hand spasmed, loosening his grip. "I thought she loved me."

Knowing every word would be repeated in her dreams, Ellender pulled away and ran out of the room as the alarms went off on the machines. In the last minutes of his life, Tate Grassley rid himself of his burden and gave it to her.

CHAPTER FORTY-SIX

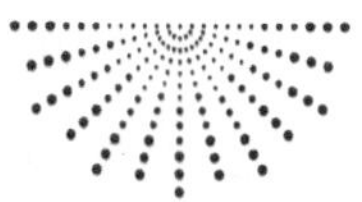

Her head hurt the worst, but Grace was afraid that was only because her other injured parts were numb. Her first twenty-four hours as a mother had been one long siege of pain interspersed with short periods of pure joy. At the moment, she was also angry, and had no patience with anyone who weighed over six and a half pounds.

When David demanded to know if she was listening to him, she snapped. "You're coming in loud and clear. How do I sound to you in Bermuda?"

"Don't start," he blustered. "I wouldn't be here if I'd known you'd get yourself in trouble again and nearly kill my child."

She dialed the animosity back. Sweet Pea was waiting down the hall in the neonatal nursery, and Grace imagined every sound to be coming from there. She wanted to be with her baby, but the other parent in their equation had to be handled first.

"Now, pay attention." David was back in lecture mode. "No caffeine, no sugar, and no alcohol. You're feeding my child and she'll be poisoned by your appalling diet. I'll be there by tomorrow morning to take her home."

"No—" Grace started, then decided to save her breath.

"And don't eat anything your so-called friends bring you. I've seen what they bring to those potluck dinners. The desserts alone would put a nursing baby into a coma. Maybe I should start Alexandra on a formula."

"I'll decide—"

"You are irresponsible," he said, cutting her off again. "I'll decide what's best for her."

"David." It was a warning. When there was only silence from his end, she said, "The baby is fine. You didn't ask, but I am not. We'll be in the hospital for at least two more days because I had some complications that need to heal. I'm happy to describe them in detail—"

"No! I believe you."

Her smile at his squeamishness vanished at his next words.

"Since Alexandra's healthy, I'll fly in and pick her up tonight. There's no need for her to be around all those germs. The nanny has everything ready."

For a moment, her only thought was gratitude that they weren't FaceTiming. She knew exactly which smug look was on his face. "I don't know who Alexandra is, but I hope you'll be happy with her. I'll call you when my baby and I are home."

"I have rights, Grace!"

His shout made her jump, and the pain took her breath away.

"Do you hear me?" he yelled. "Get used to it. That's my child."

When she could talk again, she said, "I can hear you, David. The hospital staff and everyone in Bermuda have heard about your rights. But if you don't quit bullying me, you and your rights will sit all alone on the dock of your new house."

"You found out." His chuckle made her want to scream. It had all been a game to him.

"Oh, please," she said, and managed to laugh. She hoped he never found out how long it took her to realize what he'd done. He'd paid twice for the river house, and she knew he'd hold it against her forever. But he had what he wanted—he would live across the river from Mac and there was nothing they could do about it. Nothing she'd thought of yet, anyway.

"I wanted to surprise you," he said. "Everything is set up and ready for my daughter."

It was an hour until her next round of pain medication, and that would be only acetaminophen. Grace clenched her fists, digging her prenatal vitamin strengthened nails into her palms. She wondered if he realized how much damage she could do with those ten little daggers. Or how each hateful word out of his mouth moved him further from his goal.

"Nothing to say?" he taunted her. "Aren't you going to accuse me of cheating our baby's trust fund? That's what you're thinking, isn't it? Well, *my* daughter doesn't need a loaded bank account. She has *me*. And don't even think about not signing that affidavit or leaving my name off the birth certificate. You don't want her to be illegitimate like her mother, do you?"

She didn't know how he'd found out about her father—or her lack of one—but his timing was perfect. Any regret she had for what she planned to do evaporated. "The man who sired me made a similar comment to my mother. Didn't work out so well for him."

She ended the call and groaned as she reached over to take the Affidavit of Paternity out of the bedside table. She tore it in half and called for her baby. After that, they both slept well.

When she woke, a nurse, whose name tag read "Amber," was checking her IV and smiling conspiratorially. "A beautiful flower arrangement is outside for you."

"Thanks, but if it's from someone named David, it can stay outside." Grace handed Sweet Pea over for a diaper change.

"Is he the pleasant guy who offered to help me find other employment if I didn't give him your daughter's vitals?"

"I'm so sorry." Grace had been saying that a lot to the staff.

"Oh, it's fine. We just reroute his calls to security or let him sit on hold until he gives up." When Grace had stopped laughing, Amber added, "Good news. The flowers aren't from Mr. Wonderful." She gave Sweet Pea back and left, returning a moment later bearing an enormous vase with two dozen pink roses. "Chief Mac's an old friend," she said. "I can get him up here if you want."

Grace thanked her, wondering how much the

staff knew about her personal life. Then she saw the card tucked into the middle of the arrangement. In clear block print, Mac had written, "For my girls, with love."

~

"SHE'S GORGEOUS." MAC SMILED DOWN AT THE squirming, red-faced infant he was holding and wished his words were true. His beautiful Grace had somehow produced a child who looked more like Popeye than Sweet Pea. But, if he saw nothing of Grace in her, she didn't resemble David, either, so that was something. He considered quietly asking Amber if there had been a mix-up in the nursery.

"She looks a little like Niki, don't you think?" Grace asked.

He tried to see it, but Popeye still had one eye scrunched up and was glaring at him with the other. "Yes, I believe I do. Around the eyes."

"Really? I see it around her mouth. She has my mother's eyes."

Her voice cracked with emotion, so he quickly repeated the lie about the baby's beauty. Then inspiration hit and he added, "The name is perfect, too."

"I'm so happy you approve." She gave him the smile he loved, then made a rueful face. "David is livid. I'm handling this badly, I'm afraid."

Mac realized Popeye had gone limp. He looked down in alarm to see the tiny face had relaxed and both eyes were closed.

"She feels safe with you," Grace said.

"I guess she's used to hearing my voice." Mac felt a twinge of sympathy for David. This was the father's rightful moment, but the father was an arrogant fool.

"I need to ask you something and I don't want you to think it has anything to do with the way David is acting right now."

He glanced up from his study of the sleeping baby and was startled to see she was crying. And smiling. He wanted to hold her, but he didn't want to disturb Popeye.

"This is hard." She grabbed a handful of tissues and wiped her eyes. "I wanted to ask you as soon as I knew I was pregnant, but I never knew how. I can't wait any longer, though."

His heart soared. "Grace, you know I—"

"Will you be her legal guardian if I die?"

"What?" The proposal he'd been about to make fizzled.

"There were complications, Mac. I hemorrhaged after I got to the hospital." She paused, then shrugged. "It was bad. Really bad. I'll be fine, but that's why I'll be here for a day or two. It's a good thing I'm staying at Avril's. No steps for me for a while."

He was stunned. Of course, no one had told him; he wasn't next of kin to her or the baby. She had nearly died while he was giving her space and thinking how well he was handling his unorthodox role. "My God, Grace . . ."

"I'll be fine. I'm just weak. Now, will you be her guardian if I die, which I won't."

He pulled his mind back from the unthinkable and focused on what she was saying. "What do you mean by guardian? David would never allow me to raise her."

She waved her hand as if shooing a fly. "I'll have to make a couple of modifications to my directives, but you would handle her money and have custody. It's a lot to ask."

"He'll never agree to it. She's his child." He saw an endless war with David Farquar. "He funded her trust. I can't take control of it."

"No, he didn't, and yes, you can. I set up the trust and I funded it using the proceeds from the sale of a property I owned." She smiled at his surprise. "It makes me sound awful, I know. But, it keeps the money from being a gift from David to the baby, which was never his intention when he bought the house. I'll tell you everything, but I have to get this guardian issue taken care of immediately. I was in bad shape yesterday and I can't take any more chances." She tried to sit up straighter in bed, winced, and sank back. "I'm not being fair to anyone, especially you, but it's the best thing I can do for her. As soon as she can understand, she needs to know that she has unconditional love and financial independence. She doesn't have to rely on David."

Mac thought he'd never heard anything so sad. "He's her father, Grace."

"He is, but I have to protect her. Niki has offered to be her guardian. It would be easier for her to do it, and she'll always be there, but I want my child to have a father. Not just a name on a piece of paper, or someone who only loves her when she does what he wants, but a real father. The most important thing of all is for her to have a positive male influence in her life." She stopped to get herself under control. "And to keep David from having sole custody of her if I die."

He was still confused, but he knew that look on her face. He said, "Nothing is going to happen to you, but put it all together when you're well and I'll sign whatever you need."

The smile and tears reappeared. Eventually, she said, "We should have executed the documents before she was born, but at least I prepared them. Niki has everything you'll need to sign, and she's waiting for you to call. Cyrus and Marjorie are expecting you, too, and they'll get it all filed properly."

Another jolt of panic grabbed him. "Are you sure you're okay?"

"I am, now. I have my little girl and I have you. I have everything I ever wanted, Mac."

He thought his heart would burst. The bundle in his arms wiggled, and he looked down at the rosebud lips moving with the baby's dream. Sweet Pea was beautiful. "I love you," he said, looking up at Grace, who was sleeping as peacefully as her daughter.

CHAPTER FORTY-SEVEN

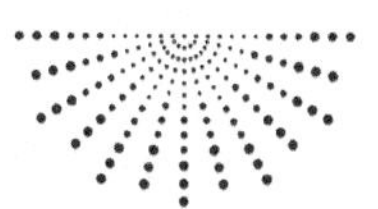

Mosley's elegant office was cozy. The elderly lawyer set a match to the kindling under a small bundle of logs in the Georgian fireplace, and Marjorie brought Ellender a mug of hot chocolate. The little bobbing marshmallows made her want to cry. This is what her mother would have done, warmed her up and fed her treats until she felt better. When Marjorie patted her shoulder, it was all she could do not to bawl.

But she'd come to discuss Grassley's final statement, not bolster her shattered ego. Since Mosley was still her attorney, and had also been Owen Wilkens's friend, she was starting her fact-finding mission with him. When he agreed to see her immediately, it didn't occur to her that he might have his own reason for opening his office on a Sunday afternoon. As it turned out, he had a good one. He took over the conversation before she could ask her first question.

"My instructions are to contact you on your twenty-fifth birthday, which I believe is in three months?"

"What? Your instructions? What do you . . ." she started, then stopped. It didn't matter how he knew her birthdate, only why.

He smiled. "Grace Reagan asked me how I knew so much about you. I was truthful, but not fully transparent with her. I only told her I had known you your entire life, which is true. Now, since you contacted me first and already know of your parentage, I can move up the time line and tell you I am the executor of Owen Wilkens's will. It contained a bequest to you which will come to you on your birthday. This is a complicated matter, but we don't need to go over everything today. You're just out of the hospital."

"All of it! You tell me all of it, now." Ellender was running on black coffee, vodka and very few calories. She knew she wasn't sober, or reasonable, but she wanted the truth.

"As you wish," he said, picking up an envelope from his desk and handing it to her. "This is a copy of the will and a current accounting of the status of the investments I made on your behalf over the last four years. The bequest was a healthy size to begin with, but it doubled two weeks ago when Natalie Wilkens died."

"*Natalie?* Natalie left me money? Why would she do that?"

Mosley sighed. "I doubt it was intentional. Owen's will states if Natalie predeceased you, any assets remaining in the trust he'd set up for her were to go to you. When she died, their house and several other properties, along with a sizable stock portfolio, became yours."

Ellender struggled to take it all in. "I don't care about the money. Tell me about my birth. I just want facts. Are you sure Owen Wilkens is my father?"

Like the rest of his kind, Mosley rarely gave a short, or unqualified answer.

He said, "I can prove these things to you." Four arthritic fingers went up, and he ticked them off. "One. Owen believed he was your father. Two. The key in the envelope I gave you is for a safe deposit box that contains an analysis of Owen's blood, a DNA report, and a letter to his physician releasing all of his medical records to you. I was entrusted with those items and I placed them in the box myself. Three. Owen wrote the letter you will find in the envelope, I watched him do it. Four. The receipt of your inheritance is not contingent upon you being his biological daughter." He paused to let her absorb what he'd said.

"So, he wasn't sure he was my father, then."

"He was sure, but he didn't want you to endure a legal battle to access your inheritance."

"Because Natalie would fight it."

"Yes."

"Did my dad know?" She tried not to whisper, but the words wouldn't come out any louder.

Mosley rubbed his bald head.

Ellender thought he was deciding how much to say. "I don't have anyone left," she said angrily. "Not a soul left to tell me the truth. I can't ask my mother, or my father. You have to tell me!"

"I'm sorry, but I can't tell you what I don't know. And I don't know what transpired between your mother and her husband."

"My father! My dad *was* my father. My mother would never cheat on him! What Tate Grassley said about me looking like Judge Wilkens is just Natalie's craziness. He was old and ugly! Mom wouldn't let him touch her!"

Mosley listened to the outburst, then walked to the far side of the room. He looked over a wall of photographs, took one down, and came back to stand in front of her. "Owen Wilkens was a fine man, Ms. York. A good and generous person. Sometimes, love blooms in inconvenient places, but that doesn't diminish its power. You asked me what I know for sure."

He handed her the photograph. Hands shaking, Ellender held the frame and looked at two men smiling and holding up a trophy. *Mallard Bay Tournament Champions, 1990.* Mosley had dark, wavy hair and a high forehead. His companion wore his straight red hair short and combed to the side, framing a familiar oval face and wide blue eyes.

After a time, she said, "Does anyone else know?"

"We're never as fascinating as we think we are, m'dear." Mosley gently took the picture back and rehung it. "Redheads aren't a rarity around here. Owen said you only had golden fuzz as a baby, while he was fading out to silver by then. But to answer your question, no. As far as I am aware, with one exception, no one other than your mother and Owen knew the truth, except me. I was his attorney and the executor of his estate. He was determined to honor your mother's decision to stay in her marriage. I wish I could tell you more about the personal aspect of this situation, but Owen was a private person."

Ellender tried hard to think rationally. She had indulged in forty-eight hours of emotional turmoil, and it was time to be an adult. "Who was the exception? Who else did Owen," she spat the name out, then stopped, ashamed. "Who else did he tell?"

Mosley grimaced. "In hindsight, it was a poor choice, but he felt he should explain himself to Natalie. He told her a few days before he died and she never spoke to him again."

"Well, that's just great, isn't it?" Ellender threw her hands up. "They all die and leave me next door to a woman who knows I'm . . . I'm a . . ."

He let her run down, then said, "I'm sorry, but I must stop our conversation at this point. I have another appointment, one I can't miss. Marjorie will set up a time for our next meeting before you leave. You won't go through this alone, I promise."

He stood, but she didn't respond. She was staring at the envelope, crumpling its edges in her grip. After a moment, she looked up and realized he was waiting for her. "What do I do?"

He smiled and said, "Why, whatever you think

is best, of course. On your birthday, you will become a wealthy young woman. Natalie tried, but she didn't spend Owen's money fast enough. I imagine she thought she had more time."

Ellender shook her head. She'd given Natalie's death a lot of thought. "Did his will say what would happen if I died before Natalie?"

"Yes," he said, taking a quick look at his watch. "In that case, your inheritance would revert to Natalie and her heirs."

"And if I were to be convicted of her murder?"

This stopped Mosley, who was halfway into his coat. "The same result," he spoke slowly, watching her. "The law would not allow you to profit from your crime. Her heirs would inherit. Why—"

But Ellender's mind was racing, and she cut him off. "Who was her heir? Tate Grassley, by any chance?"

He relaxed. "That would have been classic, wouldn't it? But no. Her will has been filed, and I have a copy. Her assets are to be divided among several charities. I don't think she shared Mr. Grassley's personal feelings."

"No," Ellender agreed. "I'm very sure she didn't." There went her neat theory that Grassley had tried to set her up. "Just one more question, please? Does anyone else know about my trust—about the inheritance?"

Mosley shook his head. "I don't want to be rude, but I can't be late. The short answer is no."

Ellender smiled.

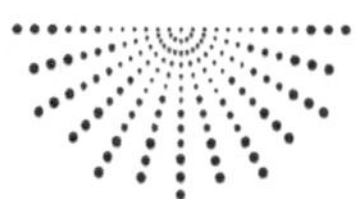

CHAPTER FORTY-EIGHT

"Oh my," Mosley said for the third time.

"Earth to Cy. It's a girl, you old fool. Say something sensible." Avril hadn't relaxed since Grace and the baby arrived, but was so happy, she chuckled as she was rude to their visitor.

"Oh my," he repeated, not taking his eyes off the baby.

"Leave him alone," Grace said as Avril opened her mouth to have another go. "This child took us all by surprise. Everyone's adjusting."

"I can't believe you don't have a name for her," Avril said and held out her arms.

Once her daughter was settled in her godmother's lap, Grace said, "Sweet Pea has a name. All nice and legal, too. I finalized everything before we left the hospital this morning."

"All right!" Avril exclaimed, startling the baby. "Does the last one start with an *F* or a *R*?"

Mosley looked appalled.

"Reagan. She has the name Mom gave me."

The godparents looked at each other, and then down at the baby, who yawned.

"Well, that's done," Avril smoothed a wrinkle from the pink blanket, then asked what they both wanted to know. "Is David named on the birth certificate?"

Mosley didn't even pretend to scold her for being rude. They both watched Grace and waited for an answer.

"No," she said. The memory of David's reaction when he realized what she had done made her sad, and she knew it always would. Breaking the news over the phone had felt cowardly, but it had been the only way to stop the barrage of instructions, demands, and threats. She sent a photocopy of the certificate by text and FaceTimed to tell him what she'd done. He'd stared at her, speechless for once, then disconnected.

"On to more pleasant topics," Cyrus said, pulling her back to her friends and sleeping baby. "What are we to call this lovely child?"

"Can't you guess? It's a family name."

"Fiona the Fourth?" A smile lit up his face when Grace nodded.

"Fiona Elizabeth Reagan."

For a moment, there was only the ambient noise from the world outside.

"That's lovely," Avril said in a too casual tone. "Is Elizabeth someone in David's family?"

"No," Grace said. "She's someone in Fiona's. You, Avril Elizabeth Oxley. She's named after all of her grandmothers."

Avril watched the baby with awe. Memories and could-have-beens flooded all of their thoughts, and the sunlit nursery felt full and peaceful until Fiona burped and broke the spell.

Taking advantage of the distraction, Mosley turned to Grace and said, "I'm so grateful you asked me to be her godfather. I was afraid that you, well, with what I said to you . . . I hope you understand I had to protect you and Ellender from Grassley and I didn't know any other way to do it. He threatened both of you."

Grace smiled to take the sting from her next words. "We're stopping this dance, Cy. We discuss our problems like adults, and handle them together. No more protecting, understand?"

His smile said, *Not in a million years.*

"I mean it," she insisted. A glance at Avril confirmed she was occupied with Fiona, but probably listening to every word of their conversation. So be it, she thought. He brought the subject up. "You're right. We're not a good fit."

"When did I say that?" he sputtered. "I would never." Then, after a moment, "So you aren't too mad at me, are you?" He leaned closer, and she saw a worrisome gleam in his eye. "Wonderful! Now, when you're ready, you can move to the second floor of the building and we'll be Mosley and Reagan, LLC. Jake will help me with the old-timers and big money downstairs, and you can save your misfits and miscreants upstairs. We might even coax Lily to come home. What do you think?"

"I'm starting my own firm, Cy. One with pro bono work, as well as misfits and miscreants. You'll hate it, and Marjorie will have a heart attack. It's best that I go it alone."

"That works! You can move in upstairs as soon as you're ready."

"No! That's not what—"

"Stop it!" Avril said and raised the baby to her shoulder for a round of gentle back patting. "No arguing around this innocent. You two can plan the great comeback in six months."

Mosley declared the matter settled and changed the subject. "Well, well, Miss Fiona Elizabeth. Lovely, of course, but my second name is Cecil. Fiona Cecilia would be nice, but I guess you have to keep her happy." He aimed a haughty nod at Avril, who stuck her tongue out.

"Her name is Fiona," Grace said, ignoring both of them and retrieving her baby.

"I'm not sure we should call her that," Avril said. "She looks like me, so let's use Eliza."

"Nice, but no." Grace nodded toward the door. "Time for you two to move along. David will be here soon and you promised to take the dogs out and give us some privacy, remember?"

The leave-taking was slow, with Avril proposing diminutives of Elizabeth, and Mosley objecting to each of them. "All right, I can agree to Liz," she said as she finally left the nursery.

"The other children will call her Lizard," Mosley protested as he trailed behind her.

They continued to pick at each other as they went through the house and rounded up the dogs. Then Avril shouted, "Goodbye! Grammy loves you, Lizzie Reagan!"

Grace recognized the signal and kissed her daughter for luck. The godmother had just announced David's arrival.

∾

"SHE HAS A LARGER NURSERY AT MY HOUSE," HE said, as he examined every nook and cranny of the room with a critical air.

"And we'll visit there," Grace said, trying to sound calm and reassuring instead of tired and irritable.

"I don't understand why she has to camp out in a stranger's house when she can be at home with her father."

One, two, three, calm, calm, calm. Grace told herself that even if he wasn't giving the argument up, he was at least being quiet with it. "We're living with Avril until January, when our new house will be ready. As soon as I think we can safely travel, we'll come see you."

"She needs a baby nurse and you need competent help."

"We're staying here, David. Besides, Avril trained as a nurse."

This had actually come as a great surprise to Grace, who received the reassuring news during her delivery. Only recently had Avril added the details of her training. Fiona had been delivered by a veterinary tech who'd helped whelp her last litter in 1990.

David snorted and said, "That old woman may be a witch, but she's no nurse."

Grace noticed he glanced at the door before making the comment. Nurse or witch, he'd never won an argument against his nemesis.

He picked up a teddy bear with "Fiona" printed on its sweater.

She waited. They had to have it out eventually, and at least she was upright now. It had been three days since she'd given birth in Avril's car and hemorrhaged in the emergency room. In that time, she and her world had changed. She was ready.

"It's a beautiful name, Grace." David's smile was insincere. "It belongs to my little girl now, and I know what it means to you. I would have agreed if you'd just asked me."

On the surface, his tone was conciliatory, but Grace knew better. *My little girl. If you'd asked me.*

She didn't know if he'd ever loved her or could love their child, but her tolerance for his behavior was spent. Ahead of them lay only negotiated truce or severed ties.

She continued to rock the sleeping baby and, keeping her voice low and matter of fact, she told David how their lives were going to be. He didn't interrupt, but stopped pacing and came to stand in front of her, planting himself with feet apart and arms crossed. His expression was one of mild amusement.

When she finished, he said, "You'll tell her I'm her father, but my name won't be on the birth certificate? That won't keep me from asserting my parental rights."

"Yes, I know."

"Then why play games? I'll petition the court to change her birth certificate."

"You can try," Grace said amiably, "but I'll fight every move you make. More than half of your practice is divorce and custody actions. You don't want to go to court on your own behalf, do you? Bad for business, I'd think."

He laughed, then his face turned hard when he saw she was smiling at him. "You can't play at my level, Grace."

"I don't have to." She fished a card from the pocket of her robe and handed it to him. His surprise told her she'd chosen well. She sent a silent thank you to Zara Wingate for connecting her to the well-known Baltimore law firm.

"You can't pay for this." He tossed the card to the floor near her feet.

"I already have, David. And I will continue to pay them until you accept that this child will not be a pawn between us. She will grow up loved and happy. You can be a part of that, as her father, or you can be in court with me for the next eighteen years."

He looked at the baby, his hands flexing nervously. "I will spend every penny I have—"

"So will I."

It took a second for her words to sink in, then his eyes widened. "You can't use the trust fund, that's a breach of the terms!"

"No. It isn't. I have full discretionary use in Fiona's behalf, and I'll use all of it to see that you never have control over her. If those funds run out, I'll sell Delaney House, and when that's gone, I'll come up with another plan. You can fight until she hates you, or, you can behave like a rational adult and have a positive relationship with our daughter on my terms. And no matter what you think right now, I will be reasonable."

When she and Fiona were alone again, Grace tried to be happy, but all she felt was relieved.

It was over. For now.

CHAPTER FORTY-NINE

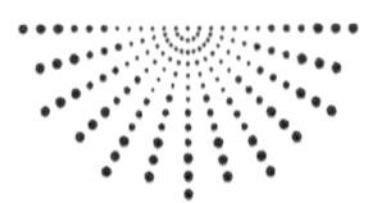

She woke to mewling sounds and momentarily thought she needed to get up and feed Leo. Reality returned with a lusty wail, and the next hour passed quickly. When Fiona was asleep again, Grace turned on the baby monitor and tiptoed away. Delicious smells were coming from the kitchen, and she was starved. She also wanted to call Mac. The short periods of sleep she'd managed during the night had allowed her to process fragments of information that had been bothering her. She had an idea about Natalie Wilkens's death, and she wanted to know if she was right.

Voices stopped her in the hallway. Mac and Avril. A third person asked for more coffee.

Cyrus. She backtracked to the bathroom to clean up, still amazed at how messy she could get by taking care of one tiny baby. When she finally reached the kitchen, she heard Mac say, "We'll have to wait for the autopsy to be sure."

Her arrival caused a momentary change of subject, but once a Fiona update was delivered and Grace had a plate of bacon and eggs in front of her, she insisted on hearing everything she'd missed.

Mac obliged, taking her through the MSP investigation, his conversations with Ellender and Tyler, and the ramifications of Tate Grassley's death.

"Ooh! Let me tell the Tyler part," Avril said, clapping her hands. "It's my favorite."

"It's Mac's story," Mosley argued.

"Someone tell me something," Grace mumbled around a mouthful of buttered biscuit.

Mac said, "Well, Mr. Forester got cocky when his meds wore off, and I mean *all* his meds. He wasn't seriously hurt when you shot him."

"Right," Avril chimed in. "He has four other toes on his left foot. We'll go out to the target range and practice when Elizabeth is older."

Mac raised his voice and continued, "Now,

when you hit him, that was a different story." He had to pause again while Grace protested she'd done no such thing, and Avril said "hit," was a kind euphemism for "squashed like a bug."

"I was in labor and I fell!" Grace insisted.

"You incapacitated him, sweetheart," Mac patted her hand. "That's all that matters. Plenty of people live full, productive lives with nine toes and three herniated discs. Here, have another biscuit."

"I won't always be distracted this easily," she groused, but took the biscuit, anyway. "So, what was he taking, and what happened when he sobered up?"

"The staff at the Detention Center did a good job of managing his meds, but when his mother bailed him out, the first thing Tyler did was treat himself to extra painkillers. Then he took uppers before he went to see Ellender. He came down hard in the hospital and had to be restrained. He says he's suing his doctors, by the way."

"Do not take that case, Grace!" Mosley wagged a finger, then pushed the last of the bacon toward her. "Here, you need protein."

"If I may continue?" Mac said, transferring the bacon to Grace's plate. "Tyler demanded to see

Ellender, which wasn't happening. Then he demanded to see you, which definitely wasn't happening. Then he got out of the restraints and ran into Tremaine Harper, who was on duty at his door. Harper held him with one hand and called Marbury with the other." He shook his head as they laughed. "I really hate that I missed seeing that."

"So where is he now?" Grace asked. "Tyler, I mean."

"Back in jail. Arraignment is today. He's being charged with first-degree murder for Tate, two counts of aggravated assault in the second degree for Ellender and Avril." He reached out and took her hand. "And one count of felony assault."

Grace stopped eating, her appetite gone. She knew the felony charge was for the risk to Fiona. "Tell me the rest. Will it all stick?"

"The SA feels good about all the charges." He let her hand go and poured fresh coffee. "But Tate was dying when Tyler shot him. The wound just speeded things up. We'll get more information from the autopsy."

"Tell them to look for the same poison that killed Natalie," Grace said. "Even if he had cancer, it could have been caused, or exacerbated, by ingesting pesticide. And, if I'm right, she was the killer as well as a victim. I think she'd been poisoning Tate all along."

Mac stared at her, ignoring Avril and Mosley, who talked over each other with questions.

"It was something David said, if you can believe it," Grace explained. "When he was ranting about my diet poisoning the baby, he was talking about chocolate and sugar, but it made me think. Mac, you told me Tate complained about Natalie's cooking. Maybe her campaign against Ellender's use of pesticides started out as just another round of complaining, but it could have given her the idea to poison Tate. If she did, she handled his contaminated food and dishes." Digging her cell phone out of the pocket of her robe, she pulled up a screen and held it up. "I googled it. Some chemicals can be absorbed through the skin and inhaled, so if she wasn't careful—"

"She'd be exposed, too," he said, breaking in.

"Yes!" Grace's excitement grew as she talked. "She poisoned herself accidentally and Tate on purpose, then she asked to borrow flour from Ellender, but didn't mind that Tyler delivered it, and why? Because she was setting a trap and needed to get the poison into the flour in Ellender's pantry. Remember, in Tyler's statement the night of the murder, he said Natalie scooped the flour from her counter back into the box, which he obligingly returned to Ellender's house."

"There's more." Mosley glowed with excitement, apparently forgetting that crimes like murder were beneath him. "You both should talk to Ellender. I met with her yesterday."

When Grace and Mac looked confused, Avril snapped, "Oh, for pity's sake, Cy, quit pussyfooting around with your confidentiality paranoia. It's just us. Natalie was a jealous, egotistical gold digger, who killed herself while she tried to poison her old boyfriend and pin it on her husband's love child." She glared at them, then shrugged. "Okay, the part about the pesticide was a surprise, but who couldn't fit the rest of it together? You people need to be more observant. And if I were in charge of this circus, I'd get the medical examiner to exhume poor Owen, and test whatever's left of him for pesticides, too. Now, no more murder talk during meals. I can't be the only one setting a good example for Beth."

"You keep us straight, Granny." Mac rose and leaned over to kiss a biscuit crumb from the corner of Grace's mouth. "Sorry to cut this short, but I'm helping Niki pack up the mountain of gifts from your baby shower."

After he left, Grace said, "He already knew, didn't he?"

"Well, my performance was mostly for you," Avril admitted. "You've missed a lot. And just so you know, Niki has promised everyone a redo on the party. She's planning a big one for Christmas."

"But—"

"Nothing for you to worry about, m'dear," Mosley said. "You need rest and we need to do the dishes."

She was full and sleepy, and more than willing to snuggle on the sunporch sofa with Leo and Louise. All three of them napped until an argument woke them.

"I'm awake," she called out.

"Told you so." Avril pushed Mosley through the doorway. "Now take that tray to her. She hasn't eaten in an hour and Lisel will be awake soon."

"My daughter's name is Fiona," Grace said, but she took the offered pound cake and hot chocolate. "You're right, though. I don't have much time before she wakes up. So, quick, tell me everything you left out earlier."

Her food team needed no encouragement.

"Finish telling her about Forester," Mosley said. "Mac left out the best part."

Avril laughed. "When he thwarted the big escape, Tremaine turned Tyler over to Desi Marbury. The fool ran his mouth, threatening everyone in sight. Desi told him it was big talk coming from a guy who was beaten up by a woman in labor and a little old lady."

"Well, that's not flattering," Grace said.

"Maybe not for you," Avril said with a sniff. "But nobody believes I'm old. Anyway, lots of people heard her, and it's flying around town. Everywhere I go, people congratulate me and ask for details."

"Oh, no!" Grace moaned. "The entire town knows how I gave birth?"

Avril laughed. "The entire town knows *we* kick fannies. Nobody will ever mess with us again."

"Nobody messes with you, anyway. I'll never live this down."

"Good for business, though," Mosley said. "When you start up your practice on the second floor, every dead-broke, downtrodden soul on the Eastern Shore will beat a path to your door. You're famous."

Grace looked at the two laughing people

across from her, and thought of the sleeping baby upstairs and the dogs next to her. Mac loved her and she had cake. Her blessings were too many to count.

She was happy.

THE END

also on Facebook and Twitter. Drop me an email — I'd love to hear from you!

Website: www.CherilThomas.com
Email: Cheril@CherilThomas.com
Amazon Author Page: www.amazon.com/author/cherilthomas

ACKNOWLEDGMENTS

The errors within these pages are my own. The fact that there aren't more of them is due to the assistance of many kind and talented people.

My wonderful story editor, Helen Chappell, made it through another round of arguing with me about murder. I didn't kill all the darlings she told me to, but I'm grateful she sticks with me, anyway. She is always kind when urging me to commit homicide. We usually meet in restaurants, and many diners have changed tables after getting an earful of our conversations. We really should stick with carryout.

Olivia Martin Hosken and Vicki Ellingson worked tirelessly to help me shape this book. As enthusiastic first readers and very talented writers in their own genres, they (among other heroic feats) caught continuity issues that resulted from my last-minute decision to rearrange the middle of the book. Why I have these harebrained ideas, I don't know - I just hope you like the final rendition.

Beta readers: Cindy Haddaway, Tara Kleinert, and Judith Hohman—you are the best! Thank you so much for the long hours you spent cleaning up

Mallard Bay and its residents. I have such kind and gifted people in my corner, and you all certainly earned your red editor's pens.

And, because I couldn't leave the manuscript alone after everyone above had finished their reviews, proofreading services were provided by Leighton Wingate. Thank you, Leighton!

As always, a thank you to my family. Ron, Patrick, Kate, James, and Jack, I don't tell you often enough how proud and grateful I am to have each of you in my life.

This book is dedicated to my wonderful aunt, Patricia McMahan Walters. Aunt Pat watched all my (oh, so bad) childhood recitals and concerts, and has read every word of my stories and books. She is a gifted businesswoman who inspires me every day with her talent, her humor and her generosity. I love you, Auntie.

July 2021
Easton, Maryland

COMING SOON IN MALLARD BAY

I didn't set out to write a mystery series. I had a story rolling around in my head about a historic, decaying old mansion and the woman who saved it. It was based on a real house, one I wanted to buy in the worst way. My husband and I walked away from that impossibly huge renovation project, but I spent several years recreating the work, and the mansion, in *Squatter's Rights.*

I finished that book, but the characters didn't take the hint when I wrote 'The End.' Two more story lines nagged at me. I decided to go for a trilogy and *A Commission on Murder* and *Bad Intent* evolved. When a life-changing event developed for Grace in *BI,* I couldn't leave her dangling, so… I started another run around the bases for a total of six books in the series.

Then, another funny thing happened. A new character blasted her way into *Death and Consequences,* and she really intrigued me. Her story was too big to be wrapped up in a subplot, so from the safety of a two book commitment cushion, I promised Ellender York her own series. I would be terrified if I weren't so excited!

I hope you'll come along for the ride, whether

the people of Mallard Bay claim six books or twenty-six. I am grateful to my readers in a way that's hard to express. Just know that I thank my lucky stars for each of you.

Thank you for reading my stories.

CHERIL
THOMAS
AN EASTERN SHORE MYSTERY
BAD
INTENT

3 Eastern Shore Mysteries
And a Holiday
Short Read!
CHERIL
THOMAS
CHERIL
THOMAS
AN EASTERN SHORE MYSTERY
SQUATTER'S
RIGHTS
COMMISSION
ON MURDER
Books
1-3
CHERIL
THOMAS
CHERIL
THOMAS
BAD
INTENT
A Little
Christmas
WAR

Want a *free* Eastern Shore Short Mystery?

Sign up to receive an email when I have news or a new release.

Just visit me here:
www.CherilThomas.com.
Scroll to the bottom of the page and send me an email with 'Sign me up' in the message, and I'll send your free copy of an Eastern Shore short story. I'm looking forward to hearing from you!

ABOUT THE AUTHOR

Cheril Thomas is the author of the Eastern Shore Mysteries series, numerous short stories and articles. When she's not writing at home in Easton, Maryland, she's traveling with her long-suffering husband, an otherwise brilliant soul who for some reason doesn't mind being married to a woman who researches methods of murder. Their lives are directed by a sassy little spaniel named Ellie Grace.

Thomas, Cheril, Death and Consequences, (An Eastern Shore Mystery) 2021. ISBN: 978-1-7334121-86

Book covers created by MiblArt .

Created with Vellum.

Published in the United States of America

Tred Avon Press
Easton, Maryland
www.TredAvonPress.com